By Mary Higgins Clark

MARY HIGGINS CLARK

Daddy's Gone A Hunting

Simon & Schuster

New York   London   Toronto   Sydney   New Delhi

Simon & Schuster
1230 Avenue of the Americas
New York, NY 10020

First Simon & Schuster hardcover edition April 2013

SIMON & SCHUSTER and colophon are registered trademarks
of Simon & Schuster, Inc.

For information about special discounts for bulk purchases,
please contact Simon & Schuster Special Sales at
1-866-506-1949 or business@simonandschuster.com.

The Simon & Schuster Speakers Bureau can bring authors
to your live event. For more information or to book an event
contact the Simon & Schuster Speakers Bureau at
1-866-248-3049 or visit our website at www.simonspeakers.com.

Designed by Jill Putorti

Manufactured in the United States of America

10 9 8 7 6 5 4 3 2 1

Library of Congress Cataloging-in-Publication Data is available.
ISBN 978-1-4516-6894-0
ISBN 978-1-4516-6896-4 (ebook)

Acknowledgments

And so it has come to pass that *Daddy's Gone A Hunting* has been tucked away in its own little bunting. It seems like a long nine months since I sent the first chapter to my forever editor, Michael Korda, with a cover sheet on which I scrawled, "Here we go again."

As always the journey can sometimes be smooth. Other days as I stare at the computer I ask myself, "Whatever made you think you could write another book?"

But whether the words are flowing or reluctantly dripping, the fact is that I love the journey, and it is time to thank the people who helped me make it.

Michael Korda suggested the DNA of the plot for this story. At first I had some doubts, but as usual I was drawn to the suggestion as a moth is to a lightbulb. Again and always, thank you, Michael. My dear friend, as our fortieth anniversary of working together looms, I can only say, it is and has been grand.

Almost three years ago, I requested that Kathy Sagan become my in-house editor. We had worked together on the *Mary Higgins Clark Mystery Magazine,* and I knew how absolutely special she is, and how she can balance a thousand details in her head as she receives the book chapter by chapter. Thank you, Kathy.

It's easy to set a fire. But when you write about it, you have to know who would be leading the investigation. For that information and guidance, I am so grateful to Fire Marshal Randy Wilson and retired Fire Marshal Richard Ruggiero. If I've done anything wrong, it's because I misunderstood what you told me, but many thanks for the kindness with which you patiently answered my questions.

Anthony Orlando, Esq., an avid tuna fisherman, was my expert about an interesting way to have an accident on a boat in the Atlantic. Many thanks, Anthony.

The behind-the-scenes production and copyediting people are vital in turning a manuscript into a book. My thanks to copy editor Gypsy da Silva, and to art director Jackie Seow for her always intriguing covers.

My readers along the way are still in place, rooting me on. Thanks to Nadine Petry, Agnes Newton, and Irene Clark. It's always good news when they tell me they're looking forward to the *next* chapter and ask how soon I'll have it.

And of course there is Himself, John Conheeney, spouse extraordinaire, who patiently abides with me as I pound the computer for hours on end as the deadline approaches. Not everyone gets a chance at having a second soul mate, and I'm grateful I'm one of the lucky few.

And now to ponder Michael's suggestion for the next book. After laying out the broad outline of a plot, he said, "I think *I'll Be Seeing You* would be a good title." I hesitated, "Michael, I think I used that title already." We both had to look it up. Yes, I did. So it won't have that title, but I love the suggestion of the plot.

But before I start I will once again follow the advice of the ancient parchment. "The book is finished. Let the writer rejoice."

Trust me, I do!

Cheers and blessings,
Mary

For John
And our Clark and Conheeney children and grandchildren
With love

Prologue

Sometimes Kate dreamed about that night, even though it wasn't a dream. It had really happened. She was three years old and had been curled up on the bed watching Mommy getting dressed. Mommy looked like a princess. She was wearing a beautiful red evening gown and the red satin high heels that Kate loved to try on. Then Daddy came into the bedroom and he picked Kate up and danced her and Mommy onto the balcony even though it was beginning to snow.

I begged him to sing my song and he did, Kate remembered.

Bye baby bunting,
Daddy's gone a-hunting,
A rosy wisp of cloud to win,
To wrap his baby bunting in.

The next night Mommy died in the accident, and Daddy never sang that song to her again.

1

Thursday, November 14

At four o'clock in the morning, Gus Schmidt dressed silently in the bedroom of his modest home on Long Island, hoping not to disturb his wife of fifty-five years. He was not successful.

Lottie Schmidt's hand shot out to fumble for the lamp on the night table. Blinking to clear eyes that were heavy with sleep, she noticed that Gus was wearing a heavy jacket, and demanded to know where he was going.

"Lottie, I'm just going over to the plant. Something came up."

"Is that why Kate called you yesterday?"

Kate was the daughter of Douglas Connelly, the owner of Connelly Fine Antique Reproductions, the furniture complex in nearby Long Island City where Gus had worked until his retirement five years earlier.

Lottie, a slight seventy-five-year-old with thinning white hair, slipped on her glasses and glanced at the clock. "Gus, are you crazy? Do you know what time it is?"

"It's four o'clock and Kate asked me to meet her there at four thirty. She must have had her reasons and that's why I'm going."

Lottie could see that he was clearly upset.

Lottie knew better than to ask the question that was on both their minds. "Gus, I've had a bad feeling lately. I know you don't want to hear me talk like this, but I sense something dark is going to happen. I don't want you to go."

In the shadowy 60-watt light of the night table lamp they glared at each other. Even as Gus spoke, he knew deep down he was frightened. Lottie's claim to be psychic both irritated and scared him. "Lottie, go back to sleep," he said angrily. "No matter what the problem is, I'll be back for breakfast."

Gus was not a demonstrative man but some instinct made him walk over to the bed, lean down, kiss his wife's forehead, and run his hand over her hair. "Don't worry," he said firmly.

They were the last words she would ever hear him say.

2

Kate Connelly hoped that she would be able to hide the restless anxiety she felt about her predawn appointment with Gus in the museum of the furniture complex. She had dinner with her father and his newest girlfriend in Zone, the fashionably new café in Manhattan's Lower East Side. Over cocktails she made the usual small talk that rolled easily off her tongue when she chatted with his "flavor of the moment."

This one was Sandra Starling, a platinum blond beauty in her midtwenties with wide-set hazel eyes, who earnestly explained that she had been a runner-up in a Miss Universe contest but became vague as to exactly how far she had been from winning the crown.

Her ambition, she confided, was to have a career in the movies and then dedicate herself to world peace. This one is even dumber than most of the others, Kate thought sardonically. Doug, as she had been instructed to call her father, was his genial and charming self, although he seemed to be drinking more heavily than usual.

Throughout the dinner, Kate realized that she was appraising her father as if she were a judge on *America's Got Talent* or *Dancing with the Stars*. He's a handsome man in his late fifties, she thought, a look-alike for legendary film star Gregory Peck. Then she reminded herself that most people her age wouldn't have any real appreciation of that comparison. Unless, like me, they're devotees of classic movies, she thought.

Was she making a mistake to bring Gus in on this? she wondered.

"Kate, I was telling Sandra that you're the brains of the family," her father said.

"I hardly think of myself as that," Kate answered with a forced smile.

"Don't be modest," Doug Connelly chided. "Kate is a certified public accountant, Sandra. Works for Wayne & Cruthers, one of the biggest accounting firms in the country." He laughed. "Only problem is, she's always telling me how to run the family business." He paused. "*My* business," he added. "She forgets that."

"Dad, I mean Doug," Kate said quietly, even as she felt her anger building. "Sandra doesn't need to hear about it."

"Sandra, look at my daughter. Thirty years old and a tall, gorgeous blonde. She takes after her mother. Her sister, Hannah, looks like me. She has my charcoal brown hair and blue eyes, but unlike me she came in a small package. Not more than five foot two. Isn't that right, Kate?"

Dad's been drinking before he got here, Kate thought. He can get nasty when he gets an edge on. She tried to steer the subject away from the family business. "My sister is in fashion, Sandra," she explained. "She's three years younger than I am. When we were growing up, she was always making dresses for her dolls while I was pretending to make money by answering the questions on *Jeopardy!* and *Wheel of Fortune.*"

Oh God, what do I do if Gus agrees with me? she asked herself as the waiter brought their entrées.

Fortunately the band, which had been on a break, came back into the crowded dining room and the earsplitting music kept conversation to a minimum.

She and Sandra passed on dessert, but then, to her dismay, Kate heard her father order a bottle of the most expensive champagne on the menu.

She began to protest. "Dad, we don't need—"

"Kate, spare me your penny-pinching." Doug Connelly's voice rose enough to get the notice of the people at the next table.

Her cheeks burning, Kate said quietly, "Dad, I'm meeting someone for a drink. I'll let you and Sandra enjoy the champagne together."

Sandra's eyes were scanning the room in search of celebrities. Then she smiled brilliantly at a man who was raising his glass to her. "That's Majestic. His album is climbing the charts," she said breathlessly. As an afterthought she murmured, "Nice to meet you, Kate. Maybe, if I make it big, you can handle my money for me."

Doug Connelly laughed. "What a great idea. Then maybe she'll leave me alone." He added a little too hastily, "Just kidding. I'm proud of my brainy little girl."

If you only knew what your brainy little girl is up to, Kate thought. Torn between anger and concern, she retrieved her coat at the cloakroom, went outside into the cold and windy November evening, and signaled a passing cab.

Her apartment was on the Upper West Side, a condominium she had bought a year earlier. It was a roomy two-bedroom, with a bird's-eye view of the Hudson River. She both loved it and regretted that the previous owner, Justin Kramer, a wealth investment advisor in his early thirties, had been forced to sell it at a bargain price after losing his job. At the closing Justin had smiled gamely and presented her with a bromeliad plant similar to the one she had admired when she saw the apartment for the first time.

"Robby told me you admired my plant," he had said, indicating the real estate agent sitting next to him. "I took that one with me, but this one is a housewarming present for you. Leave it in that same spot over the kitchen window and it will grow like a weed."

Kate was thinking about that thoughtful gift, as she sometimes did when she walked into her cheery apartment and turned on the light. The furniture in the living room was all modern. The sofa, golden beige with deep cushions, invited napping. The matching chairs in the same upholstery had been built for comfort, with wide arms and headrests. Pillows that picked up the colors in the geometric patterns on the carpet added splashes of brightness to the décor.

Kate remembered how Hannah had laughed when she came to inspect the apartment after the new furniture was delivered. "My God, Kate," she had said. "You've grown up hearing Dad explain how everything in our house was a Connelly fine reproduction—and you have gone hog wild the other way."

I agreed, Kate thought. I was sick of Dad's spiel about perfect reproductions. Maybe someday I'll change my mind, but in the meantime I'm happy.

Perfect reproductions. Just thinking the words made her mouth go dry.

3

Mark Sloane knew that his farewell dinner with his mother might be difficult and tearful. It was close to the twenty-eighth anniversary of his sister's disappearance, and he was moving to New York for a new job. Since his graduation from law school thirteen years earlier he had been practicing corporate real estate law in Chicago. It was ninety miles from Kewanee, the small Illinois town where he had been raised.

In the years he had been living in Chicago, he had made the two-hour drive at least once every few weeks to have dinner with his mother. He had been eight years old when his twenty-year-old sister, Tracey, quit the local college and moved to New York to try to break into musical comedy. After all these years he still remembered her as if she were standing in front of him. She had auburn hair that cascaded around her shoulders, and blue eyes that were usually filled with fun but could turn stormy when she was angry. His mother and Tracey had always clashed over her grades at college and the way she dressed. Then one day when he went down for breakfast, he found his mother sitting at the kitchen table and crying. "She's gone, Mark, she's gone. She left a note. She's going to New York to become a famous singer. Mark, she's so young. She's so headstrong. She'll get in trouble. I know it."

Mark remembered putting his arms around his mother and

trying to hold back his own tears. He had adored Tracey. She would pitch balls to him when he was beginning in Little League. She would take him to the movies. She would help him with his homework and tell stories of famous actors and actresses. "Do you know how many of them came from little towns like this one?" she would ask.

That morning he had warned his mother. "In her letter Tracey said she would send you her address. Mama, don't try to make her come back, because she won't. Write and tell her it's okay and how happy you'll be when she's a big star."

It had been the right move. Tracey had written regularly and called every few weeks. She had gotten a job in a restaurant. "I'm a good waitress and the tips are great. I'm taking singing lessons. I was in an off-Broadway musical. It only ran for four performances, but it was so wonderful to be onstage." She had flown back home three times for a long weekend.

Then, after Tracey had lived in New York for two years, his mother received a call one day from the police. Tracey had disappeared.

When she did not show up for work for two days and did not answer her phone, her concerned boss, Tom King, who owned the restaurant, had gone to her apartment. Everything was in order there. Her date book showed that she had an audition scheduled for the day after she had disappeared, and had another scheduled at the end of the week. "She didn't show up for the first one," King told the police. "If she doesn't show up for the other one, then something's happened to her."

The New York police listed Tracey as a missing person all those years ago. As in "just another missing person," Mark thought as he drove up to the Cape Cod–style house where he had been raised. With its charcoal shingles, white trim, and bright red door, it was a cheery and welcoming sight. He pulled into the driveway and parked. The overhead lamp at the door shed light on the front steps. He knew his mother would leave it on all night as she had for nearly twenty-eight years, just in case Tracey came home.

Roast beef, mashed potatoes, and asparagus had been his response to his mother's request for what to prepare for his farewell dinner. The minute he opened the door, the heartwarming scent of the roasting beef told him that as usual she had made exactly what he wanted.

Martha Sloane came hurrying out from the kitchen, wiping her hands on her apron. Seventy-four years old, her once-slender figure now a solid size fourteen, her white hair with its natural wave framing her even features, she threw her arms around her son and hugged him.

"You've grown another inch," she accused him.

"God forbid," Mark said fervently. "It's hard enough for me to get in and out of cabs as it is." He was six feet six. He glanced over her head to the dining room table and saw that it was set with the sterling silver and good china. "Hey, this really is a send-off."

"Well, that stuff never does get used enough," his mother said. "Make yourself a drink. On second thought, make one for me, too."

His mother seldom had a cocktail. With a stab of pain, Mark realized that she was determined not to let the upcoming anniversary of Tracey's disappearance cloud the last dinner they would have for at least a few months. Martha Sloane had been a court stenographer and understood the long hours he would probably face in his challenging new corporate job.

It was only over coffee that she talked about Tracey. "We both know what date is coming up," she said quietly. "Mark, I watch that *Cold Case File* program on television all the time," she said quietly. "When you're in New York, do you think you could get the police to reopen the investigation into Tracey's disappearance? They have so many more ways to trace what happened to missing people these days, even people who disappeared years ago. But it's much more likely they'll do that if someone like you starts asking questions."

She hesitated, then went on. "Mark, I know I have had to give up hoping that Tracey lost her memory or was in trouble and had to hide. I believe in my heart that she is dead. But if I could just bring her body back and bury her next to Dad, it would give me so much peace. Let's face it. I probably have another eight or ten years if I'm lucky. I'd like to know that when my time comes, Tracey will be there with Dad." She blinked to try to keep her eyes from tearing. "You know how it is. I always was a sucker for 'Danny Boy.' I want to be able to kneel and say a prayer over Tracey's grave."

When they rose from the table, she said briskly, "I'd love a game of Scrabble. I just found some nice twisty new words in the dictionary. But your plane is tomorrow afternoon and knowing you, you haven't started to pack yet."

"You know me too well, Mom," Mark said smiling. "And don't be talking about having eight or ten years. Willard Scott will be sending you one of those hundredth-birthday cards." At the door, he hugged her fiercely, then took a chance and asked, "When you lock up are you going to turn off the porch light?"

She shook her head. "No, I don't think so. Just in case, Mark, just in case . . ."

She did not finish the sentence. It hung unsaid in the air. But Mark knew what it was. "Just in case Tracey comes home tonight."

4

On her last visit to the family's complex, Kate had been shocked to learn that the security cameras were still not working. "Kate, your father turned thumbs down on a new system," Jack Worth, the plant manager, said. "The problem is that everything around here needs to be upgraded. And the fact is we haven't got the kind of craftsmen that were working here twenty years ago. The ones that are around are prohibitively expensive because the market is shrinking, and our new employees just aren't the same. We're starting to get returns on the furniture regularly. I can't fathom why your father is so stubborn about selling this place to a developer. The land is worth at least twenty million dollars."

Then he'd added, ruefully, "Of course, if he does that, it would put me out of a job. With so many businesses closing, there isn't too much demand for a plant manager."

Jack was fifty-six, with the burly body of the wrestler he had been in his early twenties. His full head of strawberry-blond hair was streaked with gray. Kate knew he was a strict overall manager of the factory, showroom, and the three-story private museum in which every room was furnished with incredibly valuable antiques. He had started working for the company more than thirty years ago as an assistant bookkeeper and took over the management five years ago.

Kate had changed into a running suit, set the alarm for 3:30 A.M., and settled on the couch. She did not think that she would be able to fall asleep but she did. The only problem was that her sleep was uneasy and filled with dreams, most of which she could not remember, but they left her feeling troubled. The one fragment she could remember was the same one she'd had from time to time: A terrified child in a flowered nightgown was running down a long hall, away from hands that were reaching to grab her.

I didn't need that nightmare now, she thought, as she turned off the alarm and sat up. Ten minutes later, bundled in her black down jacket, a scarf over her head, she was in the parking lot of her building and getting into her fuel-efficient Mini Cooper sedan.

Even at this early hour there was still traffic in Manhattan, but it was moving swiftly. Kate went east through Central Park at Sixty-fifth Street and a few minutes later was driving up the ramp to the Queensboro Bridge. It only took ten minutes more to get to her destination. It was four fifteen, and she knew Gus would be coming any minute. She parked her car behind the Dumpster at the back of the museum and waited.

The wind was still strong and the car quickly became cold. She was about to turn the engine on again when dim headlights came around the corner and Gus's pickup truck came to a stop near her.

In two simultaneous motions they got out of their cars and hurried to the service door of the museum. Kate had a flashlight and the key in her hands. She turned the key in the lock and pushed open the door. With a sigh of relief, she said, "Gus, it's so great of you to come at this hour." Once inside she used the beam of her flashlight to see the security keyboard. "Can you believe that even the internal security system is broken?" Gus was wearing a woolen cap pulled down over his ears. A few strands of thinning hair had escaped the cap and were plastered on his forehead. "I knew it had to be important for you to want to meet at this hour," he said. "What's up, Kate?"

"I only pray God I'm wrong, Gus, but I have to show you something in the Fontainebleau suite. I need your expertise." She reached into her pocket, brought out another flashlight, and handed one to him. "Keep it pointed to the ground."

Silently they made their way to the back staircase. As Kate ran her hand over the smooth wood of the banister, she thought of the stories she had heard about her grandfather, who had come to the United States as a penniless but educated immigrant and eventually made a fortune in the stock market. At age fifty, he had sold his investment firm and fulfilled his lifetime dream of creating fine reproductions of antique furniture. He had bought this property in Long Island City and built a complex that consisted of a factory, a showroom, and a private museum to show the antiques he had collected over the years and now would copy.

At fifty-five he had decided that he wanted an heir and married my grandmother, who was twenty years younger than he. And then my father and his brother were born.

Dad had taken over the run of the business only a year before the accident, Kate thought. After that Russ Link ran it until he retired five years ago.

Connelly Fine Antique Reproductions had flourished for sixty years, but as Kate tried repeatedly to point out to her father, the current market for expensive reproductions was shrinking. She had not had the courage to also point out to him that his heavy drinking, neglect of the business, and increasingly erratic hours at the office were other factors in why it was time to sell. Let's face it, she thought. After my grandfather died, Russ ran everything.

At the bottom of the stairs Kate began to say, "Gus, it's the writing desk I want to show you—" But then suddenly she stopped, grabbed his arm, and said, "My God, Gus, this place is reeking with gas." Reaching for his hand, she turned and headed back to the door. They had gone only a few steps when an explosion sent the staircase crashing down upon them.

Afterward Kate vaguely remembered trying to brush away the blood that was pouring down her forehead and trying to pull Gus's inert body with her as she crawled to the door. The flames were licking the walls, and the smoke was blinding and choking her. Then the door had blown open and the gusty winds rushed into the hallway. A sheer savage instinct for survival made Kate grab Gus by the wrists and drag him out a few feet into the parking lot. Then she blacked out.

When the firemen arrived, they found Kate unconscious, bleeding profusely from a wound in her head, her clothing singed.

Gus was lying a few feet away, motionless. The weight of the fallen staircase left him with crushing injuries. He was dead.

5

The highlight of Wednesday's end-of-the-day senior staff meeting at Hathaway Haute Couturier was the announcement that Hannah Connelly would receive her own designer label for a number of garments to be shown at the summer fashion shows.

Hannah's first thought was to share the wonderful news with her sister Kate, but it was almost 7 P.M., and she remembered that Kate was meeting their father and his latest girlfriend for cocktails and dinner. Instead she called her best friend, Jessie Carlson, who had been at Boston College for two years with her before Hannah had switched to the Fashion Institute of Technology. Jessie had gone on to Fordham Law School.

Jessie whooped with delight at the news. "Hannah, my God, that's great. You'll be the next Yves St. Laurent. Meet me at Mindoro's in a half hour. My treat."

At seven thirty, the two were seated across from each other in a booth. The dining room of the popular restaurant was crowded and noisy, a tribute to the excellent cooking and friendly atmosphere.

Roberto, bald and round and smiling, their favorite waiter, poured the wine. "A celebration, girls?" he asked.

"You bet it is." Jessie raised her glass. "To the world's best designer, Hannah Connelly." Then she added, "Roberto, one of these days we'll both be saying, 'We knew her when.' "

Hannah touched Jessie's glass with hers, took a sip of wine, and only wished she could stop worrying about what might be going on between her father and Kate. Because of the way the family business was floundering, their relationship was going steadily downhill.

It was as though Jessie were reading Hannah's mind. "How's that handsome father of yours?" she asked as she dipped warm Italian bread into the oil she'd poured onto her plate. "Have you told him about this yet? I know he'll be thrilled for you."

Only Jessie could have put it with such an ironic tone in her voice. Hannah looked affectionately at her former classmate. Jessie's curly red hair was pulled back in a clip, then cascaded down past her shoulders. Her vivid blue eyes were sparkling and her milk-white skin was devoid of makeup. At five feet eleven inches she towered over Hannah even sitting across from her at the table. A born athlete, Jessie's body was slim and taut. Totally indifferent to fashion, she depended on Hannah when she needed to have something to wear for a special occasion.

Hannah shrugged. "Oh you know how excited he will be." She imitated her father's voice. " 'Hannah, that's wonderful. Wonderful!' And then he'll forget what I told him. And a few days later he'll ask how the designer business is going. The playboy of the Western world never did have much time for Kate or me, and the older he gets the less he has to do with us."

Jessie nodded. "I caught the tension the last time I had dinner with you guys. Kate let off a few zingers to your father."

Roberto was heading back to the table, menus in hand. "Do you want to order now or wait a few minutes?" he asked.

"Linguine with clam sauce and the house salad." It was Hannah's favorite pasta.

"Salmon, with tricolor salad," was Jessie's choice.

"I shouldn't have bothered to ask," Roberto said. He had been there for fifteen years and knew every customer's favorite meal.

When he was out of earshot, Hannah took another sip of wine and shrugged her shoulders. "Jessie, you've been around us since college. You've seen enough and heard enough to get the picture. The market has changed. People aren't buying fine reproductions of antique furniture that much anymore, and the fact is that our productions are no longer all that fine. Up until five years ago or so, we still had a few of the great craftsmen, but now they're all retired. After my grandfather died thirty years ago, my father took over the reins with the help of Russ Link, who had been my grandfather's right-hand man. But after the accident, my father took a long time to recover, and when he did, he had lost interest in the business. From what I gather, neither he nor his brother ever really got involved with the day-to-day workings of the business. I really think it's the old tale of the hardworking immigrant who wants his sons to have every advantage he didn't have."

Hannah realized it was good to talk so openly to the friend she could absolutely trust. "Jess, it's absolutely coming to a head. I can't understand it. Dad is getting more and more reckless with money. Can you believe that last summer he leased a yacht for a month? Fifty thousand a week! He's leasing yachts while the family ship is sinking. I wish to God he'd met someone and gotten married when we were young. Maybe a sensible woman could have kept him in bounds."

"I'll be honest. I've wondered about that. He was only thirty when your mother died and that's nearly twenty-eight years ago. Do you think he was so in love with her that he could never replace her?"

"I suppose she *was* the love of his life. I only wish I could remember her. How old was I? Eight months? Kate was only three. And of course it was a terrible tragedy. He lost my mother, his brother Connor, and four close friends. And he was at the helm of the boat. But I must say any guilt didn't keep him from having a succession of girlfriends or whatever you want to call them. But enough of the

family woes. Let's enjoy the dinner you're paying for and hope that
Kate and Dad and whoever-she-is are being civil to each other."

Two hours later, on the way home to her condo on Downing
Street in Greenwich Village, Hannah was again reflecting on the
past. I was just a baby when we lost our mother, she was thinking
as she got out of the cab. She thought of Rosemary "Rosie" Masse,
their nanny, who had retired to her native Ireland ten years ago.

God love Rosie. She raised us, but she always told us that she
wished Dad would get married again. "Marry a nice lady who will
love your two beautiful little girls and be a mother to them," was
her advice to Dad, Hannah thought with a faint smile, as inside her
apartment, she settled into her favorite chair and turned on the television and DVR to watch a few of the shows that she recorded.

The fatal fishing accident that had killed her mother, her uncle,
and four other people had happened because her father's boat hit a
cable between a tanker and a barge in the predawn darkness. They
were headed seventy miles out into the Atlantic to where tuna often
gathered at daybreak. Her father, Douglas Connelly, was the only
survivor. He was found lying unconscious and badly injured in a life
raft by a coast guard helicopter crew when the sun came up. He had
been hit in the head by debris of the sinking boat.

He wasn't totally an absentee father, Hannah mused as she fast-
forwarded through the commercials. It was just that he wasn't there
a lot—either traveling for business or just too busy with his social
life. Russ Link ran the business and Russ was a perfectionist. The
guys who worked there, like Gus Schmidt, weren't just craftsmen.
They were artists. Rosie lived with us on East Eighty-second Street
and was always there for summers and holidays when we came home
on school vacations. God knows Dad sent us to boarding schools as
soon as they'd take us.

Hannah was not sleepy and did not turn off the television until midnight. Then she undressed quickly and slipped between the covers at 12:20 A.M.

At 5 A.M. the phone rang. It was Jack Worth. "Hannah, there's been an accident—some kind of explosion at the plant. Gus Schmidt and Kate were there. God knows why. Gus is dead and Kate is in an ambulance on the way to Manhattan Midtown Hospital."

He anticipated her next question. "Hannah, I don't know why the hell she and Gus were in the museum at that hour. I'm on my way to the hospital. Should I call your father or will you?"

"You call Dad," Hannah said as she bolted out of bed. "I'm on my way. I'll see you there."

"Oh God," she prayed. "Don't let this be Kate's fault. Don't let it be Kate's fault. . . ."

6

Even before she started openly flirting with Majestic, Douglas Connelly had become thoroughly bored with Sandra. He knew that her story of being runner-up to Miss Universe was total fiction. He had looked her up on the Internet and learned that she had been runner-up in a local beauty contest in her hometown of Wilbur, North Dakota.

He had been faintly amused by her fantasizing until at dinner he had seen the scorn in Kate's face and knew she was contemptuous of him and his lifestyle.

He also knew that he deserved that contempt.

A favorite expression his own father used when he had a difficult decision to make ran constantly through his mind. *I feel as though I'm between the devil and the deep blue sea, and be damned to them both.* No matter how much I drink, I feel that way all the time, Doug thought as he sipped the last of the champagne.

Between the devil and the deep blue sea. It was a singsong refrain that he could not turn off.

"I like to go to places like this," Sandra was saying. "I mean you might meet someone who's casting a movie or something like that."

How much bleach does it take to get her hair that color? Doug wondered.

The maître d' was approaching with a fresh bottle of champagne. "Compliments to the beautiful lady from Majestic," he said.

Sandra gasped. "Oh my goodness."

As she leaped from the chair and hurried across the room, Douglas Connelly got up to slip out. "The usual tip," he said, hoping he wasn't slurring his words. "But be sure *that* bottle gets charged to Majestic or whatever he calls himself."

"Certainly, Mr. Connelly. Is your car outside?"

"Yes."

That's another thing that drives Kate nuts—my having a chauffeur, Doug thought as a few minutes later he slumped in his limo and closed his eyes. The next thing he knew, Bernard, his driver, was opening the door at his East Eighty-second Street building and saying, "We're here, Mr. Connelly."

Even with the doorman's arm guiding him through the lobby, it was an effort for Doug to keep his legs moving in the same direction. Danny, the elevator operator, took the key from Doug's hand after he had fumbled it out of his pocket. On the sixteenth floor, Danny escorted him to his apartment, unlocked and opened the door, and led him to the couch. "Why not rest here for a little while, Mr. Connelly?" he suggested.

Doug felt a pillow being placed under his head and the top button of his shirt being opened and his shoes being removed.

"Just a little under the weather," he mumbled.

"You're fine, Mr. Connelly. Your keys are on the table. Good night, sir."

"'Night, Danny. Thanks." Doug fell asleep before he could say anything else.

Five hours later he did not hear the constant ringing of the landline phone on a table only a few feet away from the couch or the equally insistent buzzing of the cell phone in his breast pocket.

Finally, in the waiting room reserved for families with patients in surgery, Hannah, her face ashen, put her cell phone away and folded her hands in her lap to keep them from trembling. "I'm not going to try him again," she said to Jack. "Let him sleep it off."

7

Douglas Connelly woke up at nine Thursday morning. He grunted and opened his eyes, momentarily disoriented. The last thing he remembered was getting into the car. Then blurry images formed in his mind. The doorman holding his arm . . . Danny taking the keys from him . . . Danny putting a pillow under his head.

The head that was splitting now.

Awkwardly, Doug sat up and swung his feet onto the floor. Leaning his hands on the coffee table for balance, he managed to pull himself up to a standing position. For a moment he waited until the room stopped spinning, then he made his way into the kitchen, where he took a half-empty bottle of vodka and a can of tomato juice from the refrigerator. He poured them half and half into a juice glass and gulped it down.

Kate was right, he thought. I shouldn't have bought that bottle of champagne last night. Another possibility pushed through the fog in his head. I've got to be sure that the bottle that jerk Majestic sent over to the runner-up beauty queen didn't end up on my bill.

Doug moved slowly into his bedroom, shedding his clothes with every step. It was only after he'd showered, shaved, and dressed that he bothered to check his phone messages.

At 2 A.M. Sandra had tried to reach him. "Oh, Doug, I feel terrible. I just went over to thank Majestic for the champagne and the sweet things he said about me, and he begged me to sit with him and his friends for just a minute. Before I knew it, the sos-men-elee, I mean whatever they call that guy who opens the wine, came over with the bottle Majestic had sent over and said you had to leave. I had a lovely time with you an—"

Connelly pressed the delete button before Sandra had finished speaking. He could see that the next message was from Jack, and the one after was from his daughter, Hannah. Well, at least *she* doesn't ride me about how I should sell the plant every time she talks to me, he thought.

When he realized that Jack's call had come in at 5:10 A.M. and Hannah's call twenty minutes later, he knew something was wrong. Blinking his eyes to try to focus and sound sober, his finger unsteady, he pushed the button to return the call.

Hannah answered on the first ring. In a monotone she told him about the explosion, about Gus and about Kate's severe injuries. "Kate just came out of surgery to relieve the pressure on her brain. I can't see her yet. I'm waiting to speak to her surgeon."

"The plant is gone!" Doug exclaimed. "Everything? You mean everything, the factory, the showroom, the museum, all the antiques?"

Hannah's voice unleashed her pent-up anger and heartbreak. "Didn't you get our calls? Your daughter may not survive!" she screamed. "If she does, she may be brain damaged. Kate may be dying . . . And you, her father, ask about your godforsaken business."

Her voice became icy. "Just in case you want to stop by, your daughter is in Manhattan Midtown Hospital. If you're sober enough to get here, ask for the post-op waiting room. You'll find me there praying that my only sister is still alive."

8

At six o'clock, as Lottie Schmidt was having coffee at her kitchen table and desperately worrying about why Gus had left to meet Kate Connelly at the ungodly hour of 4:30 A.M., the doorbell rang. When she answered the door and saw her minister and a policeman standing together on the porch, she almost fainted. Before they could say a word, she knew that Gus was dead.

The rest of the day passed in a haze of disbelief. She was vaguely aware of neighbors coming in and out and of talking to her daughter, Gretchen, on the phone.

Had Gretchen said that she would fly in from Minneapolis today or tomorrow? Lottie couldn't remember. Did she warn Gretchen not to be flaunting pictures of her beautiful home in Minnetonka? Lottie wasn't sure.

Lottie left the television on all day. She needed to see the video of the destruction of the plant, needed the comfort of knowing that at least Gus hadn't been burned to death.

Charley Walters, the director of Walters Funeral Home, had made the arrangements for most of the people in their congregation and was reminding her that Gus always said he wanted to be cremated. Later Lottie remembered that she responded to Charley by saying something like, "Well, he was almost cremated in that fire, but luckily was not."

Her neighbor and close friend, Gertrude Peterson, came by and urged her to have a cup of tea, a taste of muffin. The tea she could swallow, but she waved off the muffin.

Sitting hunched in the fireside chair in the living room, her small frame diminished by the chair's high back and wide seat, Lottie huddled under a blanket. The cop had told her that Kate Connelly had been gravely injured. Lottie had known Kate from the day she was born. She had mourned for the motherless little girls after the terrible accident their parents were in.

Oh God, she prayed. No matter what she's done, let her live. And forgive Gus. I told him he was making a mistake. I warned him. Oh God, please have mercy on him. He was a good man.

9

Jack Worth stayed with Hannah until Douglas Connelly reached the hospital. Jack found it hard to hide his contempt when he saw Connelly's bloodshot eyes. But his tone was deferential when he said, "Mr. Connelly, I can't tell you how sorry I am about this."

Doug nodded as he walked past him to go to Hannah. "What is the latest word about Kate?" he asked her quietly.

"Nothing more than what I told you. She's in a deep coma. They don't know if she'll make it and if she does, there may be brain damage." Hannah pulled back from her father's embrace. "There were people from the fire department here earlier. They took my number. They wanted to talk to Kate, but of course that was impossible. She and Gus were found just outside the back entrance to the museum after the explosion. Jack is afraid the police might think they set it off deliberately."

Pushing her father away, her tone low but furious, Hannah said, "Dad, the plant was losing money. Kate knew it. Jack knew it. You knew it. Why didn't you take that offer for the land? We wouldn't be sitting here right now if you had."

In the cab on the way to the hospital, Douglas Connelly had prepared himself for the question. Despite the throbbing headache that the early-morning drink and three aspirin had not been able to overcome, he forced himself to sound firm and authoritative as he answered.

"Hannah, your sister exaggerates the problems the business is having, and the land is worth a lot more than the offer we got for it. Kate simply wouldn't listen to reason." Without attempting to touch Hannah again, he walked across the small waiting room, sank into a chair, and buried his face in his hands. A moment later his muffled sobs shook his body.

That was when Jack Worth stood up. "I think it's better that you two are alone," he said. "Hannah, will you let me know if there is any change in Kate's condition?"

"Of course. Thanks, Jack."

For long minutes after he left, Hannah sat unmoving in the gray waiting room armchair. Her thoughts drifted as she studied her father sitting opposite her in the matching chair. His sobs quieted as suddenly as they had begun. He leaned his head back and closed his eyes.

I wonder if all the chairs in the waiting rooms are exactly like these, Hannah thought . . . Will Kate live? . . . If she does, will she be the same person? I can't imagine Kate not being just the way she always was . . . She had dinner with Dad last night. Did she give him any hint that she was meeting Gus at the museum?

It was a question she had to ask. "Dad, did Kate mention she was going to the museum this morning?"

Doug sat up, nervously clenched and unclenched his hand, then rubbed his forehead. "Of course she didn't tell me that, Hannah. But God help us, when she called me last week and started ranting again about selling the complex, she told me that she'd love to blow it up to kingdom come and be finished with it."

The last sentence was spoken just as a grave-faced doctor was opening the door of the waiting room.

10

Dr. Ravi Patel gave no sign that he had heard Doug Connelly's shocking outburst. Instead, ignoring Doug, he addressed Hannah. "Ms. Connelly, as I told you before we operated on your sister, she has a severe head injury and brain swelling. At this point we cannot know if she has suffered any permanent brain damage, and we won't know that until she comes out of the coma, which could be in a few days, or a month."

Her throat dry, her lips barely forming the words, Hannah asked, "Then you think she is going to live?"

"The first twenty-four hours are crucial. I would certainly say that you do not have to wait here. You're better off getting some rest yourself. I promise if there is any change I will—"

"Doctor, I want the best possible care for my daughter," Doug interrupted. "I want a consultation and private nurses."

"Mr. Connelly, Kate is in the intensive care unit. Later you may want private nurses, but now is not the time. Of course I will be happy to consult with any doctor you choose about her condition." Dr. Patel turned back to Hannah and verified her cell phone number. Then, with understanding in his eyes and manner, he said, "If Kate makes it through the next few days, she may have a long road to recovery. The best thing you can do is to begin to preserve your own strength."

Hannah nodded. "Can I see her?"

"You can certainly look in on her."

Doug took Hannah's arm as they followed the doctor out of the waiting room. "Nothing's going to happen to her," he said in a low voice. "Kate's tough. She'll come through this better than ever."

If she doesn't get arrested for arson and possibly even murder, Hannah thought. By now her anger at her father had faded into a kind of resignation. He certainly could not have anticipated that Dr. Patel would walk into the room just as he blurted out Kate's comment.

At the end of the long corridor Dr. Patel pushed the button for the heavy doors that opened into the intensive care unit. "Be prepared," he told them. "Kate's head is bandaged. She's on a breathing tube and has all kinds of wires attached to her."

Even with that warning Hannah was shocked to see the still figure of her sister on the bed. I guess I have to take Dr. Patel's word for it that it's Kate, she thought as she searched for anything that would help her recognize her. The hands on the bed were totally bandaged, and she remembered that when she first arrived at the hospital she had been told that Kate had suffered second-degree burns to her hands. The breathing tube covered most of her face, and there was no hint of Kate's blond hair escaping from the wrappings around her head.

Hannah bent down and kissed her sister's forehead. Was it Hannah's imagination, or could she detect a faint scent of the perfume Kate always wore? "I love you," Hannah whispered. "Don't leave me, Kate." She almost added, "You're all I've got," but managed not to say it.

Even though it's true, she thought sadly. We certainly haven't had much fathering over the years from a dad who always insisted, "Call me Doug." She stepped back, and it was her father's turn to lean over Kate's bed. "My little girl," he said, his voice trembling, "You've got to get better. You can't let us down."

With a final glance at Kate, they turned to go. At the door of the recovery room Dr. Patel once again promised to call if there was any change in Kate's condition.

At one thirty, when they were about to leave the hospital, to forestall any suggestion of having lunch Hannah said, "Dad, I'm going to the office. There are a few things I should do, and I'm much better off being busy than sitting home."

When they stepped onto the street, they found a media crush awaiting them.

"What is Kate Connelly's condition?" reporters demanded to know. "Why was she in the museum with Gus Schmidt at that hour of the morning? Did she tell you she was going there?"

"My daughter's condition is very serious. Please respect our privacy." A cab was dropping someone off at the curb. His arm around Hannah, Doug forced their way through the crowd and pushed Hannah into the backseat. He jumped in himself and pulled the door shut. "Get going," he snapped to the driver.

"My God!" Hannah exclaimed. "They're like a pack of vultures!"

"It's only the beginning," Douglas Connelly said grimly. "It's only the beginning."

11

Despite her father's urging to go home and get some rest, Hannah firmly insisted on being dropped off at her office across town on West Thirty-second Street. "The company is planning a press release to announce a new designer's line," she said. She did not mention that the new line would have her name on it.

At the corner of her office building, she opened the cab door and gave Doug a peck on the cheek. "I'll call you the minute I hear anything. I promise."

"Are you going back to the hospital tonight?"

"Yes. And unless the doctor calls and there's a reason to go earlier, I'll get there around seven."

The tap of the horn from the car behind them made Hannah realize that she was holding up the traffic. "I'll talk to you later," she said hurriedly as she stepped onto the sidewalk. The busy street, packed with pedestrians shoulder to shoulder and racks of clothes being ferried from one building to another, was a sight that Hannah usually loved, but today it offered no comfort to her. Though it was not raining, the raw, damp wind made her hurry into the building.

Luther, the security guard, was at the lobby desk. "How is your sister, Ms. Connelly?" he asked. After the media crush outside the hospital, Hannah had realized that the fire was breaking news and she needed to be prepared to answer questions about it and about Kate.

"She was gravely injured," she said quietly. "We can only pray that she will make it." She felt as though she could read Luther's mind. What was Kate doing in that place at that hour? Without giving him time to ask her anything else, Hannah moved quickly to the elevator. It was only when she got to her office and dealt with the surprised reactions of her fellow workers that she realized that no one had expected to see her today.

Farah Zulaikha, the company's head designer, tried to send her home. "We're putting off the announcement for a better time, Hannah," she said. "There's going to be a lot of publicity about the fire for at least a few days. Some people who live near the East River told me they could see the flames from their windows."

Hannah insisted on staying. She told her that it was better to be here than just sitting in the hospital or at her apartment. But once she was in her small and cluttered office with the door shut, she sat at her desk and buried her face in her hands. I don't know what to do, she thought. I don't know where to turn. If Kate doesn't make it, or if she lives but is brain damaged, she won't be able to defend herself if they try to say she was responsible for setting off the explosion.

How many times in the last year or so had Kate openly said that the plant should be closed and the property sold? All our friends knew it, Hannah thought. Kate and I each own 10 percent of the assets, but every quarter for two years we've been running at a loss. Thank God we had enough in dividends to buy our apartments when we did.

Did Kate use the words "blow it up" to anyone other than Dad?

The doctor heard him say that.

But why would she want to blow the whole place up with priceless antiques in it? It doesn't make any sense.

That thought gave Hannah a measure of comfort. But then, with a sinking heart, she remembered that there was a $20 million insurance policy on the antiques alone.

She had recently seen the video of a car racing down the highway with the driver twisting and turning to avoid a crash. The woman had made a call to 911 and was screaming, "I can't stop it! I can't stop it!"

That was the way Hannah's mind felt now, racing from one fearful possibility to the other. Suppose the explosion was an accident, and it was just a coincidence that Kate and Gus were there when it had occurred. Was that so impossible? Even at four thirty in the morning? But why would Kate have met Gus?

Five years ago Jack Worth said it was time to retire Gus, that it was clear that with the tremor in his hands and his increasingly poor vision, he simply couldn't do the job anymore. Gus had been angry and had gotten nasty even when Kate had insisted he receive a year's salary as a bonus. He and Kate remained good friends.

Oh God, there has to be a reasonable explanation. Kate would never commit a crime to get money. I know her too well. I can't believe that I'd even consider that possibility, Hannah thought. She pushed back her chair. What am I doing here? I have to go back to the hospital. I have to be there with her.

Hannah said good-bye to the others in the office with the simple statement, "I'll call you if anything changes." She had turned off her cell phone in the hospital and had forgotten to turn it on until now. She checked her messages. There were a dozen calls from their friends and from Kate's boss and coworkers. All of them expressed shock and concern. Three of the calls were from Jessie. "Hannah, call me," she had said.

I'll wait to call Jessie until I see Kate again, Hannah thought. Is it possible that it was just last night that Jessie and I had such a good time celebrating that I had my own label? Does that matter anymore? Does anything matter if Kate doesn't recover?

When Hannah got to the hospital she was told to go to the ICU waiting room, that Dr. Patel would meet her there. But when she opened the door, someone else was standing at the window, her back to Hannah. One glance at Jessie's flaming red hair and Hannah was able to release the fear that kept building up inside her.

A moment later, sobbing and shaking, she was enveloped in Jessie's arms.

12

Doug Connelly was not sure where he wanted to go after he dropped Hannah off. When she got out of the cab, it had pulled away from the curb and now the cabbie was asking, "Where to, sir?"

All Doug wanted was to go home and get a couple of aspirin and some coffee, but he wondered if he shouldn't go out to Long Island City to see the damage for himself. Would it seem strange for the owner not to show up when there was such a massive fire?

On the other hand, it would be better to go home and call for his own car. Or maybe he didn't really have to go right away, or at all. He gave the cabbie his address on East Eighty-second Street, then leaned back and closed his eyes. He was trying to calculate the appropriate move to make next.

Was it clear that the fire was deliberately set? Did it look as if Kate teamed up with Gus to set it? And did something go wrong and it went off too soon, before they could escape? Five years ago, when we made Gus retire, he was mighty nasty about it. The girls were always friendly with him. It wouldn't be impossible to make a case that he got her help to set some sort of explosion and then it went off sooner than they planned.

But where would that leave the insurance payout? If the insurance company can prove arson by a disgruntled member of the family, would that be an excuse for the insurance company not to pay?

Sure the land is valuable, but there is a $20 million policy on the antiques alone.

Well, no one could ever say I had anything to do with it. Doug took refuge in the knowledge that he had had too much to drink last night and plenty of witnesses to prove it. He vaguely remembered that Bernard, his driver, had helped him out of the car and that Danny, the elevator operator, had taken him into the apartment and made him lie down on the couch. If it came to that, they would testify about his condition and the all-night doorman would swear that he never left the building.

At least I'm in the clear, Doug comforted himself. If necessary we can start building a case against Gus. Especially if Kate doesn't pull through, he thought. But then he was ashamed to even consider that possibility.

The cab finally reached the door of his apartment building. The fare had come to twenty-two dollars. Doug peeled off two twenties from the bills in his wallet and shoved them into the opening between the front and back sections of the cab. "Keep the change."

That was something else that drove Kate crazy, he thought. "Dad, why do you find it necessary to give tips that are practically the price of the ride? If you think you're making a big impression, you're wrong."

Was it only last night that Kate had a sour look when he ordered the champagne? Seems like years ago. Ralph, the day doorman, was holding the door open for him. When he got out, the man's first question was, "How is your daughter, Mr. Connelly?"

The disapproving look on Kate's face from the night before was in Doug Connelly's mind when he said, "It's too soon to tell."

"There's a young lady waiting for you in the lobby, sir. She's been here for an hour."

"A young lady?" Startled, Doug walked swiftly to the door of the building. Just as swiftly Ralph was there to hold it open for him. Sandra was sitting upright on one of the armless canvas chairs in the modernistic lobby. She jumped up when she saw him.

"Oh, Doug. I'm so sorry. You must be in agony. How awful for you!"

"Ah, the beauty queen tears herself away from Majestic," Doug said. But then, as her hands reached out to massage his fingers and she kissed his cheek, the demons in his head began to retreat. Sandra was another witness as to where he was last night. He'd go over to the complex tomorrow, or the next day, or never . . . I don't want to see it, he thought.

He put his hand under her arm. "Let's go upstairs," he said.

13

When he knew he was going to move permanently to New York, Mark Sloane made some carefully considered decisions. He signed up with a well-recommended real estate agent and told her what he wanted. A roomy two-bedroom, two-bath condo in the Greenwich Village area. His law office was in the Pershing Square Building, opposite Grand Central Terminal, so the commute would be easy by subway or foot.

The furniture he had gathered in his post–law school days had seen better days. He decided to pitch it and start from scratch. It also gave him a chance to completely eliminate any traces of the several ladies along the way who had been more than willing to move in with him.

The real estate agent had introduced him to a decorator who had helped him select a comfortable couch and chairs, a coffee table and end tables for the living room, a bed, dresser, and lounge chair for the bedroom, and a small table and two chairs that fit perfectly below the unusual luxury of a kitchen window.

Mark had shipped the bulk of his clothes, his bookcases, books, the native art he had collected over the years, and the hand-woven rug in vivid shades and intricate designs he had bought in India.

"The rest we'll fill in as I get the feel of the place," he had told the decorator, who had been all too anxious to plan window treatments and accessories.

He left Chicago that Thursday morning in a heavy snowstorm. His plane was three hours delayed in taking off. Not an auspicious start, he thought as he disembarked into the gloomy late afternoon at LaGuardia Airport. But then as he waited for the luggage at the carousel, he acknowledged that he was glad to be here in this place at this time. The job he'd been in for the past five years had lost its challenge.

He planned on Skypeing with his mother regularly. That way he wouldn't have to take her word for it that she was "just fine." And he had plenty of old friends in New York who were fellow graduates of Cornell. Time for a new beginning.

And time for something else to be resolved, he thought, as he reached down and with an easy movement lifted his one heavy suitcase from the carousel. With fellow passengers who also had been fortunate enough to have their bags among the first to come tumbling down the chute, he made his way to the cab stand outside and stood patiently in line. His height had made him a star basketball player in college. His hair had once been auburn like his sister Tracey's, but it had darkened to a deep brown shade. His somewhat irregular features, caused by a badly broken nose during a game, were complemented by warm brown eyes and a strong mouth and chin. To strangers, Mark Sloane gave the immediate impression of being the kind of guy you'd like to know better.

Finally he was in a cab and on the way to the apartment. On previous visits to New York City, Mark had observed that many drivers talked on their hands-free cell phones and were not likely to strike up a conversation. This cabbie was different. He had a classic New York accent and wanted to talk. "Business or tourist?" he asked.

"Actually as of today I'm a resident," Mark answered.

"No kidding. Welcome to the Big Apple. I don't see how anyone who comes here would ever want to go home. Always something going on. Day and night. I mean it's not like living in some burb where the most exciting thing you can do is watch somebody get a haircut."

Mark was sorry he'd let himself in for a dialogue. "I've been living in Chicago. Some people consider that a pretty good town, too."

"Yeah. Maybe."

Fortunately the traffic got heavier and the driver turned his attention to it. Mark found himself wondering what his sister Tracey's reactions were when she first arrived in New York. She hadn't flown, probably because she didn't want to spend the money. Instead she'd come by bus and moved into a YWCA rooming house before finally getting the apartment where she was living when she disappeared.

I'll get settled at the job quickly, he thought, and then figure out how I can get the detectives interested in her case again. I guess the best place to start is the district attorney's office in Manhattan. Those detectives were the ones who investigated the case. I have the name of the lead guy, Nick Greco. I should be able to track him down.

With his plan set, he tipped the driver generously when he arrived at his newly purchased apartment on Downing Street, took his shiny new keys from his wallet, let himself into the vestibule, and then entered the lobby. It was just a few long strides to the elevator, where two attractive women were waiting, one tall with vivid red hair, the other dark-haired, small-boned, and with heavy sunglasses covering most of her face. It was obvious she was crying.

The redhead had certainly noticed Mark's suitcase. "If you're here for the first time, you'll notice that the elevator is slow," she told him. "When they renovated these old buildings, they didn't bother to replace the elevators."

Mark had the feeling that she was making conversation to divert his attention from her tearful friend.

There was a ring at the vestibule door and in a moment, the only apartment door in the lobby opened. The superintendent, whom Mark had met before, stepped out and let two men in. Mark could clearly hear the voice of one of them. "We have an appointment with a Ms. Hannah Connelly." Mark recognized the voice of authority, and he instinctively felt that even though neither of the men was in uniform, both were in law enforcement.

"She's right there," the superintendent said, pointing to the young woman with the dark glasses. "She must have just come in."

"Oh, for heaven's sake, they're here already. You didn't even get a chance to get something to eat," the redhead said, her voice low.

The other young woman's voice sounded faltering and resigned as she said, "Jessie, whether they come now or later, there's no difference. Whether they believe it or not, I can't add a single thing to what I told them this morning."

What is this about? Mark wondered as the elevator door opened and side by side, he, the two women, and the two men got into it.

14

Fire Marshals Frank Ramsey and Nathan Klein had been on duty at their desks in Fort Totten in Queens when they received the early-morning phone call about the fire at the Connelly complex in Long Island City. They had rushed to it to find squads from two companies battling the flames. The fact that two people had barely escaped the building after the explosion suggested that others might have been trapped inside, even at that unusual hour. At that time they could not tell if Gus Schmidt had managed to crawl out on his own before he died. When they learned that the one survivor had been rushed to Manhattan Midtown Hospital, they immediately followed, hoping to be able to interview her. She was already in surgery, and her sister and the plant manager had no idea why she had gone to the complex.

The marshals had returned to the fire and then changed into the gear they always carried in their car. After they had battled the flames for four hours, the fire was finally extinguished and it became clear that no one else had been in any of the buildings. The back wall of the museum had been the first to collapse, but by then the searchers had gotten out of the conflagration.

Ramsey and Klein, their heavy boots protecting them from the heat of the scorched remains of the complex, methodically searched for the source of the fire.

The first eyewitness, a watchman from a neighboring warehouse, had come running over at the sound of the explosion and verified that the flames were originally shooting straight up from the museum. The fact that its back wall had collapsed was the second clue that it was there that the fire had started.

Next was the painstaking search for evidence of causation, including possible arson.

By eleven o'clock on Thursday morning, Marshals Ramsey and Klein had found a partially unscrewed gas pipe that had leaked gas into the museum. The wall that had fallen had covered the remains of the charred outlet that had the wires exposed. The two veteran fire marshals did not need to look any further. The fire was of an incendiary nature and had been deliberately set.

Before they could finalize their crime report, Jack Worth, the plant manager, had arrived on the scene.

15

When he drove into what had been the Connelly complex, Jack Worth was shocked at the amount of destruction. Even though it was a cold, damp day, a crowd of onlookers, kept at a distance by lines of yellow tape, were watching as firefighters continued to walk through the rubble, their heavy boots protecting them from the heat of the cluttered ruins. The hoses they were holding sent forceful gallons of water onto the smoldering pockets throughout the wreckage. Jack pushed his way to the front and caught the attention of a policeman who was on guard to keep anyone from slipping through the ropes. When Jack identified himself, he was taken to see one of the fire marshals, Frank Ramsey.

Ramsey did not waste his words. "I know we spoke to you at the hospital and I'd like to verify a few of the statements you made. How long have you been working here?"

"Over thirty years. I have an accounting degree from Pace University and was hired as an assistant bookkeeper." Anticipating further questions, he explained, "Old Mr. Connelly was still alive then, but he died shortly after I started to work here. It was two years before the boating accident that took the lives of one of his sons and his daughter-in-law as well as four other passengers. By then, even though I was pretty young, I was head accountant."

"When were you put in charge of the whole operation?"

"Five years ago. There was a big turnover then. The former plant manager retired. His name is Russ Link. He lives in Florida now. I can give you his address there. Over the past ten years our craftsmen have been retiring. Gus was the last to go, just as I took over, and quite frankly it had to be forced. He simply wasn't capable of doing the work anymore."

"Do you have an outside accounting firm?"

"Absolutely. They can verify that the business was going downhill."

"Is the business insured?"

"Of course it is. There is a separate policy for the antiques."

"How much is that policy?"

"Twenty million dollars."

"Why weren't the security cameras working?"

"As I told you, the company hasn't been doing well lately. As a matter of fact, we're losing money hand over fist."

"You mean you couldn't afford to fix the security cameras?"

Jack Worth had been sitting in a folding chair facing Marshal Ramsey in the back of a mobile police van. For a moment he broke the eye contact he had been making with Ramsey, then said, "Mr. Connelly was looking into several security systems, but didn't want to commit to one of them yet. He said to hold off because he was expecting to sell the business as soon as he got the right offer for the land."

"And, once again: Did you know that Kate Connelly was meeting the former employee, Gus Schmidt, here early this morning?"

"Absolutely not," Jack said forcefully.

"Mr. Worth, we will be speaking to you at length again. Do you have a business card?"

Jack fished in the pocket of his trousers. "I'm sorry. I ran out without my wallet." He hesitated and then added, "Which means I'm not carrying my driver's license. I'd better not get stopped by a cop on my way home."

Frank Ramsey did not respond to the attempted touch of levity. "Please leave your address and phone number or numbers with me. You're not planning to leave the area, are you?"

"Absolutely not." Now Jack Worth bristled. "You have to understand, all of this is overwhelmingly shocking to me. I've worked for this company for over thirty years. Gus Schmidt was my friend. I've watched Kate Connelly grow up. Now Gus is dead and Kate may not make it. How do you think I feel?"

"I am sure that you're very upset."

Jack Worth knew what the fire marshal was thinking. As plant manager, Jack should have insisted that the complex be protected by security cameras. And Ramsey was right. But wait till this guy gets a handle on Doug Connelly, he thought grimly. Ramsey might get some idea of the kind of boss I was dealing with.

A policeman was handing Jack a pad and pen. He scrawled his name, address, and cell phone number on the paper and handed it over to the cop and turned abruptly. They can't charge me for not fixing equipment, he thought, as, hands in pockets, he made his way back to his car.

The curiosity seekers were beginning to disperse. The few burning embers were smaller and scattered.

Jack's car was a three-year-old BMW. He had been planning to buy a new one, but that couldn't happen now. He didn't have a job and he'd have to be careful about appearances.

It wasn't even one o'clock in the afternoon, but he felt as though it were midnight. He'd gone to bed late and then the phone call had come about the plant. Less than three hours' sleep, he thought, as he drove toward his home in nearby Forest Hills. The traffic was heavy and he realized he had had nothing to eat since last night. When he got home, he'd fix something for himself and take a nap.

But a half hour later, when he was sitting at the breakfast counter in the kitchen his ex-wife had so lovingly planned fifteen years ago, a beer and ham-and-cheese sandwich in front of him, his phone rang. It was Gus Schmidt's daughter, Gretchen, calling from Minneapolis. "I'm at the airport," she said, her voice trembling. "Jack, you have got to promise me that when the police start digging into my father's past, you will stand up for him and say you never believed he meant it when he said he'd like to blow up the plant."

Jack reached for the beer as he promised with a fervent tone, "Gretchen, I will tell anyone who asks that Gus was a fine, good man who is the unfortunate victim of circumstances."

16

After questioning Jack Worth in the mobile unit, Marshals Frank Ramsey and Nathan Klein called the people who had dialed 911 when they heard the neighborhood explosion. They also called Lottie Schmidt and spoke to some of Kate's coworkers.

Then they went to the local police station to make their crime report that the fire was of an incendiary nature and involved the death of Gus Schmidt. They spent the rest of the afternoon at the scene of the fire, searching for any further evidence they might find.

The next person they wanted to talk with was Hannah Connelly. They called her on her cell phone. She told them that she would be leaving the hospital shortly, and they could meet her at her apartment. They stopped to pick up Gus Schmidt's clothing from the medical examiner for testing, then headed to Downing Street. That was when they caught Hannah at the elevator.

They did not stay long in her apartment. "Ms. Connelly, I know how distraught you were this morning, and we didn't want to burden you. But now we'd like to go over some facts with you," Ramsey began. "You said that you did not know that your sister was meeting Mr. Schmidt in the museum early this morning?"

"No, she didn't mention it to me. I knew that she was meeting my father for dinner last night. Kate and I talk almost every day, but I was busy at work yesterday and I knew she was going out in the early evening."

"A few of your sister's coworkers mentioned that she was concerned and quite vocal about the fact that the family business was going downhill and should be sold."

Jessie had made Hannah a cup of tea, then sat next to her on the couch, her manner protective. She had not intended to butt in, but now her instincts as a criminal lawyer were warning her that the way the investigators were zeroing in indicated they believed that Kate may have deliberately set the fire.

Jessie addressed Nathan Klein. "Marshal Klein, it seems clear that Hannah did not know of her sister's plan to go to the complex. Knowing Kate, I am very sure there is a perfectly reasonable explanation for her being there, but I do think you should defer any further questions until Ms. Connelly has a chance to rest."

Klein was clearly unimpressed. "I don't think it will burden Ms. Connelly too much"—he nodded in Hannah's direction—"to answer a few more questions while her memory is still fresh about the circumstances leading up to the explosion that took a person's life."

Jessica looked at Hannah. "I don't agree. I am an attorney and a close friend of both Hannah and Kate Connelly. I detect an air of both suspicion and accusation." She looked at Hannah. "May I put myself forward as Kate's legal representative at least for the present, Hannah?"

Hannah looked at Jessie, her mind a kaleidoscope. When she had gone back to the hospital this afternoon, she had been thankful Jessie was there. The doctor had taken both of them in again to see Kate.

"Is she totally unresponsive, or is there some level of consciousness?" Hannah had asked Dr. Patel.

"We have her heavily sedated," the doctor said.

She and Jessie had stayed for a few more hours. When they were almost about to leave, Douglas Connelly had arrived again, this time accompanied by a young woman. "Sandra met Kate last night," Doug explained. "She wanted to come with me to see her."

"You are not bringing a stranger in to look at my sister." Hannah remembered that her voice had become high-pitched.

"I don't want to intrude," Sandra had said, her voice soothing.

Doug had gone alone into the ICU. After a moment Hannah had decided to follow him. She watched carefully as he bent over Kate. It appeared her sister's lips were moving. Then as her father straightened up, Hannah saw the way the color was draining from his face. "Dad, did she say anything that you could make out?" Hannah had asked, frantic to hear that Kate was able to communicate.

"She said, 'I love you, Daddy, I love you.' "

Something inside Hannah made her sure her father was not telling the truth. But why would he lie?

Jessie was looking at Hannah.

What was the question Jessie asked me? Hannah thought. About representing her and Kate. "Of course, I want my trusted friend Jessie to represent my sister in this situation," she said.

"Then as Kate Connelly's lawyer, I must insist that there be no attempt to see her at the hospital or talk to her unless I am present."

The fire marshals left soon after that, saying they would be in touch. Relieved for the moment, she and Jessie sent out for sandwiches from the local deli. Then they went back to the hospital. Kate, deep in a coma, did not speak again.

While at the hospital, Hannah called Lottie Schmidt and gave her her heartfelt condolences, and promised to be at the services for Gus. Lottie said they would take place the next afternoon.

After that Hannah insisted that Jessie take her own cab home.

"You've had a long enough day with the Connellys," she insisted. Then she hailed herself a cab.

Finally back home in her apartment, Hannah went straight to bed. She left her cell phone on the night table with the volume set to the highest pitch. She knew she needed to sleep but was afraid she might miss a call. Instead for over an hour she lay there, her eyes closed, her mind demanding to know what Kate might have said that made her father react like that. What was the expression that she had seen on his face?

As she drifted off to sleep, the answer came. Fear. Dad had been terrified by what Kate whispered to him.

Was it that she admitted she had set the fire?

17

Kate was trapped in a well. There was no water in it but somehow she knew that it was a well. Her whole body was weighted down and her head was detached from her neck. Sometimes she heard the rustle of voices, some of them familiar.

Mommy. Kate tried to pay attention. Mommy kissing her goodbye and promising that someday she could go out at night on the boat, too.

Daddy kissing her good-bye. "I love you, Baby Bunting."

Did that happen? Or was it a dream?

Hannah's voice, "Hang in there, Kate. I need you."

The nightmare. The flowered nightgown and running down the hall. It was very important to remember what happened. She was almost there. For a moment she had remembered. She was sure of it.

But then everything was dark again.

18

⸙

The fire marshals did not catch up with Doug Connelly until later Thursday evening.

They called the hospital and learned that he had made a second visit there in the late afternoon. He had been accompanied by a young woman and had gone in with his daughter Hannah for a brief visit with Kate in the ICU.

The marshals had grabbed something to eat, then had gone to Doug's apartment building and waited, but he did not show up until after nine o'clock, with the young woman, Sandra, on his arm.

He invited them upstairs and promptly prepared a drink for himself and Sandra. "I know when you're on duty you can't have any," he said.

"That's right." Neither Ramsey nor Klein was unhappy to see the already slightly drunk man pour himself a strong scotch. *In vino veritas*, Ramsey thought. In scotch even more truth may come out.

As they sat down Sandra explained, "Poor Doug completely fell apart after seeing Kate. So I insisted we go out to dinner. He hardly had a bite all day."

Unmoved, Ramsey and Klein began to question Douglas Connelly. His voice was slurred and hesitant as he groped to explain his differences with Kate. "The business hasn't been doing that well, but I tried to tell Kate that's not a big problem. Think how much all that land was worth in Long Island City thirty years ago. Peanuts compared to now. Long Island City is changing. People are moving there. They finally figured out how close it is to Manhattan. The arty types are flocking there, just like they settled in Williamsburg. Not long ago you could live in Williamsburg for next to nothing. Now it's hot. Long Island City is the same way. Sure we have an offer on the land. Take it now and we'd be kicking ourselves in five years for all the money we lost."

"But it seems from what others have said that your daughter Kate felt the company was losing money hand over fist," Ramsey said.

"Kate's stubborn. Even when she was a kid she wanted everything now . . . this minute . . . not tomorrow."

"Do you think that in her frustration she might have teamed up with Gus Schmidt to destroy the complex?"

"Kate would never do that!"

To both marshals, Doug's blustery tone was masking fear. They were sure they knew what he was thinking. If a member of the family set the fire and would benefit from the insurance, it was certain that the insurance company would refuse to pay the claim.

They switched to questions about Kate's relationship with Gus. "We understand that she was very sympathetic to him when he was forced to retire."

"Talk to the plant manager, Jack Worth. Gus's work was getting downright sloppy. Everybody else his age had retired. He just didn't want to give up. With all his other benefits, we even threw in a full year's salary. He still wasn't satisfied. He was a bitter old man."

"Wasn't it at Kate's insistence that he got that year's salary?" Ramsey shot the question at Doug.

"She may have suggested it."

"Mr. Connelly, some other of your employees have come forth to volunteer what they know. Gus Schmidt was quoted as saying that there's nothing he wouldn't do for Kate . . ."

"Certainly Gus was very fond of Kate," Doug replied.

At the end of the questioning, as they left, the marshals, even though they were keeping an open mind, had a gut feeling that Kate had found a willing partner to help her do what she had told several people she wanted to do.

Blow up the entire Connelly complex.

19

After leaving Douglas Connelly, Frank Ramsey and Nathan Klein decided to call it a day. They drove back to Fort Totten, called their supervisor, completed their reports, then each left for home. They had been on the job almost twenty-four hours.

Ramsey lived in Manhasset, a pretty suburban town on Long Island. He sighed with relief when he turned into his own driveway and pressed the garage opener. He was used to bad weather but the hours outside on a cold, damp, windy day had penetrated even his warm outerwear. He wanted to get into a hot shower, put on some comfortable clothes, and have a drink. And much as he missed his son Ted, who was a freshman at Purdue University, he wouldn't mind just being with Celia tonight, he thought.

No matter how long you're in the business, it still affected you when a dead man was taken to the medical examiner's office and a young woman rushed away in an ambulance, he thought.

Frank Ramsey was a solidly built six-footer. At forty-eight, although he weighed nearly two hundred pounds, his body was strong and muscular thanks to meticulous workouts. Judging from the men in his family, he knew that genetically he would probably be white-haired by the age of fifty, but to his surprise and pleasure, his hair was pretty much still salt-and-pepper. His manner was naturally easygoing but that changed swiftly if he spotted any incompetence among his underlings. In the department he was universally well liked.

His wife, Celia, had heard the car pulling into the garage and had the door to the kitchen open for him. She had had a double mastectomy five years earlier and even though her doctor had now given her a clean bill of health, Frank was always fearful that one day when he opened the door, she might not be there. Now the sight of her, with her light brown hair caught in a ponytail, a sweater and slacks enhancing her slender body, a welcoming smile on her face, made a lump form in his throat.

If anything ever happened to her . . . He pushed away the thought as he kissed her.

"You've had some day," she observed.

"You could call it that," Frank confirmed as he inhaled the welcoming scent of pot roast coming from the Crock-Pot. It was the meal Celia often prepared when there was a major fire and she knew that there was no way of telling when her husband would get home. "Give me ten minutes," he said. "And I'll have a drink before I eat."

"Sure."

Fifteen minutes later he was sitting side by side with her on the couch facing the fireplace in the family room. He took a sip of the vodka martini he was holding and fished out the olive. The television was set to a news station. "They've been showing the fire all day," Celia said, "and they've dug up the coverage of the boating accident that killed Kate Connelly's mother and uncle years ago. Have you heard any more about how she's doing?"

"She's in a coma," Frank said.

"It's such a shame about Gus Schmidt. I met him a couple of times, you now."

At her husband's surprised expression, she explained: "It was when I was in chemotherapy at Sloan-Kettering. His wife, Lottie, was in treatment, too. I'm so sorry for her. It was obvious they were really close. She must be devastated. As I remember, they have a daughter, but she lives in Minnesota somewhere."

She paused, then added, "I think I'll try and find out what the funeral arrangements are. If there's a service, I'd like to go to it."

That's just like Celia, Frank thought. If there's a service, she will go to it. Most people think about doing something like that but never follow through. He took another sip of the martini, totally unaware that his wife's coincidental acquaintance with Lottie Schmidt would unlock one aspect of the investigation surrounding the destruction of the Connelly Fine Antique Reproductions plant.

20

Mark Sloane's curiosity about his neighbor was quickly satisfied the next day when he picked up Friday's morning newspapers and stopped for coffee and a bagel at the counter of a coffee shop on his way to the office. The burning complex was on the first page of the papers and on the inside pages he saw a picture of Hannah Connelly outside the hospital, being rushed to a taxi by her father. Ironic, he thought. The firm he left and the one where he was now dealt with corporate real estate. He had seen his share of buildings conveniently being burned down when they became a financial liability.

He remembered the time Billy Owens, a restaurant owner in Chicago, had collected on a large insurance policy after a second suspicious fire, and an investigator for the insurance company had sarcastically suggested that the next time Billy needed to unload some property he should try flooding it.

As he bit into a bagel, Mark read that the widow of the dead man, Gus Schmidt, was adamant that Kate Connelly, the daughter of the owner, had been the one to make the predawn appointment at the complex. But according to the papers, Schmidt had been a disgruntled former employee of the firm. Mark's analytical mind toyed with the idea that Schmidt might have been a logical person to involve if someone wanted to burn the complex down. There was a picture of Kate Connelly in the paper. She was a stunning blond.

In any case, it was an interesting coincidence that the sister lived on the floor below him. He hadn't gotten a good look at her because of her dark glasses and the way she turned away from him, probably embarrassed to be seen crying. But it was clear that she didn't resemble her sister at all. The friend who was with her with the blazing red hair and fiercely protective attitude was the one who had made the strongest impression on him.

As he accepted a second cup of coffee from the waitress at the counter, he turned his attention to his own situation. He'd been back and forth from Chicago to the new office enough times in the previous weeks to feel comfortable with his coworkers. So as soon as possible, he intended to attempt to reopen Tracey's missing person's file. It's not just Mom, he thought. Tracey has never been out of my mind, either. When that woman who'd been missing since she was fourteen escaped captivity twelve or fourteen years later, I wondered if maybe Tracey was possibly being held somewhere against her will.

She'd be fifty this month. But she hasn't aged in my mind, he thought. She'll always be twenty-two.

He paid his bill and walked out onto the street. At 8 A.M., Greenwich Village was bustling with people heading for the subway. Even though it was cold, there was no feel of rain in the air and Mark was happy to stretch his legs and walk to work. He did not officially start at the new office until Monday, but going there today would give him a chance to settle early. On the way he thought about the detective who his mother had said had worked so hard on Tracey's case. Nick Greco. Mom said he was in his late thirties then, so he'd be in his sixties now. He's sure to be retired, he thought. I can always try to Google him.

21

On Friday morning, a clerk at the medical examiner's office was set to release the body of Gus Schmidt to Charley Walters, the funeral director whom Lottie had chosen to handle the arrangements. "If it's any comfort for the widow," the clerk said, "death was instantaneous when the staircase collapsed. He never felt the burns on his hands when he was dragged outside."

Gus's body was to be taken to the funeral parlor for one day of visitation that afternoon, and then cremated the next day.

The clerk, a slightly built thirty-something lab technician, was new on the job and loving the excitement that frequently accompanied it. He had voraciously devoured the story of the explosion that had destroyed the Connelly complex and pondered the reason why Gus Schmidt and Kate Connelly had been there in the predawn hour just as the fire started. Knowing he had no business asking the question, his curiosity still got the better of him. "Did you hear why Schmidt and the daughter were there?"

Recognizing a fellow gossip, Walters replied, "Nobody's said anything. But everyone knows Gus Schmidt never got over being fired."

"A couple of fire marshals were here yesterday to pick up his clothes. When they have a suspicious fire, the first thing they do is gather the clothes of any victims for evidence."

"Whenever we have a funeral with a fire involved, there's always an investigation," Walters said. "Some of them are caused by acts of God, like lightning. Some of them are accidents, like kids playing with matches. We had one where a three-year-old did that. He ran outside but his grandmother ended up dying of smoke inhalation looking for him. Or you get someone who can't sell a house or a business property and the insurance looks good to them. Rumor is that Connelly's business was on the way downhill."

Walters realized that he was talking out of turn and that it would be prudent to sign the necessary papers to obtain the release of the body of Gus Schmidt and be on his way.

22

After a sleepless night, Lottie Schmidt dozed briefly in the early hours on Friday morning. The last time she looked at the clock it had been 4:05, just the time that Gus had left only yesterday. Gus had never been a demonstrative man. He had bent over and kissed her good-bye. Did he have a premonition that he would never come back home? she wondered.

That was the last thought she had before she mercifully drifted off. Later she was awakened by the sound of the shower running in the bathroom. For one hopeful moment she thought it was Gus there, but then she realized that of course it was Gretchen, who had arrived from Minneapolis late the afternoon before.

Lottie sighed and with a weary gesture sat up in bed. She fumbled for her ten-year-old robe and then stuffed her feet into her slippers. The robe had been a Christmas present from Gus. He'd bought it at Victoria's Secret. Lottie remembered thinking that when she saw the package she hoped that Gus hadn't wasted his money on silly skimpy nightgowns that she'd never wear. Instead she had found inside the wrapping a pretty blue-patterned robe with a satin exterior and cozy warm lining. And it was washable.

They didn't make those robes anymore, but as soon as the weather turned cold she trotted this one out and loved to slip into it first thing in the morning. Both she and Gus were early risers, never later than seven thirty. Gus usually was up ahead of her and had the coffee ready when she came down.

He'd have the papers collected, too, and they'd eat in contented silence. Lottie always got to read the *Post* first. Gus liked the *News*. They both had orange juice and cereal with a banana because the doctor had said it was the best way to start the day.

But there wouldn't be any coffee waiting for her today. And she'd have to go out to the end of the driveway to pick up the newspapers. The guy who delivered them wouldn't come down and leave them at the side door, because he didn't like to back out onto the street.

The shower was still running when Lottie passed the bathroom. Gus would have had a fit that Gretchen's using up so much hot water, she thought. He always hated waste.

As she walked down the stairs, she tried to push back her worry that Gretchen would be tempted to show neighbors and friends pictures of her expensive house in Minnesota during the viewing for Gus. People who know us would wonder how Gretchen could afford such a lavish place. Divorced and childless, after working for the telephone company for years, Gretchen had become a masseuse. And a good one, Lottie thought loyally. Even if she didn't make a lot of money, she had a nice circle of friends out there. She's active in the Presbyterian Church. But she doesn't think. She's a talker. All she needed to say was . . .

Lottie did not finish the thought. Instead she went into the kitchen, started the coffeepot, and opened the door.

At least it wasn't raining. She walked down to the edge of the driveway and, bending slowly to keep her balance, picked up the three newspapers, the *Post*, the *News*, and the *Long Island Daily*, and carried them back to the house.

Inside she took off the protective wrappings and then unrolled them. All three had pictures on the front page of the Connelly fire. With trembling fingers she opened the *Post* to page three. There was a picture of Gus under the headline FIRE VICTIM A DISGRUNTLED EX-EMPLOYEE OF CONNELLY FINE ANTIQUE REPRODUCTIONS.

23

"It's not for nothing you have red hair" was the oft-repeated comment of Jessica's father, Steve, in her growing years. At twenty-one Steve Carlson had graduated from the police academy in New York and spent the next thirty years rising through the ranks until he retired as a captain. He had married his high school sweetheart, Annie, and when it became obvious that the large family they had planned was not to happen, he made his only offspring, Jessica, his companion at sports events.

As close as he and Annie were, his wife vastly preferred reading a book to sitting out in the hot or cold and watching any kind of game.

At age two Jessica had been on Steve's shoulders at Yankee Stadium in the summer and Giants Stadium in the fall. She had been a star soccer goalie in school and was a fiercely competitive tennis player.

Her decision to go into law had thrilled her parents, although when she chose to become a criminal defense attorney, her father was less than pleased. "Ninety percent of the ones who are indicted are guilty as sin," was his comment. Her answer: "What about the other ten percent and what about extenuating circumstances?"

Jessie had worked for two years as a public defender in criminal court in Manhattan, then accepted a job offer from a growing firm specializing in criminal defense practice.

On Friday morning Jessie went into the office of her boss, Margaret Kane, a former federal prosecutor, and told her that she had taken on the job of defending Kate Connelly against a potential criminal charge of arson. "It may not stop there," she told Kane. "The way I see it, they may try to say Kate was an accessory to Gus Schmidt's death."

Margaret Kane listened to the details of the case. "Go ahead," she said. "Send the family the usual contract and retainer fee." Then she added dryly, "The presumption of innocence sounds like a stretch in this case, Jess. But see what you can do for your friend."

24

Clyde Hotchkiss had been living on the streets of various cities since the mid-1970s. A decorated veteran of the Vietnam War, he had come home to Staten Island with a hero's welcome but was haunted by his wartime experience. There were memories he could talk about to the VA hospital psychiatrist, and the one he could never discuss, even though it was vivid in his mind—the night in Vietnam when he and Joey Kelly, the youngest kid in their platoon, huddled together, caught in a barrage of enemy artillery fire.

Joey had always talked about his mother, how close they were, how his father had died when he was a baby. Clyde and Joey were shoulder to shoulder trying to crawl toward a clump of trees that offered some shelter when Joey was hit.

Clyde had put his arms around him as Joey, holding together his own guts, whispered, "Tell Mama how much I love her," and started to cry, "Mama . . . Mama . . . Mama." Then, his blood soaking through Clyde's uniform, Joey had died in Clyde's arms.

Clyde had married his high school sweetheart, Peggy, "the beauteous Margaret Monica Farley," as the local Staten Island paper reported. They had a good laugh over that one. Sometimes when Clyde called to tell her he'd be late from work, he would say, "Am I having the privilege of speaking to the beauteous Margaret Monica Farley?"

Always instinctively good at any construction task, he had gotten a job with a local builder and quickly became his right-hand man.

Three years later Clyde Jr. was born, and they promptly nicknamed him Skippy.

Clyde loved his wife and son with a deep, abiding love, but the baby's crying brought back memories of Joey, especially the one he had tried his hardest to leave in the past.

He began to drink, a cocktail with Peggy after a hard day's work, wine at dinner, wine after dinner. When Peggy expressed concern, he began to skillfully find places to hide the wine. When he became short-tempered, she begged him to go for help. "It's the war hitting you again," she told him. "Clyde, you need to go to the VA hospital and talk about it to the doctor."

But it was when Skippy began teething and would wake them up in the middle of the night, screaming, "Mama . . . Mama . . . Mama," that Clyde knew he could never belong to a normal life, that he needed to be alone.

One night when Peggy and the baby were away on a pre-Christmas visit to her mother and father in Delray Beach, Florida, where, happy to retire early, they had relocated, Clyde knew it was over. He had drunk a bottle of good red wine, then put on his flannel shirt, winter jeans, and his thick boots. He had stuffed his insulated gloves into the pocket of his warm denim jacket and written a note. "My beauteous Margaret Monica, my little guy, Skippy. I'm sorry. I love you so much but I can't handle this life. All the money in our savings is for you and our Skippy. But please don't spend it on looking for me."

Clyde did not sign the note. But he took his always polished medals out of the breakfront in the dining room and laid them on the table. Then he remembered to take the framed picture of him and Peggy and Skippy and put it in the knapsack that already was filled with a couple of bottles of wine.

He made sure the front door was locked on their small ranch house on Staten Island and began his forty-year walk to nowhere . . .

Now sixty-eight years old, nearly bald under his skullcap, his gait unsteady from an old fall down subway stairs that had cracked his hip bone, his face unshaven unless he happened to find a used razor in a garbage can, Clyde lived his solitary life.

He spent his days panhandling on the streets, just enough to keep a steady supply of drink. First he went to Philly and managed to survive for several years there, even picking up a few regular handyman gigs for pocket money. But eventually he began to grow wary when the vagrants he holed up with at night started to become too friendly. So he set out for Baltimore and spent some years there, too. Finally one day he just got the urge to head back up to the city. By this time decades had slipped away.

When he finally came back to New York, he wandered around the five boroughs but had a few regular routines. He frequently had a meal at the St. Francis of Assisi breadline, and came to know other shelters where he could get food in any of the boroughs. The only one he avoided was Staten Island, even though his guess was that Peggy had long ago taken Skippy to Florida to be with her parents.

Clyde's rod and his staff were those bottles of wine that dulled pain and warmed his aging body on the many cold nights that he spent outdoors escaping the unwanted caring of the volunteers who tried to save him from the blustery winds of winter. He had always been ingenious at squatting in church cemeteries or shuttered buildings no matter what city he called home, and now he sought shelter in abandoned subway stations or between cars in parking lots after the attendant had locked up for the night.

Over the years he had developed a hair-trigger temper. Once when he was in Philadelphia he had swung at a cop who tried to force him into a shelter and had almost spent the night in jail. He agreed to go to the shelter, but he didn't want that to happen ever again. So many people. So much talk.

Clyde's new life began in the Connelly complex a little more than two years ago. He had gotten on the subway with his shopping cart at about eleven o'clock one night, rode back and forth until he woke up, then got off the subway at the nearest station. It was in Long Island City. Clyde vaguely remembered that he had been in that area before and there were old warehouses, some vacant, some under construction. His sense of direction, one of the few acute senses he still possessed, kicked in, and he had dragged his cart until he happened upon the Connelly complex, the landscaped jewel in the midst of its grimy neighbors.

The few lights he saw led up the driveway to the buildings. Clyde had walked cautiously around the perimeter of the property, not wanting to be caught by any security cameras. He did not go near the buildings. Probably some sleepy watchman on duty, he figured. But then at the back of the property, past where he guessed cars were parked during the day, he came upon a large enclosure that reminded him of the carport he once had at home on Staten Island. Only a lot bigger. Lots and lots bigger, he whispered quietly to himself.

One by one he counted the vans there. Three big ones, the size you could move everything you owned in. Two maybe half that size. One by one he tested the handles. All of them were locked.

Then he saw it. The very last one. The night was overcast but there was enough for him to see that this one had been in a crash. The hood was crumpled, the side door jammed, the windshield shattered, the tires flat.

But it wouldn't be too bad to sleep under it, and then get out in the morning before anybody showed up. Then Clyde had an inspiration. Try the big back doors. He was getting really cold and the cart was heavy. When he turned the latch that connected those doors they swung open. The sound they made was like a welcome to him.

He fished his pencil flashlight out from his grimy pocket, pointed its beam, then gave off a grunt of joy. The walls and floor of the back of the van were covered with heavy cotton padding. Clyde climbed in, lifted his cart, dragged it inside, then pulled the doors closed.

He sniffed and was glad when a stale smell filled his nostrils. It told him that no one had bothered to open those doors for a long time. Trembling with anticipation, Clyde fished out of his cart the newspapers that were his mattress and the odds and ends and rags that served as his blanket. He had not been so comfortable in years. Totally secure in the knowledge that he was alone, he sucked on his bottle of wine and fell asleep.

No matter how late it was when he found a place to squat, his internal clock always woke him at 6 A.M. He shoved his newspapers and rags into his cart, buttoned up his coat, and opened the back doors. In a few minutes he was blocks away, just another homeless man shuffling along on his endless trip to nowhere.

That night he was back in the van again and after that it became his nocturnal retreat.

Sometimes Clyde heard one of the vans pull out and figured it was on a delivery to a faraway place. Sometimes he could even hear the murmur of voices, but he quickly realized that they were no danger to him.

And always he left by six o'clock with all his belongings, leaving no trace of himself behind, except for the newspapers that had begun to pile up.

Only one bad thing had happened in the two years before the morning explosion that had sent him scurrying away barely in time to escape the police and the fire trucks. That was the night early on when that girl had followed him from the subway and wouldn't leave him alone and got into the van before he had closed the door. She had been a college kid and told him she just wanted to talk to him. He had spread out his newspapers and covered himself with his blanket and closed his eyes. But she wouldn't stop talking. And he couldn't suck his wine bottle in peace. He remembered that he had sat up and punched her in the face.

But then what happened? He didn't know. He'd had a lot of wine, so he fell asleep fast, and she was gone when he woke up. So she must have been all right. Or did she start yelling? Did I put her in the cart and push her away? No. I don't think so. But anyway she was gone.

He didn't come back to the van for days, but when he did it was all right. She mustn't have told anyone about it, he decided.

But then the explosion happened and he had had to rush out of the van before the fire trucks came and try to get everything in his cart, but he worried he had missed some of his belongings.

I'll miss my secret space, Clyde thought sadly. When I was there I felt so safe that I never dreamed about Joey.

He knew enough not to go near the burned-out complex the following day, because in a newspaper he fished out of the garbage can in Brooklyn he read that some old guy who had worked at the plant and the daughter of the owner were there when it happened and were suspected of setting the fire. Funny he never heard them that night. But now there'd be cops all over the place.

He probably could never go back to his van. Even when he realized on Friday that somehow, in his rush to get out, he had lost the picture of Peggy and Skippy and him. He just shrugged. He almost never looked at the picture anymore, so what was the difference? He could hardly remember his family. If only he could forget Joey, too.

25

Terrified to miss a call from Dr. Patel, Hannah had slept with her cell phone on at its highest volume. Her exhaustion was so great that she slept deeply. When she woke at seven on Friday morning she had called the hospital. The nurse in intensive care had told her that Kate had had a quiet night.

"Did she try to say anything?" Hannah asked.

"No. The sedation is very strong."

"But late yesterday afternoon she *did* say something to my father." Oh God, if she ever says anything about setting the fire and they hear her, Hannah agonized. What will happen?

"I would doubt that she said anything coherent, Ms. Connelly." The nurse tried to be reassuring. "There is no change in her condition, which, I'm sure the doctor has explained, is a good sign."

"Yes, yes. Thank you. I'll be over soon."

Hannah hung up the phone and for a long moment lay back on the pillow. What day is it? she asked herself, then began to sort out the events of the past day and a half. Wednesday had been the big day at work, when they told her she would have her own line. I didn't call Kate, she remembered, because she was meeting Dad and his latest girlfriend, Sandra. Jessie and I went out for dinner. I came home, watched TV, and went to bed. Then I got the call from

Jack at about five yesterday morning. That was Thursday? Was it *really* only yesterday?

She tried to put the events of Thursday in order. The rush to the hospital. Waiting for Dad to show up. Staying at the hospital until Kate was out of surgery, then going to work. That was silly, she told herself now. What did I think I was going to accomplish? Going back to the hospital and thankfully finding Jessie there. Then Dad and Sandra showing up there in the late afternoon, and Kate appearing to say something to Dad. Going home after that and having to deal with the fire marshals again. After they left, Jessie had fixed something for us to eat and then they had gone back to see Kate.

Dad went in ahead of me to see Kate in the afternoon, she remembered. When I got near the bed, Dad was bent over Kate, and he was clearly frightened by what she had said to him.

Does she know Gus is dead? Did she try to apologize to him for setting the fire?

I won't, *I can't* believe that.

She pressed the television remote, then was sorry she did. The lead news was the fire. "The question is why was Kate Connelly, the owner's daughter, in the complex at that hour with Gus Schmidt, an ex-employee who was fired five years ago?" the anchor was asking.

It was the first time Hannah had seen a picture of the ruined complex. How did Kate ever make it out alive? she asked herself. Dear God, how did she ever make it out alive?

She turned off the television, swung her legs to the floor, then realized she was wearing a nightshirt that Kate had given her. "*Ma petite soeur,* on you it should fit perfect," she had said. "It's too short for me."

From the minute she was in her first French class, Kate always called me that, Hannah thought. *My little sister.* She's always looked out for me. Now I've got to look out for her.

Jessie is right. Those fire marshals are going to try to hang this on Kate. Well, I won't let them.

A long hot shower made her feel better. She plugged in her new coffeemaker, which served up one cup at a time; it was another thoughtful gift from Kate. She decided to put on a sweater and slacks and change later to go to the funeral home where Gus was to be laid out.

Hannah dreaded the prospect of seeing Lottie. What can I possibly say to her that can help lessen her grief? she wondered. "I'm sorry the media is calling Gus a disgruntled former employee with a grudge against the company and a possible conspirator?" No matter what I say, Lottie is going to tell me and everyone else that Kate phoned him to meet her, not the other way around.

Her boots had three-inch heels, which barely brought her up to five feet five. With all those tall models, I always feel like a dwarf at the fashion shows, she thought as she ran a brush through her hair. I always wanted to be as tall as Kate. And I wish I looked like our mother, the way she does. Their pictures are just about interchangeable.

But I'm a chip off the old block of Dad—or Doug, as he wants us to call him now that we are grown. I pray to God I'm not like him in any other way!

When she went out into the hall and rang for the elevator, she remembered with embarrassment how she had been crying when the tall guy with the suitcase had ridden up in it yesterday with her and Jess and the fire marshals. I hope he didn't think I'd had too much to drink and was on a crying jag, she thought.

Not that it mattered. Not that *anything* mattered except that Kate recover fully and not be accused of setting the fire.

Thankfully she was alone in the elevator, and out on the street was able to hail a cab immediately. On the way to the hospital she could feel her chest tightening. The doctor had warned that Kate's condition could change in a minute. Even the relatively good news the nurse had given her on the phone wouldn't necessarily still be true.

At the hospital she got out of the cab and realized for the first time that the rain and dampness of the past few days had been replaced by a sun-flooded sky.

I'll take it as a sign, Hannah thought. Please let it be a sign that everything will work out.

When she got to the ICU, it was a shock to see her father at Kate's bedside so early. When he turned his head, his red-rimmed eyes told her that he had had another boozy night. "Did they call you? Is that why you're here?" she asked in a frightened whisper.

"No, no. Don't get scared. I just couldn't sleep and had to see her."

Almost limp with relief, Hannah looked down at her sister. Nothing was different. Kate's head was totally bandaged. The breathing tube still covered her face. The wires and tubes were still in place. She was a wax doll, inert, impassive.

Hannah was standing on the right side of the bed. She took Kate's bandaged right hand in both of hers, bent down, and kissed her sister's forehead. Can she feel anything through all those bandages? she wondered. "Katie, Dad and I are here," she said, her voice low but deliberate and clear. "You're going to get well. We love you."

Was she feeling the slightest response on her palms? Hannah turned to Doug. "Dad, I swear she can hear me. I know she can hear me. Say something to her."

Glancing to see if a nurse was near enough to hear him, Doug leaned over Kate, his voice a whisper. "Baby, you're safe. I'll never tell, I promise I'll never tell."

Then he looked up at Hannah and mouthed the words, "Yesterday she told me she was sorry about the fire."

Hannah was afraid to ask him anything more, but from the look on his face it was clear to her that Kate must have apologized for setting the fire.

26

By noon on Friday Mark Sloane knew he had made the right decision to join his new law firm, Holden, Sparks & West. Specialists in commercial litigation law, they represented international real estate firms, investment companies, and worldwide banks. In a litigious world, they had a formidable reputation. Their three floors of sleekly modern offices were a visible sign of their success.

Mark had been back and forth enough in the last few months so that he had no sense of being a total newcomer. He already knew that the receptionist, the first employee to be seen through the glass doors after he walked down the hall from the elevator, was the mother of three high school boys. He was very pleased that he would be one of the top aides to the president of the firm, the renowned Nelson Sparks, and work on the most important cases with him. A partnership in two years had been promised.

But he was not aware that from his first visit he had become a man of intense interest to the single women in the firm and had been the subject of lively discussion among them.

He liked his new office, which looked over East Forty-second Street and Grand Central Terminal. And above all, he was glad to be in New York. Maybe I got that from Tracey, he mused as he stood at the window and observed the panorama below of one of the busiest streets in the world. Coming to New York was always his sister's dream. She talked about it to me so many times. I wonder if she ever would have made it big in the theater. So many try and it doesn't work out . . . And then somebody gets blessed with stardust.

Enough of that, he decided. Time to begin to earn my keep here. Very considerable keep, he acknowledged to himself, as he settled at his desk and picked up the employee telephone book. He had long ago realized that for him the best way to get to know everyone in a company was to match their names to the positions they held. He had already been working on achieving that goal, but now that he was here, he intended to complete the learning process fast.

But despite his eagerness to delve into his new job, he was a bit distracted by the realization that he could now begin his real search for Tracey, or at least bring some closure to his mother about her disappearance. At four fifteen that afternoon he did a search on the Internet for the name of the detective on the case, Nick Greco.

The information he wanted came up immediately. Greco had a website for his own private detective agency. He was sixty-four years old, married with two daughters, and lived in Oyster Bay, Long Island, his profile stated. He had retired as a detective first grade in Manhattan after thirty-five years of service and opened his own investigative agency on East Forty-eighth Street in Manhattan. Just a few blocks away, Mark thought. Almost without knowing he was doing it, Mark dialed the phone number listed on the site.

To Mark's surprise a live receptionist answered the phone instead of one of those annoying, automated voice instructions. Press one for this, press two for that, press three . . .

When Mark asked for Greco and the receptionist requested the reason for the call, Mark realized that his throat was dry. He tried to clear it but it felt hoarse and rushed as he said, "My name is Mark Sloane. My sister, Tracey Sloane, disappeared twenty-eight years ago. Mr. Greco was the detective from the district attorney's office who handled the case. I have just moved to New York and would like a chance to talk with him."

"Hold on, please."

Seconds later, a firm male voice said, "Mark Sloane, I would be very pleased to meet with you. Not being able to solve your sister's disappearance all these years has continued to be a great frustration to me. When can we get together?"

27

"Mama, I don't know why you're insisting on having visitation for Poppa at the funeral home for only a few hours this afternoon," Gretchen complained. She was watching her mother remove her father's dark blue suit from the closet.

"I know what I'm doing," Lottie said firmly. "Your father is not going to be embalmed, so I want you to take these clothes over to the funeral home now. They were picking up his body from the medical examiner's office early this morning. They will have him ready for anyone who wants to visit by four o'clock. I spoke to the minister. He'll have a prayer service tonight at eight. And in the morning Poppa will be cremated, as he always wished."

Lottie's voice was detached as she spoke. Not *that* tie, she was thinking. I liked it on him but Gus never did. The blue one is nice. His good shoes are polished. Gus was such a perfectionist.

"I mean my friends growing up always liked Poppa, and there isn't even enough time to call all of them."

Gretchen was sitting on the edge of the bed, still wearing a robe and with curlers in her hair. At age fifty-four her round face was virtually unlined. Unlike both her parents, she had always been chubby, but her body was well proportioned. Divorced for twenty years, Gretchen did not miss her husband, or *any* husband, at all. She was an excellent masseuse and had a full clientele. Active in the

Presbyterian Church in Minnetonka, a suburb of Minnesota, she kept a vegetable garden and loved to cook. On weekends she often had friends in for dinner.

The joy of her life was the home her mother and father had bought for her five years ago. A builder's spec house, it was a large, handsome one-story, stone-and-shingled structure with a chef's kitchen and a conservatory. The grounds sloped down to the lake and the landscaping accentuated the house's charm and surroundings. An annuity Gus and Lottie had bought for Gretchen assured her of the ability to pay taxes, insurance, and any necessary repairs in the years to come.

Gretchen loved that house the way other women loved their children. In a moment's notice she would pull out pictures of it to show off: inside and out, pictures in every season. "It's like I'm living in heaven," she would say to any new admiring audience.

That kind of happiness was what Lottie and Gus had wanted for their only child, especially as they themselves aged. But it was also exactly why Lottie now told Gretchen not to talk about her house at the wake and to leave her pictures home. "I don't want to see you show them to anyone," she cautioned. "I don't want anyone to wonder where your father and I got that kind of money to help you out. And you know, Poppa should have paid gift taxes on everything he gave you." Lottie draped the blue tie over the suit hanger and laid it on the bed, next to where Gretchen was sitting. "I know he didn't pay enough, so if you don't want to be socked with taxes you can't pay yourself, just keep your mouth shut."

"Mama, I know you're upset, but you don't have to talk to me like that," Gretchen snapped back. "I don't know why you're rushing poor Poppa into his grave. Why don't you have a proper funeral service for him at church? He went every week and was an usher there."

As she spoke, Gretchen had moved slightly and was now sitting on the arm of the blue suit that Lottie had just put down.

"Get up," Lottie snapped. "And get dressed." Her voice broke. "It's bad enough having to put Poppa's clothes together. It's bad enough to know that he won't be here tomorrow or next week or ever. I don't want to argue with you, but I also don't want you to lose your home. Poppa gave up too much for you to do that."

As Gretchen stood up, Lottie opened the dresser drawer to get out underwear and socks and a shirt to send to the funeral parlor for Gus. In a torrent of words, she asked bitterly, "And as far as rushing your father into his grave, can't you see what you're reading in the papers? They're all but saying that Poppa met Kate to set that fire. He was upset about being fired. His work was as good as it ever was when that Jack Worth let him go. Kate was the one who insisted he be given a year's salary beside his pension. The way the media and those fire marshals see it, Kate wanted the place burned down and she asked Poppa to make it happen. If reporters get wind that there's a wake today, they'll be all over the place with their cameras, and crowds of gawkers will come just because it's exciting to try to get in the media pictures. Now *get dressed*."

Finally alone after Gretchen went back to get dressed, Lottie closed the door. Oh, Gus, Gus, why did you go meet her? she lamented as she selected an undershirt and boxer shorts. I told you it would be trouble. I knew it. I warned you. Why didn't you listen? What's going to happen to us now? I don't know what to do. I don't know what to do.

At three thirty Lottie arrived alone at the Walters Funeral Home. "When I spoke to you earlier I said that I wanted the casket closed," she said quietly to Charley Walters, the funeral director. "But I've changed my mind. I do want to see him." She was wearing her good black dress and the string of pearls Gus had given her for their twenty-fifth anniversary. "And did you remember to order flowers from me and Gretchen?"

"Yes, I did. Everything is ready. Shall I take you to him?"

"Yes." Lottie followed Walters into the viewing room and walked to the casket. She nodded in satisfaction when she saw the floral arrangement with the ribbon that read BELOVED HUSBAND.

She waited silently while the director lifted it off, laid it on a chair, and opened the top half of the casket. Without saying anything else he walked out of the room and closed the door behind him. Lottie sank onto the kneeler and carefully studied her husband's face. Only his hands were burned in that fire, she thought. He looks so peaceful, but he must have been so frightened. She ran her fingers along his face. "Did you know it was dangerous to go there when you kissed me good-bye?" She whispered the question. "Oh Gus, Gus."

Ten minutes later, she got up, walked to the door, and opened it. Charley Walters was waiting for her. "Close the casket now," she directed. "And put the flowers back on it."

"When your daughter delivered Mr. Schmidt's clothing she said that she wanted to see him," Walters said.

"I know. I convinced her it would be a mistake. She'd be hysterical, and she admitted it. She'll be coming in a little while."

Lottie did not add that it would be just like Gretchen to blubber her thanks to her father for his generosity to her. When Lottie had gotten out of the car, she had spotted two men sitting in a car parked across the street from the funeral home. She could see an official-looking placard attached to the visor on the driver's side. They're not here to pay their respects, she thought. They want to get a line on who shows up here and maybe question them about Gus.

I have got to keep them away from Gretchen.

28

After seeing Kate in intensive care and running into Hannah in the hospital Friday morning, Douglas Connelly had gone home. Sandra had left the apartment sometime during the night. He wouldn't be surprised if she'd gotten a text from Majestic or whoever that scruffy-looking rapper was, but he didn't care.

Should he have told Hannah that Kate had apologized to him for the fire? Would it have been better to say nothing? But Hannah had known right away that he had been lying when he said that Kate had whispered to him she loved him. But then Hannah had looked aghast when he told her that Kate had said she was sorry about the fire.

Hannah told him that she had hired her friend Jessie to represent Kate if she was accused of setting the explosion.

What about Gus? Would his wife hire a lawyer to defend his reputation as well?

Doug pondered these questions when he returned from the hospital shortly after nine o'clock. The spacious eight-room apartment on East Eighty-second Street where he had raised the girls was just off Fifth Avenue and around the corner from the Metropolitan Museum of Art. Now both girls had their own apartment. He didn't need all the space, but he liked the location on Museum Mile, and the restaurant in the building. The apartment was filled with Connelly

Fine Antique Reproductions and exquisite in its own way, although even he admitted he found the totally formal atmosphere and the furniture not particularly comfortable.

In fact, it was a daily reminder that Kate was entirely right. Either multimillionaires bought original antiques for investment, or they chose a mixture of antiques and comfort. Decorating with reproductions of fine furniture, even high-quality ones, just was going out of fashion, even for five-star hotel chains that had been their best customers. Doug recognized the truth of this when Kate furnished her own apartment, even if it was done in a sense of rebellion. Not even one end table had come from the plant.

Doug reflexively clenched and unclenched his hand. To steady his nerves, he went into the library and poured himself a vodka despite the early hour. Sipping it slowly, he settled in his one comfortable chair, a leather recliner, and tried to make sense of what was going on. Should he get a lawyer? He didn't need one to know that the insurance company wouldn't pay any claims on the original antiques or the whole complex if it was proven that a member of the family had set the fire.

Without the business, even if it is losing money, I'll run out of cash in two months, he thought. Maybe I can take a deposit on the property with the understanding it won't be available until any lawsuits are settled. A sudden shiver made his body go clammy with sweat. Not now, he thought as he closed his eyes knowing he was about to relive the moment years ago that changed his life forever— the moment the boat he was steering hit that cable. It was as though they had sailed off the end of the earth. The bow of the boat was sliced off and the rest of it slipped under the water. He was at the helm. The others were in the cabin below.

They never knew what happened, he thought to himself. The crew on the tanker never knew we'd hit the cable. He had grabbed a life jacket and pulled it on. Then he had managed to throw out the life raft, grab the bag with his wallet, and jump in as the boat sank. Doug closed his eyes, willing the memory to pass. And it did as suddenly as it had come over him. He resisted the impulse to pour a second vodka. Instead he reached for his cell phone and called Jack Worth. They had not spoken at all since yesterday, when they met at the hospital.

Jack answered on the first ring. When they had been at the complex, he always called Doug "Mr. Connelly," but when they were alone it was "Doug."

"How is Kate?"

"No change."

"Did you get over to the property yesterday?"

"No, I intended to. But I went to the hospital twice and then the fire marshals were here last night. You went over, didn't you?"

"I went straight there from the hospital. Those marshals got pretty rough about the lack of security on the premises." Jack Worth's voice was worried. "I got the feeling that since I was running the place, they think I should have insisted on having security cameras. I told them the place was up for sale for the right price."

Doug didn't like the undercurrent of panic he heard in Jack's voice.

"Some of the guys at the plant called Gus's wife," Jack said. "You know how popular he was with them. She told them that there'll be visitation today at the Walters Funeral Home in Little Neck between four and eight. Gus had no use for me or you after he was fired, so I don't know whether or not to go."

"I think you should go," Doug said adamantly. "And I will, too. It will show our respect for Gus." He looked at his watch. "I'll get there around six." He considered for a moment, then knew he was not interested in having dinner with any of the women listed in his address book. "Why don't you get there around the same time and we'll grab a bite to eat afterward?"

"Fine with me." Jack Worth hesitated, then added, "Doug, watch what you drink today. You tend to run off at the mouth when you have too much."

Knowing it was true, but angry at the suggestion, Douglas Connelly said curtly, "I'll see you around six," and turned off his phone.

29

Lawrence Gordon, chairman and CEO of Gordon Global Investments, whose college-aged daughter, Jamie, was murdered two years ago, had directed Lou, his chauffeur, to pick him up at his Park Avenue office at three fifteen on Friday afternoon, but it was more than an hour later before he was able to get away.

The breaking news had been that three major companies were planning to make public their fourth-quarter projections and all had fallen seriously short of their expectations. This revelation had sent the stock market into a sudden plunge.

Lawrence had stayed glued to his desk to monitor the developments. By late afternoon, the market had stabilized.

With a sigh of relief, Lawrence Gordon finally got into his car and commented to Lou, "At least we're a shade ahead of the five o'clock rush."

"Mr. Gordon, the five o'clock rush starts at four o'clock, but you'll be home in plenty of time before the rest of the family arrives," Lou replied.

Bedford, in the heart of Westchester County, was an hour's drive away. Lawrence often used that time to read reports or catch up on the news. But today he reclined the seat, leaned back, and closed his eyes.

Sixty-seven years old, he had once been six feet two but was now just below six feet tall. His thinning head of pure white hair, his patrician features, and the aura of authority he emitted to those around him were the reasons that he was inevitably described as "distinguished" in the many articles that had been written about him.

Tonight Lawrence and his wife, Veronica, were marking their forty-fifth wedding anniversary. Until two years ago they had celebrated it by going to Paris or London or to their villa in Tortola.

That was, until their daughter, Jamie, disappeared. The familiar knifelike pain bolted through Lawrence's body as he thought of his youngest child, his only daughter. He and Veronica had believed their family to be complete with their three sons, Lawrence Jr., Edward, and Robert. Then, when Rob was ten, Jamie was born. He and Veronica were both forty-three years old but were delighted and thrilled to welcome their daughter.

Lawrence remembered how enchanted he had been the first time he held the newborn Jamie in his arms, with her beautiful little face and wide brown eyes. Then she had wrapped her fingers around his thumb and he had felt a moment of exquisite happiness. He had thought of his Pilgrim ancestors and the fact that they believed there was a "tortience" between a father and a baby daughter, a special unbreakable bond of love.

Jamie, the golden child. She could easily have been spoiled rotten by all of us but she never let that happen, Lawrence remembered sadly. Even as a child she had a social conscience. By the time she was in high school she was volunteering at a food pantry and helping to organize clothing drives. While at Barnard College she had spent two summers with Habitat, one in South America and one in Africa.

She had been a senior at Barnard when, for her sociology class, she had decided to write a paper about street people. She had explained to them that this would involve talking to the homeless who were literally living on the streets.

Lawrence and Veronica had tried to talk her out of the project, but Jamie was always headstrong. She did promise to be very careful, joking that she certainly didn't want to put herself in danger. "I've got good radar about people and, trust me, I have no intention of getting myself into a situation I can't handle," she had assured them. But three weeks after she started the project, nearly two years ago, Jamie had disappeared. A month later, a coast guard vessel had fished her body out of the East River. There was a black-and-blue mark on her jaw, her hands and feet were tied together, and she had been strangled.

There was absolutely no clue as to where she had been or who had been her murderer. Because she had been caught on security cameras talking to street people in lower Manhattan the day before she vanished, the case was in the jurisdiction of the Manhattan district attorney's office. John Cruse, the detective in charge of the investigation, called Lawrence regularly. "I promise that this case stays open and active until we track down the animal who did this to your daughter," Cruse said.

Lawrence shook his head. He didn't want to think about Jamie right now, about the fresh clean smell of the sun-streaked brown hair that tumbled past her shoulders. "If you keep washing it every day, it'll start to fall out," he would tease her. Even when she was in college she loved to curl up on the couch next to him to watch the evening news when she came home for a weekend.

As the car made its slow journey across Manhattan to the West Side Highway, Lawrence tried to concentrate on the gift he was giving Veronica for their anniversary. He was endowing a $2 million chair in sociology at Barnard in Jamie's name. He knew that that would please Veronica. She missed Jamie so terribly. We both do, he thought.

When they turned north on the West Side Highway, he glanced

at the Hudson River. On this gloomy day it seemed to be a shifting shade of dirty gray. Lawrence quickly looked away from it. No matter whether he drove past the Hudson River or the East River, he could envision Jamie's body bobbing in it, her long hair tangled with muck.

Shaking his head to dispel the horrifying image, he leaned forward and turned on the radio.

It was five thirty when Lou pushed the button that opened the gates to their property. Lawrence was already unbuckling his seat belt before they were halfway down the long driveway. His sons and daughters-in-law were expected at six, and he wanted a chance to change into something more comfortable.

When he got out of the car, Lou already had the front door of the luxurious brick mansion open for him. Lawrence was about to hurry up the curving stairs in the imposing foyer when he glanced into the living room. Veronica was sitting there in a fireside chair, already dressed for the evening in a colorful silk blouse and long black skirt.

If Lawrence was considered distinguished, Veronica was described by the media as the "lovely and elegant Veronica Gordon," but that was usually accompanied by a list of the charities with which she had been tirelessly involved. In the last year, the articles would include the Foundation for the Homeless, which she and Lawrence had also established in Jamie's memory.

She always tried to keep up a brave front, but on so many nights he woke up to hear her trying to stifle sobs in her pillow. There was nothing he could do except wrap his arms around her and say, "It's okay to let it out, Ronnie. It's worse if you try to hold it in."

But now, as he entered the living room, she hurried over to meet him. He could see that her eyes were bright. "Lawrence, you won't believe this. You won't believe it."

Before he could ask her a question, she rushed on: "I know

you'll think it's crazy but I heard about a psychic who is absolutely amazing."

"Ronnie, you didn't go to see her!" Lawrence exclaimed incredulously.

"I knew you'd think I was crazy. That's why I didn't tell you that I had made an appointment with her. She was seeing people at Lee's house this afternoon. Lawrence, do you know what she told me?"

Lawrence waited. Whatever it was, if it gave Veronica comfort it was all right with him.

"Lawrence, she told me that I had suffered a tragedy, a terrible tragedy, that I had lost a daughter named Jamie. She said that Jamie is in heaven, that she was not supposed to live a long life, and that all the good that we are doing in her memory makes her very happy. But she is distressed when she sees how grief-stricken we are and tells us to please try to be happy for her sake."

Lee probably put this psychic up to this, bless her, Lawrence thought.

"And she said that the new baby will be a girl and Jamie is so happy that they're going to name it after her."

Their youngest son, Rob, and his wife were expecting their third child around Christmas. They already had two little boys and had decided not to find out what this one would be. If it was a girl they were planning to call her Jamie.

Lee knew that, too, Lawrence thought.

Veronica's expression changed. "Lawrence, you know how hard it is for us not to see Jamie's killer arrested before the same thing happens to another girl."

"And it is also hard because I haven't yet sat in a courtroom to see that monster sentenced to rot in prison for the rest of his life," Lawrence snapped.

"It's going to happen. The psychic said that very, very soon something belonging to Jamie will be found and it will help lead the police to her murderer."

Lawrence stared at his wife. Lee certainly didn't tell the psychic to say that, he thought. Good God, was the psychic for real? Is it possible that this is going to happen?

A few days later, he received his answer.

30

At four thirty Friday afternoon Jessica picked up Hannah for the drive out the island to the funeral home in Little Neck where the wake for Gus Schmidt was being held. Hannah had changed into a black and white tweed suit, one of her own designs. As Hannah got into the car, Jessie said approvingly, "You always look so put-together. I, on the other hand, manage to give the appearance of someone who closed her eyes, reached into the closet, and grabbed for the nearest hanger."

"Not true," Hannah said matter-of-factly, "and in fact it's insulting. I helped you pick out that suit in Saks and it looks great on you." She tossed her rain cape over to the backseat, where it landed next to Jessie's trench coat.

"My mistake. I forgot that you helped me pick it out," Jessie said ruefully as she stepped on the gas and skillfully maneuvered her Volkswagen between two double-parked cars.

"Anyway, you were just making conversation, which is very nice of you," Hannah said, "but it isn't necessary. I admit I'm nervous about seeing Lottie Schmidt. But it has to be done."

"You know and she knows that there has to be a reasonable explanation for Kate and Gus to have gone to the complex the other night. As soon as Kate comes out of the coma, we'll find out what it is," Jessie said firmly.

Hannah did not answer.

Jessie waited until she had turned the car onto Thirty-fourth Street, heading to the Queens-Midtown Tunnel, before she said, "Hannah, have you learned something that you're not telling me?" Then she added, "I am Kate's lawyer. It is absolutely critical that you tell me what you know so that I can properly represent her. Do you understand how important this is? And don't worry, should Kate be charged with a crime, I don't have to tell the DA anything I find out on my own."

As Hannah listened, she felt almost paralyzed with fear. Kate was still in critical condition. At any moment she could die or, if she recovered, she could be brain damaged. If she did recover and was found guilty of blowing up the complex and causing Gus's death, she could end up spending most of the rest of her life in prison. It was a scenario that, like a drum banging mournfully, was always repeating itself in her mind.

"Okay, Jessie, I understand." Kate did not volunteer anything more.

Jessie gave her a worried glance but decided not to press her further. They drove the rest of the way in awkward silence and arrived at the funeral home in forty-five minutes.

As Jessie pulled into the driveway to the parking lot, she said, "Look who's going inside!" Hannah turned her head quickly and was dismayed to see the two fire marshals opening the door of the funeral home. "Do you think we should wait a while in the car and try to avoid them?"

Jessie shook her head. "My guess is that they'll stay around and strike up a conversation with any of the people who worked with Gus who may be here. Let's go."

In the entrance room, a solemn-faced attendant directed them to the room where Gus Schmidt's casket had been placed. Hannah was surprised to see the room already filled. A long line had formed to greet Lottie and Gretchen, who were standing by the closed, flower-covered casket.

Jessie touched her arm. "Let a few more people get in the line. I don't want to be directly behind the marshals."

Hannah nodded. They moved to the left behind the last row of chairs, most of which were occupied. From where she was standing, she could see that Lottie was composed, but Gretchen had a handkerchief balled in her hand and was frequently raising it to dab her eyes.

A few minutes later, Jessie whispered, "There are more people in line behind the marshals. We can go over there now."

A moment after they took their place in line, a woman came up behind them and said to Hannah, "I recognize you from your picture in the newspapers. How is your sister?"

Hannah turned and looked into the concerned eyes of a slender woman who appeared to be in her late forties. "She's holding her own. Thank you for asking."

"My husband came separately. Would you mind if I went ahead and joined him?" She pointed to Fire Marshal Frank Ramsey.

It was Jessie who answered, "Of course not." They watched as the woman asked the same question of the men directly ahead of them and then slipped into the line between her husband and Nathan Klein.

"There's no way she's here just because he's investigating the explosion," Jessie whispered. "She's got to have some connection with the family. I want to try to hear what she has to say to them."

Jessie moved to the side and stepped forward until she was at the foot of the casket. She heard both fire marshals extend their sympathy to Lottie and Gretchen. Then she heard Ramsey's wife say, "Lottie, I'm Celia Ramsey. I don't know if you remember me, but you and I were in chemotherapy together at Sloan-Kettering five years ago. We went through a lot together. I'm so sorry about your loss. I could always see how devoted Gus was to you."

Celia turned to Gretchen. "Gretchen, I'm so sorry. I remember when I met you at Sloan, you had just bought your new home. You were showing me pictures of it."

Gretchen's face lit up. She shoved the soggy handkerchief into the pocket of her black pantsuit. "You can't imagine how even more beautiful it is with all the work I've done, both inside and out. And I'm growing plants and vegetables in my conservatory," she said enthusiastically. She looked over at her mother, whose expression did not change. "Mama, it doesn't matter if I show Celia some pictures, does it? I mean she's already seen pictures of the house."

Lottie did not answer. She simply watched as her daughter stepped out of the receiving line, hurried over to a seat in the front row, and reached for her pocketbook. Then Lottie turned her attention back to the people in line. Soon Hannah was before her.

Before Hannah could express her sympathy, Lottie, her voice so low that Hannah had to lean forward to hear her, said, "The police are convinced that Gus and Kate intentionally set that fire."

"They're suspicious, yes," Hannah said quietly. "I don't think they're convinced by any means."

"I don't know what to think," Lottie replied fiercely, "but I do know my husband is dead. If your sister convinced him to set this fire, it would be better off if she dies, unless she would prefer to spend years in prison."

Heartsick, Hannah realized that Lottie was afraid that Gus and Kate *had* set the fire. Was she telling that to the fire marshals? Knowing now that Lottie wanted no part of her sympathy, Hannah turned away. Gretchen, seated in the first row with Celia Ramsey beside her, had her iPad on her lap and was enthusiastically pointing out details in the pictures she was displaying on the screen.

Marshal Frank Ramsey had quietly slipped into the seat on Gretchen's other side so that he, too, could see the pictures of her beautiful home in Minnetonka, Minnesota.

At that moment Hannah heard a plaintive moan and spun around in time to see Jessie try to grab and hold on to Lottie Schmidt as the frail woman collapsed to the ground in a faint.

31

As Clyde Hotchkiss had scrambled to get away from the complex early Thursday morning before the cops and fire engines arrived, he frantically threw just about everything into his cart and opened the back door of the van.

He could see that all the buildings in the complex were on fire. Thick clouds of smoke were being blown around by the wind. His eyes began to water and he began to cough. In the distance he heard the sound of sirens. Sobered up by the shock of the explosion, he had been desperate to get out of there and reach the subway station. He was pretty sure that he smelled of smoke. But he was lucky. He always kept a fare card for one subway ride and he was able to lift his cart over the turnstile gate and get down the stairs and onto the subway platform just as a Manhattan-bound train was pulling in. With a sigh of relief Clyde got on. The train was almost empty.

He closed his eyes and began to think. I can never go back to that place in Long Island City. When the fire is over, they'll surely move the vans and if they look inside the wrecked one, they will know someone had been holed up in it. They might even try to blame the explosion on me. He'd read enough papers to know that street people were often blamed if they had been hanging out in an abandoned house or building where a fire occurred.

Then he had begun to think about the girl who climbed in his van that time. For some reason he had been dreaming about her when the explosion happened. I don't think I hurt her, he thought. I did take a swing at her when she kept talking and asking questions and I needed her to be quiet. But I don't know . . . I just don't know . . . I think I punched her . . .

He panhandled all that day on Lexington Avenue. That night he went back to one of his old spots. It was a garage on West Forty-sixth Street that had a ramp from the street to the underground parking area. Between 1 A.M. and 6 A.M. the garage was closed and the overhead door at the end of the ramp was lowered and locked. Clyde could sleep next to the door, protected from the wind and out of sight of the street.

He hung around about half a block away until he saw the attendant come up the ramp, then he scurried to settle in there. It worked out okay because he usually didn't need much sleep, but he realized how much he missed the comfort of the van.

On Friday morning he left before dawn and wandered down to panhandle on West Twenty-third Street. Enough quarters and dollar bills were dropped into his cap that he was able to buy four bottles of cheap wine. Two of them he drank in the late afternoon. That evening, he dragged his cart back up Eighth Avenue to Forty-sixth Street, keeping a sharp eye out for the do-gooders who might try to force him into a shelter.

He had drunk even more wine than usual and he grew impatient waiting for the parking attendant to leave. It was nearly 1:15 A.M. before Clyde heard the slam of the overhead grate as it hit the ground. Seconds later the attendant came up the ramp and disappeared down the street.

Five minutes after that, Clyde was settled by the grate, newspapers beneath and over him, sipping the wine with his eyes closed. But then he heard the sound of another cart coming down the ramp.

Furious, he opened his eyes and in the dim light saw that it was a real old street guy whose name was Sammy.

"Get out of here!" Clyde shouted.

"Get out of here yourself, Clyde!" a raspy voice shouted back, the words slurred. Then Clyde felt the bottle he was holding yanked out of his hand and the contents spilling on his face. In an instant his fist shot up and caught Sammy on the jaw. Sammy staggered back and fell, but then managed to get to his feet. "Okay, okay, you don't want company," he mumbled. "I'm going." Sammy put his hand on his cart, started forward, but then paused long enough to knock over Clyde's cart before hurrying up the ramp.

Clyde's last bottle of wine rolled out of the cart and landed next to him. He'd been about to spring up and chase Sammy. He knew he could catch him and he was aching to get his hands around Sammy's throat. Instead he paused and reached for the wine bottle, unscrewed the top, and settled back onto the newspapers. With the sleeve of his filthy outer jacket, he wiped the wine Sammy had spilled on him from his face.

Then he closed his eyes and began to sip from the bottle. Finally, when it was empty, with a satisfied sigh Clyde fell into a deep sleep.

32

Early Friday evening, Doug Connelly and Jack Worth met in the parking lot of the funeral home and went in to pay their respects to the late Gus Schmidt. Lottie, ghostly pale, who had returned to the receiving line after a brief rest, greeted them with the same coldness she had shown to Hannah.

"Gus never was himself after he was let go from Connelly's," she told Jack. "He wasn't too old to work. He was a perfectionist and you know it." To Doug she said, "Kate took advantage of him. He was devoted to her because she fought for him to have a year's salary when he was fired."

Both men listened, then Doug said, "Lottie, we know what the media is saying. It's public knowledge that Gus hated Jack and me. We have no idea why Kate met him at that hour in the museum. For all we know, she may have reached out to him to see how he was doing. They were good friends. The truth will out. And now, again, I extend my deepest sympathy for your loss and this whole tragic situation."

Recognizing that it was time to leave, Doug simply nodded to Gretchen and began to walk toward the door. But he didn't get far, because most of the people there were his own employees, and many of them had worked with Gus. They were all extremely anxious to know if Doug was planning to rebuild the complex.

"I am moving heaven and earth to make that happen," Doug assured them.

He's lying through his teeth, but he does it with style, Jack Worth thought. He knew it was his own turn to step in. "Mr. Connelly," he said, his tone respectful, "you've had an exhausting day at the hospital at your daughter's bedside. I know you want to talk to everyone, but they'll understand if you have to leave now." His firm tone conveyed a clear message to the men whom, until yesterday morning, he had supervised on a daily basis.

"Of course . . . certainly . . . we're praying for your daughter Kate, Mr. Connelly."

Followed by Jack Worth, Doug left the funeral home and walked across the driveway to the parking lot.

Jack opened the door of his Mercedes for him. "No driver tonight?" he asked.

"It's going to be an early night and I don't intend to have more than one scotch at dinner. Did you make a reservation at Peter Luger's?"

"Yes, I did, Mr. Connelly."

"Good. See you there in ten minutes."

It was less than a half hour later that they were seated at a corner table in the famous Peter Luger Steak House. They both ordered a scotch on the rocks, then Doug said, "Lottie just gave me a very good idea—in fact a perfect idea. Kate's cell phone will show that she called Gus on Wednesday afternoon, but nobody knows what they said to each other. Maybe Gus planned to trap her in the explosion."

Jack looked across the table at the handsome face of his boss. "Doug, do you think that anyone would believe that?"

"I don't see why not," Doug said promptly. "Anyone who knows Kate would vouch for the fact that she was prone to exaggerate for emphasis. For example, did she ever say to you that she'd like to blow up the whole damned complex?"

"Yes, she did, when she was out there a couple of weeks ago and saw that the security cameras still weren't working."

"Did you think she meant it?"

"No, of course not."

"There you are." The drinks arrived. Doug Connelly took the first sip of his and smiled. "Perfect."

"You can't do much to foul up a scotch on the rocks," Jack remarked.

"Sorry, but I think you're wrong about that, Jack. Too much ice in a drink can ruin it."

There were some subjects that Doug had forbidden Jack to ever bring up. "Don't even think about them," Doug had ordered.

That was why Jack carefully phrased his next question before he asked it. "If Kate recovers, do you think she would go along with saying that Gus set her up by asking her to meet him?"

"Jack, Kate is a very smart young woman. She's a CPA. She also has been extremely anxious to receive her ten percent share of the proceeds of any sale of the property. If Gus is blamed for everything, the insurance will be paid, including the insurance on the antiques. Arson by a disgruntled former employee is hardly unusual."

Dismissing the topic, Doug looked up to catch the waiter's eye. "I'm having steak, Jack," he said. "How about you?"

33

Kate's condition did not improve over the weekend. Hannah knew that Dr. Patel considered that to be a setback. Hannah spent most of Saturday in the hospital, finally leaving when Jessie dragged her out for dinner.

Sunday morning she was back. Dr. Patel had also stopped in to check on Kate. Seeing the dark circles under Hannah's eyes, he said emphatically, "Hannah, you can't sit here all day again. If there is any meaningful change in your sister's condition you will be notified promptly. After all the rain we've had, it's a beautiful day. Go for a walk and then go home and rest. I doubt if you've had much sleep since Thursday."

"I've already decided that I'll leave, at least for a few hours," she told him.

That was not enough to satisfy the doctor. "Hannah, Kate could go on in this condition for months. I've had other cases like this, patients in a deep coma, and I tell all families to live as normally as possible. Go to work tomorrow. Don't cancel your usual activities."

"But Kate spoke to my father on Thursday afternoon."

"Even if she seemed to be able to say a few words, I would suggest that they were probably meaningless."

If they were meaningless, Kate didn't know what she was doing when it sounded as if she admitted to setting the fire, Hannah thought with a faint ray of hope. Is that possible?

She realized she was fighting back tears of exhaustion and worry when she thanked the doctor for his care of Kate.

"I'll stop by again in late afternoon," he assured her. Then with a smile he asked, "Which part of my advice are you taking, a long walk or a rest at home?"

"I'm afraid neither," Hannah said. "It occurred to me that I had better check Kate's apartment. There's probably food in the refrigerator that should be thrown out."

"Yes, I suppose there is." As Dr. Patel nodded, his cell phone rang and with a slight wave of his hand, he stepped outside.

For thirty agonizing seconds, Hannah was sure that he was being summoned back to Kate's bedside, but then through the large interior window she could see out to the corridor. She watched as the doctor, speaking on his cell phone, broke into a smile as he walked away. It is time I got some fresh air, she thought. I'll walk through the park to the West Side. It will do me good. Then I'll come back here later to check on Kate.

After the mostly cold and rainy week, Central Park was filled with joggers, strollers, and bicyclists enjoying the sunshine even though the temperature was still a brisk fifty-four degrees. As she walked, Hannah inhaled deeply, trying to force her mind to restore some sense of balance. As Dr. Patel had warned, Kate's condition might stay the same for a long time, she reminded herself. If the police try to blame the explosion on Kate, I've got to have a clear head to work with Jessie to defend her. Yesterday Jessie gently suggested that I might want to have my own lawyer in case they try to drag me in, too. She recommended another attorney that she says is tops. I'll look into it if I need to in the next few days.

Involuntarily she smiled at the sight of a pretty young mother pushing her two children in a double stroller. The smaller one was about two years old, the taller one about a year older. Hannah thought about the pictures of her and Kate with their own mother when they were little. Some of them had been with her in Central Park. In all of them, their mom, like this young mother, had been so pretty and looked so proudly happy of her babies.

What would it have been like if she had lived? Certainly Dad would have been much more involved with us instead of being out or away so much. Yesterday he had stopped at the hospital in the late afternoon, staying only a half hour or so. He had told her then that his big concern has been whether Kate might have muttered anything more about the fire within hearing of the hospital staff. If he shows up when I'm there this afternoon, she reminded herself, I'll tell him that Dr. Patel said that anything Kate might say while she is still in the coma is probably meaningless.

She left the park at West Sixty-seventh Street and walked up Central Park West to Sixty-ninth, then turned left. A block and a half later, she was in front of Kate's building, a few doors west of Columbus Avenue. She and Kate had given each other a spare set of keys to their apartments, and it was a good thing we did, she thought. Kate's shoulder bag with her keys inside had not been found. It had probably been torn from her and destroyed by the force of the explosion.

The doorman opened the door for Hannah. She did not recognize him. Over the past year she had gotten to know some of the regular staff. The desk clerk recognized her at once, and by rote, she gave him the same answer she was giving to everybody: "Kate's condition is serious. We're hoping and praying for the best."

She picked up Kate's mail and stuffed it in her shoulder bag, then took the elevator up to the apartment. At first glance everything was still in its usual pristine order. Jessie had warned her that it was very probable that, as the investigation developed, the police would regard Kate as an active suspect in setting or planning the fire. In that case, they would certainly obtain a warrant to search her apartment. And Gus's home, too. Poor Lottie if that happens, she thought.

She shook off her coat, and as she walked around the living room, she saw a folded blanket and pillow on the couch. The Bose radio that was usually in the kitchen was on the end table next to the couch. She pushed the alarm button and could see that it had last been set for 3:30 A.M. That made sense, she thought. The explosion happened an hour later. She walked into the bedroom. It was in immaculate order. She opened the walk-in closet. At the hospital they told her that Kate had been wearing a running suit and an outer jacket when she was found in the parking lot of the complex.

She must have changed into the running suit when she came back from dinner with Doug, Hannah thought. Then she got a blanket and pillow, set the alarm, and lay down on the couch. But why did she meet Gus at that ungodly hour?

She looked around Kate's bedroom seeking answers. Even the way it was furnished was a rebellion against the Connelly fine reproductions décor. There were three white throw rugs on the polished fruitwood floor. The four-poster metal bed held a white comforter. The navy blue and white dust ruffle was repeated on the pillows that were propped on the headboard. White valances with narrow blue and white panels framed the two wide windows, one of which gave Kate a bird's-eye view of the Hudson River.

Modern bedside tables, a television set on a swivel, a desk, and a large club chair with an ottoman were the only other furnishings in the room. The walk-in closet had been custom-designed to hold shelves of sweaters, scarves, and gloves, and racks of shoes. And God knows what else, Hannah thought. Kate could not abide clutter.

Feeling like an intruder, Hannah walked over to Kate's desk. The narrow drawer under the surface was a study in perfection. The usual trappings were there. A letter opener, an extra pen, a roll of stamps, personal writing paper, an address book, the kind people used before email and text messaging.

The large bottom drawer contained the kind of files used by any bill-paying adult, except the last file. It was marked WILL — COPY.

Her hands trembling, Hannah took out the file and opened it. On the inside cover was the name and address of the attorney Kate had used for estate planning purposes. She had written underneath it "original in safe deposit box." Besides the copy of her will, there was a sealed envelope marked HANNAH in the file.

Careful to open the envelope so slowly that she could reseal it, Hannah began to read:

Dearest Hannah,

If you are reading this it is probably because I am dead. Except for some charities, I have left everything I have to you, including, of course, my ten percent interest in the company.

I hope this will be read by your eyes only but I must warn you that I don't trust Dad. He is a spender and out for himself always. If anything happens to me, be sure to have my fellow CPA, Richard Rose, keep an eye on the company books. I don't want you to be cheated.

I cannot understand why Doug will not face reality, unless by forcing the company into bankruptcy he hopes to have a financial gain for himself at the expense of the employees. The antiques in the museum are separately owned, eighty percent by him and ten percent each by you and me, and would not be an asset of the company.

I know you have always been glad to let me handle our business interests but now you must take over.

Hope you don't read this for fifty years or so.

Love you my little sister,

Kate

Her eyes brimming with tears, Hannah put the letter back in the envelope and resealed it. Then she hesitated. Face it, she told herself fiercely. What if Kate doesn't fully recover? Who will be her guardian? I wouldn't put it past Dad to come over here and take a look at her personal records. I don't think he has a key, but the desk clerk might let him in.

She took the envelope out. I can't wait to put this back if Kate gets well, Hannah thought, but until then it's safer with me. She had the combination to Kate's small safe. It was on a wall in the closet. She opened it and took out Kate's jewelry from their boxes. In her will their mother had left all of her jewelry to her daughters, to be given to them at age twenty-one. Kate had rings and necklaces and bracelets that were quite valuable. Anyone knowing that the apartment was empty indefinitely might find a way to get in. Hannah knew these small safes were easy prey for a professional thief.

She did not allow herself to complete the thought that her father might try to make a claim on the jewelry, given his out-of-control spending habits. Hannah put the letter and the jewelry inside her large shoulder bag. She then went to check on the second bedroom, which Kate used as a den.

The room contained a pullout couch, a comfortable chair, end tables, and a sixty-inch television. Hannah knew that after a long day at her office, Kate loved to sink into her favorite chair, relax, and have a late supper as she watched TV. I hope so much that she gets home soon, Hannah thought, her eyes stinging with tears.

Her last check was the kitchen. She looked for the phone number for Kate's every-other-week cleaning woman, Marina, to ask her to take all of the perishables out of the refrigerator. She found it on the refrigerator and called her. Since she said she would not be in until Thursday, Hannah glanced into the refrigerator to make sure nothing was already spoiling. Her final concern was the leafy plant

Kate had on the windowsill. In the four days since Kate was last at home it had begun to wilt without water.

That's another thing I know nothing about, Hannah thought. Kate has a green thumb. I look at a plant and it dies. It was at that moment that Kate's phone in the kitchen rang. Hannah picked it up. It was the desk clerk. "Ms. Connelly," he said, "a Mr. Justin Kramer is here. He sold his condo to your sister. He was inquiring about how to reach you and I told him that you were here. It seems he gave a plant to your sister as a housewarming gift, and he wanted to offer to take care of it until she gets back home."

Until she gets back home! Words Hannah desperately needed to hear from someone else's lips.

"Please send Mr. Kramer right up," she said.

34

When Justin Kramer came upstairs to Kate's apartment, Hannah had immediately liked what she was seeing. He looked to be in his early thirties. Trim, about five feet ten, with hazel eyes, a firm jaw, and a head of curly dark brown hair, he reminded her of a boy she'd had a crush on when she was sixteen.

His concern for Kate was genuine. He explained, "I got in over my head when I bought this condo. Then when I lost my job in the Wall Street fallout two years ago, I knew it would be wise to sell it. My father drilled into us that you trim your sails when there's a financial pinch and you don't dip into savings. The investment firm I'm with now is even better than the one I was with before. But I'll never forget how concerned your sister was about me. That was why when I read about the accident, I thought of the plant I had given her and that if she still had it, it would need care. I know that with everything that has happened, it's a very small gesture, but I wanted to do something."

"That's just like Kate to be concerned about the other guy," Hannah said simply. "She's that kind of person."

"I understand that she's badly injured, but, for whatever it's worth, I have a strong feeling that she'll make it through. I obviously have seen the hints in the media that Kate might be implicated in the explosion. As little as I know her, I absolutely cannot believe that Kate could ever be involved with something like this."

"Thank you for that," Hannah said, "and thank you for believing that she'll make it through all this. Right now, being in her home and wondering if she'll ever see it again, I needed to hear that."

They left the apartment together, Justin carrying the plant. When they were outside the building, standing on the sidewalk, and before she could say good-bye, Justin said, "Hannah, it's one thirty. If you haven't had lunch yet, would you like to grab a bite with me?"

Hesitating for only a couple of seconds, Hannah said, "I'd like that."

"Italian food okay?"

"My favorite."

They walked three blocks to a small restaurant called Tony's Kitchen. It was obvious that Justin was well-known there. He seemed to sense that she did not want to talk about Kate or the explosion and so, instead, he told her about himself. "I was raised in Princeton," he said. "Both my parents teach at Princeton."

"Then you've got to be very smart," Hannah smiled.

"I don't know about that. I went to Princeton, but for my master's I was ready for a new setting so I went to business school in Chicago."

They both had a salad. Hannah had an appetizer-size penne with vodka sauce. Justin decided on lasagna and ordered a half bottle of Simi chardonnay. Hannah realized it was the first time since the dinner she had with Jessie, celebrating her new designer label, that she could taste food. Justin asked her about her job, another safe subject. When they left the restaurant, he asked if he could call a cab for her.

"No. I'll walk across the park to the hospital and check on Kate. I don't think she knows that I'm there, but I just need to be with her."

"Of course, but first please give me your cell phone number. I'd like to keep in touch and find out how Kate is doing." He smiled, then added, "And report on the progress of her plant."

When Hannah reached the hospital and went up to the intensive care unit, her father was sitting at Kate's bedside. He looked up when he heard her footsteps. "She's the same," he said. "No change at all. She hasn't said anything else." He looked around, careful to see that neither a doctor nor nurse was within earshot. "Hannah, I've been thinking. The other day when Kate said to me that she was sorry about the explosion, I took it to mean she had set it."

Hannah looked at him in astonishment. "You implied that Kate said she *had* set it."

"I realize that. I wasn't thinking straight. I meant that she said she was sorry about it, not sorry that she actually caused it."

"I have never believed that Kate set that explosion," Hannah whispered vehemently, "and you could have saved me a lot of heartache if you hadn't implied the other day that she virtually admitted it. And anyhow the doctor said that anything she mumbled was probably meaningless."

"I know. It's just that what has happened in these last few days has brought back everything of the time I lost your mother and . . ." Douglas Connelly buried his face in his hands as tears began to form in his eyes.

Composing himself, he slowly got to his feet. "Sandra is in the waiting room," he explained. "I know you didn't want her to come in here."

"I don't."

Hannah stayed for an hour and then went home. She later watched the evening news while she ate a peanut butter sandwich, all that she wanted for dinner. She started to watch the next episode of a television series that she enjoyed but fell asleep on the couch. Waking up at midnight, she stripped off her clothes, put on pajamas, washed her face, brushed her teeth, and fell into bed.

The alarm woke her at seven on Monday morning. At eight she visited Kate for a half hour, then she spent a long day at work trying to concentrate on new designs for sportswear. It's one thing for your name to be put on a fashion line. It's another thing to keep it on, she reminded herself.

After work she visited Kate again, holding her hand, smoothing her forehead, speaking to her in the hope that somehow she would understand. She was about to leave when Dr. Patel came in. The deep concern in his voice was obvious when he said, "I'm afraid she's developed a fever."

35

On Monday morning, Frank Ramsey and Nathan Klein were back at the scene of the explosion. They found insurance investigators meticulously sifting through the rubble. Frank knew both of them. Over the years they had been at other fires where arson was suspected. The difference in this case, Frank thought, is that if the fire can be attributed to Gus Schmidt acting alone, they'll have to pay on the insurance claim. Even if Kate Connelly was involved, a good lawyer could lay the blame squarely on Schmidt. Unless, of course, she recovers and admits she put him up to it. Which is highly unlikely, Frank thought.

At the funeral home Friday, he and Klein had jumped up to assist when they witnessed Lottie Schmidt faint. They had carried her to the couch in the office. She had recovered quickly, but both they and her daughter had insisted that she rest on the couch in a back room for at least twenty minutes. An assistant at the funeral home had made a cup of tea for her.

Lottie's absence had given Frank and Nathan a chance to speak with others at the wake who had worked with Gus. Speaking as one, they told the fire marshals that Gus had been fired after Jack Worth became manager, and that Gus hated both him and Douglas Connelly.

"Gus was a perfectionist," was the way one of them put it. "It would take a team of experts to tell the difference between the original pieces and the copies of the furniture he made. For them to tell him his work wasn't up to par was a terrible insult."

"Did he ever talk about blowing up the complex?" Ramsey had asked.

One of the men had nodded. "In a manner of speaking. I'm on a bowling team with Gus. I mean I *was* on a bowling team with him. He always asked how things were going at the complex. When I told him we were getting a lot of returns, he said something like, 'I'm not surprised. Do me a favor and set a match to the whole place for me.' "

All of this meant that the fire could end up being blamed solely on Gus, which the worried insurance investigators admitted to Frank Ramsey on Monday morning. While they were speaking, drivers began to move the big furniture vans from under the shelter to be placed in storage. Except for the damage from smoke and flying debris, they seemed to be in pretty good shape.

"Connelly will never try to rebuild this place," Jim Casey, the older of the insurance investigators, said. "If he gets the insurance money, he can live like a king. On top of that, the property alone is worth a fortune. Why would he bother to rebuild?"

Four undamaged vans, all bearing the name CONNELLY FINE ANTIQUE REPRODUCTIONS, slowly exited past them up the driveway to the main road. Frank Ramsey saw that there was still one left in the far back area where the vans had been kept. That area had an overhead roof and open sides. He walked over to inspect the remaining van and observed the battered doors, the cracked windshield, the rusting exterior, the flat tires. It was obvious to him that this damage had preceded the explosion and that this useless van had been left there for a long time. Why didn't they just get rid of this thing? he wondered. Jack Worth impressed me as the kind who would be a good manager. On the other hand, he had not insisted on the need for security cameras, so maybe he was all show. But Worth had told them that it was Douglas Connelly who wouldn't let the money be spent. Either way, it wouldn't have cost much to have this thing towed to a junkyard.

Frank walked around to the back of the van and then, not anticipating that it would open, turned the handle of the rear door. To his astonishment, he saw unmistakable signs that the van had been occupied. Empty wine bottles were scattered on the floor. Newspapers were haphazardly strewn throughout the deep interior. He picked up the newspaper nearest to the door and looked at the date on it.

It was Wednesday, the day before the explosion.

This meant that whatever vagrant was using this place to sleep might have been here that night. Frank Ramsey did not venture farther but closed the door of the van.

It was abundantly clear to him that the whole complex had become a complicated crime scene.

36

Mark Sloane had made an appointment with Nick Greco for one o'clock on Monday afternoon. He had explained to Greco that he had just relocated to start a new job and did not want to take much more than a usual lunch hour to meet with him. The alternative would be to meet after 5 P.M.

"I get in very early but then I catch a five-twenty train home," Greco told him. "May I suggest you come at lunchtime and we can order in from the deli?"

A man in his early sixties, Nick Greco was of average height with the disciplined body of a lifetime runner. His once-dark hair was mostly gray. Rimless glasses accentuated dark brown eyes that looked out on the world with a calm but piercing appraisal. A hopeless insomniac, Greco frequently rose at three or four in the morning and walked across to the room that his wife called his nocturnal den. There he would read a book or a magazine or turn on the television to catch the latest news.

Just after 5 A.M. last Thursday, he had been watching an early news program and had seen the first pictures of the fire that was ravaging the Connelly Fine Antique Reproductions complex in Long Island City. As always, Nick's mind had gone into search-and-retrieve. His near-photographic memory had been immediately flooded with details of the tragedy, almost three decades ago, when

Douglas Connelly, his wife, Susan, his brother, Connor, and four friends had been involved in a boating accident. Only Douglas had survived.

Tragedy seems to follow some people, Greco had thought. First, the guy loses his wife, his brother, and his friends. Now his daughter is in a coma and his business is destroyed. Then the media began to insinuate that Kate Connelly and a former employee, Gus Schmidt, might have conspired to set the explosion. Greco's reaction was that he couldn't think of anything worse than to lose your daughter, unless it was to discover that your daughter had not only destroyed your life's work, but in the process had also contributed to someone else's death.

But that was not on his mind when the receptionist announced the arrival of Mark Sloane, brother of the long-missing Tracey Sloane. "Send him in," Greco said as he got up and walked to the door. A moment later he was shaking hands with Mark and inviting him to sit at the conference table in his roomy office.

They agreed on ham-and-cheese sandwiches on rye. Greco asked the receptionist to phone the order in. "I have a good coffee machine," he explained to Mark. "So as long as we're both having it black, we might as well have it as hot as possible rather than wait for a delivery."

He liked the look of Mark Sloane with his firm handshake and direct eye contact even though the younger man was very tall. But he could also see that Sloane was somewhat tense. Who wouldn't be? Nick Greco thought sympathetically. It's got to be so tough to relive his sister's disappearance. That was why he chatted about Mark's new job for a few minutes before he opened the file that he had reviewed earlier in the day.

"As you know, I was one of the detectives assigned to the case when Tracey disappeared," Greco began. "At first, by law, she was considered a missing person, but then when she didn't show up for work, missed two important auditions, and did not contact any of her friends, it was concluded that foul play was almost certainly involved."

He read aloud from his file: "Tracey Sloane, age twenty-two, left Tommy's Bistro in Greenwich Village, where she was employed as a waitress, at eleven P.M. She refused the suggestion of having a nightcap with several fellow employees, saying that she was going directly home. She wanted to get plenty of sleep before an audition scheduled for the next morning. Apparently she never got back to her apartment on Twenty-third Street. When she didn't show up for work the next two days, Tom King, the owner of the restaurant, fearing she had had an accident, went to her apartment. Accompanied by the building superintendent, he went inside. Everything was in order but Tracey was not there. Neither her family nor her friends ever saw or heard from her again."

Greco looked across the table at Mark. He saw the pain in his eyes, the same kind of pain he had seen so many times over the years in other people who were trying to trace a missing loved one. "Your sister dated, but from all the feedback we received, her career came first and she was not ready for a serious relationship. After acting classes, she would have a hamburger and a glass of wine with some of her fellow students, but that was usually it. We drew a wide circle, questioning her neighbors and friends, people in her acting classes, and coworkers, but without any success. She had simply disappeared."

The sandwiches arrived. Greco poured the coffee for both of them. When he noticed that Mark was barely touching his food, he said, "Mark, please eat. I guarantee the sandwich is good, and you have a big frame to fill. I know you came here hoping for answers but I don't have any. Your sister's case is always in the back of my mind. When I retired I took a copy of her file with me. I never thought this was a random abduction and murder. Unless the weather was very bad, Tracey always walked home. She told coworkers she wanted the exercise. I don't think she was dragged off the street. I think she met someone she knew who may have been waiting for her to leave the restaurant."

"You mean someone intended to kill her!" Mark exclaimed.

"Or picked her up at least—and then something went wrong. It could be someone whom she considered a friend but that person might have developed an obsession for her. She might have accepted a ride if that person pulled up in a car. Maybe she rebuffed his advances and he lost control. I can tell you that even after nearly twenty-eight years the case is never considered closed. Recently the bodies of four women, some of whom had been missing for more than twenty years, were found buried together, the work of a serial killer. DNA was retrieved from the bodies and identified by comparison with DNA that their family members had contributed in recent years to the police database that is maintained just for circumstances like this."

"Neither my mother nor I have ever been asked to give DNA," Mark said. "That doesn't say much to me about her case remaining open."

Greco nodded. "I fully agree, but it's really never too late. I'll call the detective bureau and make sure it is arranged for both of you. Your mother will be contacted to give the sample. Tell her not to worry about it. It's just a swab inside your mouth with something like a Q-tip."

"So right now you're not aware of anyone ever having been a suspect?"

"No, there never has been. Even though I'm retired, the guys at the bureau would have let me know if there had been any developments. The only question we had—and still have—is the significance of this picture that Tracey had on top of her dresser."

Mark looked. Tracey, beautiful, with her long hair and vivacious smile, was sitting at a table with two women and two men.

"This was apparently taken one of the nights when Tracey joined her friends at Bobbie's Joint," Nick said. "We checked all four out and saw no connection. But somehow I always felt that this picture is telling us something and I'm missing it."

37

In one way Clyde Hotchkiss was very careful. He always tried to save enough money from panhandling to have enough subway fare for at least one ride. Where he was going didn't matter. He would get on a train late at night and get off to go to his van, or wherever he wanted. Sometimes if he fell asleep he rode to the end of the line and then back to Manhattan.

After the fight with Sammy, and then being thrown out of the garage driveway on Sunday morning, he had pulled his cart to Thirty-first Street to join the St. Francis bread line. Then, because he knew Sammy would talk to his homeless friends about what had happened and they might gang up on him, he decided to do the one thing he hated to do: stay at a homeless shelter on Sunday night. But when he got there, being near so many other people nearly drove him crazy. It was as though Joey Kelly's body were again pressing against his in Vietnam, but even so he stayed. He was coughing a lot and the pain from his old hip injury was getting worse and worse. And the fact that he had forgotten the picture of him and Peggy and Skippy when he had fled the van was now bothering him a lot. At first he hadn't cared, but now he knew that he needed the comfort the picture gave him, the feeling of being loved. He hadn't seen Peggy or Skippy in all these years, but their faces were suddenly so clear in his head.

And then Joey's face and the face of that girl began to follow the faces of Peggy and Skippy, going round and round like in a carousel.

On Monday it began to rain again. Clyde's cough got deeper as he shivered, crouching against a building on Broadway. Almost no one in the hurrying crowd stopped to drop a coin or a dollar bill in the ragged cap he had placed near his feet. His luck was changing and he knew it. He had become so used to the nightly protection of the van that he couldn't last much longer in the streets without it.

Cold and wet, he dragged his cart downtown to another shelter that night. As he arrived at its door, he fainted.

38

"Mommy dancing in her red satin shoes." The memory was so clear to Kate as, again, pictures began to form in her mind while she lay deep in the induced coma that the doctors hoped would save her life. Mommy was wearing a red gown and the red shoes. Then Daddy had come into the room and said how beautiful Mommy looked, and he picked me up and danced Mommy and me out onto the terrace even though it was beginning to snow. And he sang to me. Then he danced Mommy and me around the bedroom. The next night Daddy and Mommy had gone out on the fishing trip.

Kate remembered that after Mommy died, she had taken those red satin shoes and hugged them over and over because when she did she could feel Mommy's and Daddy's arms around her. Then Daddy had taken them away from her. He seemed different. He was crying and said it was too sad to look at them and that it wasn't good for me to hug them anymore. And then he said that he would never dance with anyone else as long as he lived.

The memory disappeared and Kate slipped back into a deep sleep. After a while she heard the murmur of a familiar voice and felt lips kissing her forehead. She knew it was Hannah but she couldn't reach her. Why was Hannah crying?

39

By noon, the wrecked van had been taken to the crime lab to be examined, inch by inch, to try to learn who had been using it as a shelter. And if that person had been there the night of the explosion, could he or she have had anything to do with it?

"It certainly opens up another possibility," Frank Ramsey told Nathan Klein. They were on their way to talk to Lottie Schmidt. "We know that whoever stayed there had Wednesday's newspaper with him. Probably fished it out of a trash barrel. There were pieces of food stuck to it. My guess is that he or she, but I'll bet it was a he, would get onto the complex at night. No watchman. No security cameras. And probably would leave early in the morning before anybody came to work. And it's been going on a long time. The earliest newspapers are nearly two years old."

"And if he didn't have anything to do with the fire, he may have heard or seen something or someone there." Klein was thinking aloud. "It will be interesting to see if any DNA or fingerprints match anyone on file."

"You know that there are two guys who won't be happy to hear that the explosion might have been set off by a vagrant. Our friends the insurance investigators," Frank observed. "They'll have a hell of a time denying payment to the Connellys if this guy is identified as having a criminal history, especially if it includes arson."

Frank had called ahead to Lottie and asked if they could drop in on her for a few minutes. He had heard the resignation in her voice when she said, "I was expecting that you would want to see me again."

Thirty-five minutes later they were ringing the bell of her modest home in Little Neck. With a practiced eye, both men observed that the shrubs were neatly cut, the mature Japanese maple tree in the front yard had obviously been recently pruned, and the driveway appeared to have been resurfaced.

"Looks like Gus Schmidt took great care of his house and property," Nathan observed. "I bet those shutters have all been freshly painted, and you can see where he touched up the shingles on the right side."

Lottie Schmidt opened the door in time to hear the last comment. "My husband was a meticulous man in every way," she said. "Come in." She opened the door wider and stepped aside to admit them. Then she closed it and led them into the living room.

With one glance, Ramsey could see that it was furnished in exactly the same way as his own mother and father had furnished their own living room fifty years ago. A couch, a club chair, a wing chair, and end tables that matched the coffee table. Framed family pictures on the mantel and another grouping of them on the wall. The rug, an imitation Oriental, was threadbare in a number of spots.

Lottie was wearing a black wool skirt, a white high-neck sweater, and a black cardigan. Her thinning white hair was pulled into a neat bun. There was a weary expression in her eyes and both marshals noticed that her hands were trembling.

"Mrs. Schmidt, we're so sorry to have to see you again. We certainly don't want to upset you any more than you already are. But we do want you to be aware that the investigation into the cause of the explosion is not over, not by a long shot," Frank Ramsey said.

Lottie's expression became wary. "That's not what I'm reading in the newspapers. Some reporter from the *Post* has been talking to Gus's friends. One of them from the bowling team, who still works at Connelly's, told the reporter that only a few weeks ago, Gus told him to throw a match onto the complex and do it for him."

"Let's go back a little. When your husband was fired, was it completely unexpected?"

"Yes and no. They had had a wonderful manager for years. His name was Russ Link. He was running the business ever since the boating accident. Douglas Connelly virtually handed the daily operations over to him. Douglas would show up maybe two or three times a week when he wasn't on some kind of vacation."

"Was the business doing well under Russ Link?"

"Gus said that the problems were beginning even before he left. Their sales were really falling off. People just weren't into that kind of furniture the way they used to be. People want comfort and easy upkeep, not baroque-style couches or Florentine credenzas."

Lottie paused, her eyes brimming with rage. "Gus was their finest craftsman. Everybody knew that. The market was dwindling, but no one could copy a piece of furniture like him. He put loving care into every piece of furniture. Then that miserable Jack Worth replaced Russ and in a few months Gus was gone."

"How well did you know Jack Worth?"

"Personally, not very well at all. The annual Christmas party was usually it. Gus told me that Jack was always hitting on the young women who worked there. That was why his wife divorced him. And he has a nasty temper. If he was in a bad mood, he lit into anyone around him."

"Under those circumstances I would think Gus might have been glad to leave Connelly's," Nathan Klein observed.

"Gus loved what he was doing. He knew how to stay out of Jack's way."

Frank Ramsey and Nathan Klein were sitting on the couch. Lottie was sitting in the wing chair. Frank leaned forward, his hands clasped. He looked directly into Lottie's eyes. "Is your daughter still staying with you?"

"No. Gretchen went back to Minnesota yesterday. She is a masseuse and has a very active clientele."

"She told me she is divorced."

"For many years. Gretchen is one of those people who is naturally single. She's perfectly happy with her job and friends, and she's very active in the Presbyterian Church out there."

"From the pictures we have seen, she has a very beautiful home," Klein remarked. "I would say it's probably worth at least a million dollars. She told us that her father had bought it for her around five years ago, a few months after he was fired. Where did Gus get the money for that?"

Lottie was ready for the question. "If you examine our checkbook, you will see that Gus ruled the roost as far as money was concerned. He paid the bills and gave me cash for groceries and incidentals. He was very thrifty. Some people would even say that he was cheap. Five years ago, around the time I was in the hospital, he bought a lottery ticket and won three million dollars. I forget which state the lottery was in. He was always buying twenty dollars' worth of lottery tickets every week."

"He won a lottery! Did he pay taxes on that money?"

"Oh, I'm sure he did!" Lottie insisted. She began to explain: "Gus was always worried about Gretchen, that when something happened to us, she might go through any money we could leave her. When he won the lottery, he did what he thought was the best way to make sure she would be okay. He bought her that house and she loves it. With the rest of the lottery money, he bought an annuity for her so that she'll always have an income to keep it up."

Lottie looked directly at both marshals. "I am quite weary, as I think you can understand." She stood up. "And now may I ask you to leave?"

Silently the men followed her to the door. After she closed it behind them, they looked at each other. They did not need to exchange words. They both knew that Lottie Schmidt was lying.

Then Frank said, "No matter where he supposedly won the lottery, the state would automatically keep part of it as a tax payment. We can easily check this. But I predict that we'll soon find out that Gus Schmidt never won any big lottery."

40

At the crime lab, both the interior and the exterior of the wrecked van were methodically examined for evidence that might lead the police to the vagrant who had spent so many nights there. The empty bottles of cheap wine and the stacks of yellowing newspapers were brought out and methodically dusted for fingerprints. Ragged pieces of clothing were studied for stains of blood or other bodily fluids, as well as identifying labels. The padded floor and walls of the van were scrutinized under special lab lamps to make sure that no possible clue would be missed. Strands of human hair were placed in plastic bags.

Of enormous interest was the family picture in the battered silver frame that had been found in a corner of the interior, covered by a shabby sweater. "That picture was obviously taken decades ago," Len Armstrong, the senior chemist, commented to his assistant, Carlos Lopez. "Look at the way those people are dressed. My mother wore her hair like that when I was a kid. The father's shaggy haircut, with those long sideburns, are like the pictures I've seen of my uncle in the seventies. And this frame has been around for a long, long time."

"The question is whether the picture has anything to do with the guy who was squatting here, or is it something he found in the garbage," Lopez replied. "The marshals might want to try posting it on the Internet to see if anyone recognizes it."

They were nearing the end of the stacks of newspapers. "We're going to get enough prints off these to keep the FBI busy for a month," Lopez observed. Then, his voice suddenly crisp, he said, "Wait a minute. Look at this!" He had uncovered a spiral notebook in the midsection of one of the newspapers and opened it.

The first page contained only a few sentences: "Property of Jamie Gordon. If found, please call me at 555-425-3795."

The two chemists looked at each other. "Jamie Gordon!" Len exclaimed. "Isn't she the college kid whose body was dragged out of the East River about two years ago?"

"Yes, she is," Lopez said grimly. "And we may have just found the place where she was murdered."

41

After his lunchtime meeting with Nick Greco, Mark Sloane stayed at his desk until after 6 P.M., trying to put off the moment when he would call his mother to ask her to have a DNA swab taken to help in the search for Tracey. Talking to Greco had brought back so many memories for him. He had been only ten years old, but he remembered his mother's heartbroken crying when she learned that his sister was missing. He had stayed with neighbors while she went to New York. She had stayed a week in Tracey's apartment as the intensive police search went on.

Then, taking the sympathetic advice of the police, she had flown home. Her face ravaged with grief, she had told him that the police thought that something bad had happened to Tracey. "I'm going to hope and pray," she had told him. "I still think that maybe Tracey had some sort of memory loss. She was working so hard and taking all those classes. Or she may have had a breakdown."

His mother had even continued to pay the rent on Tracey's apartment for six months. Then, no longer able to keep it up, she had gone to New York again, that time to pack up Tracey's clothes and other personal items and bring them home. For another year she had stored Tracey's furniture in a warehouse but then had told the owners of the facility to give everything to the Salvation Army.

All of this was running through Mark's mind before he finally made the phone call home. To his surprise and relief, his mother told him that she had already been contacted by Detective Greco. "He was so nice," she said. "He said that you were going to call me, but he wanted to first assure me that this was an important step to help the process of bringing Tracey home someday. I told him that I remembered how kind he had been all those years ago and that I've always been so grateful."

She changed the subject to ask about his new job and his apartment. When their conversation ended, somewhat heartened by having spoken to her, Mark left the office. He had planned to sign up at the gym in his neighborhood, but instead he decided to go straight home. In the lobby, again waiting for the elevator, he saw the tall, attractive redhead who had been with Hannah Connelly when the marshals had arrived.

She gave him a brief smile, then turned her head away.

It doesn't take a genius to see that she's terribly upset, he thought. "I'm Mark Sloane," he said. "We rode up in the elevator together the other day. Since then I've read the story of the explosion at the Connelly factory. How is the sister who was injured doing?"

"She's developed a fever," Jessie said, quietly. "Hannah is going to stay overnight in the hospital and asked me to pick up some of her personal things."

The elevator arrived and they got into it. Mark fished out his business card and handed it to Jessie. "Look, I'm Hannah's new neighbor. If there's anything I can ever do to help out, I hope she or you will call on me."

Jessie looked at the card. "Jessie Carlson. And I'm a lawyer, too. You read about the explosion, so I guess you know that Hannah's sister, Kate, may be accused of setting it. I'm representing her."

The distress in her expression gave way to a look of fierce determination. "She is innocent and can't defend herself." Then the elevator stopped at Mark's floor and reluctantly he got off. The lawyer in him wanted to know more about how strong a case was being built against a gravely wounded young woman. The thought of the pain that her sister, who was now his neighbor, was undergoing reinforced his own personal grief about Tracey.

He had no way of knowing that the answer to his own sister Tracey's disappearance would be found in the rubble of the Connelly complex explosion.

42

Over the weekend, Jack Worth had called Douglas Connelly every day to inquire about Kate's condition and had received the same answer: "No change."

On Monday evening when Jack made the call, Doug's new girl-friend, Sandra, had answered. "Kate has a fever," she explained. "Doug is staying there with Hannah for a while. We'll have a late dinner. The poor man is so upset and, between you and me and the lamppost, I think Hannah is being rotten to him. I've seen it. You'd think she was the only one heartsick about her sister. I told Doug that he should out and out tell her that they should be emotionally supporting each other."

"I couldn't agree more," Jack Worth said, even as he sarcastically raised his eyes. "Douglas Connelly loves his girls to death."

"I mean he told me that he never remarried, because he was afraid that a stepmother might resent them. Now, I ask you, wasn't that a big sacrifice for a handsome, generous man like Doug to make?"

Sandra's voice had become indignant.

He couldn't have had a carload of bimbos all these years if he had been married, Worth thought. Just the way I got stuck, he'd have been divorced and would have had to split his assets. Doug was never going to do that. "He made a great sacrifice for his girls," was his answer to Sandra, his voice dripping with sincerity.

When he hung up, Jack Worth felt uneasy. It was all very well that Doug had figured out a scenario where Kate had been lured to the complex by Gus Schmidt because Gus intended to let her die in the explosion, but would it hold water? And if Kate came out of the coma with all her senses, would she go along with that story? If she did, everything would be A-OK. But if she didn't, Doug would be out the millions in insurance for the antiques, to say nothing of the value of the rest of the complex. He'd be left with a piece of land that was worth lots of money but nothing compared to the total value of the furniture, the buildings, the equipment, and whatever else he could throw at the insurance adjustor.

But Gus Schmidt's wife had practically admitted that she thought Gus and Kate had planned the explosion. The ironic part of what Lottie had said is that if Kate recovers and can wiggle out of it, Gus will be blamed. And Lottie's mouthing off about how bitter Gus had been at the Connellys will end up helping them collect the insurance.

Jack Worth looked around at his colonial-style home, which had been tastefully decorated by his then-wife, Linda, before she had walked out fifteen years ago, when Johnny was three years old. She hadn't told him she was leaving him. She had just cleared out, taking Johnny with her. She'd left a note on the table. "Dear Jack, I've struggled to make this work, but it can't, and it won't because you're always having your dirty little affairs with employees at Connelly's. I'm filing for divorce. My parents back me up completely. I'll stay with them for a while until I get my own place. My mother is happy to mind Johnny while I'm at work and when he's not in preschool. Good-bye, Linda."

Linda was a nurse in the neonatal unit at Columbia Presbyterian Hospital. She was still there, but now she was married to a gynecologist, Theodore Stedman. When he was twelve, Johnny, John William Worth Jr., had asked that his name be changed to John William Stedman so that he wouldn't feel different from his two little brothers.

"And besides, Dad," he had explained to Jack, "I don't see very much of you."

"Well, you know how it is, Johnny. I'm a pretty busy guy."

Johnny was eighteen now and was the quarterback on his high school football team. Jack knew that his son was playing a big game tonight and he momentarily debated about attending it. Then he shrugged. It was getting colder and he didn't feel much like sitting on freezing metal bleachers, rah-rahing for the home team. Especially since his son couldn't care less if he was there.

He debated about taking a ride up to his condo in Connecticut near the Mohegan Sun Casino, where he could try his luck at the blackjack table. But he didn't feel lucky tonight and instead decided to go out to the local pub, where he could sit at the bar, get a good steak, have a couple of drinks, and watch the ball game on the oversized television. And who knows? He might get lucky with one of the many women who hung out at the pub.

Jack smiled and thought that this would be a satisfactory answer to a very unsettling day. He was reaching into the hall closet for his jacket when the phone rang. It was Fire Marshal Frank Ramsey. "I'm very glad I caught you, Mr. Worth," he said. "We can be over at your place in twenty minutes. It's very important."

"Of course, come right over," Worth said. Slowly he hung up the phone and sank into a chair. He stared straight ahead as he tried to guess what was so urgent that those marshals needed to see him right away. Keep cool, he told himself. You have nothing to worry about. Absolutely nothing.

43

Fire Marshals Frank Ramsey and Nathan Klein had rushed to the crime lab when they received the call telling them a spiral notebook that belonged to Jamie Gordon, the murdered college student, had been found in the damaged van. It had been tested for fingerprints and hairs and blood by the time they arrived. The fingerprints matched the ones on file for Jamie. Her prints had been obtained after she disappeared by the original detectives who tested personal articles from her home and off-campus apartment.

Soberly, with gloved hands, Frank and Nathan, both fathers, had looked through the notebook. There were four accounts of homeless men and women whom she had interviewed at length. There was also a list of people whom she had tried to interview. Sometimes she didn't know their names and only gave descriptions, noting that they wouldn't talk to her at all. Other times her observations were more detailed:

"Woman in her seventies, long gray hair, missing most of her teeth . . . clearly delusional . . . said she was a nomad in the Middle Ages and is destined to live that life again now. I believe she was well educated. She goes to shelters at night but doesn't stay during the day unless the weather is really terrible. She calls herself Naomi. From what I could learn about her, she used to squat in one of the abandoned apartment buildings on the Lower East Side but they've been pretty much cleared out now. Heavy drugs were her problem. Now she begs marijuana from other street people. They all like her and most are willing to share. Then she blesses them so that in their next incarnation, they'll come back as a king or a queen or a sheikh."

The three additional case accounts were described in their own substantial detail.

"The notebook is in pretty good condition," Frank Ramsey had observed. "So maybe she carried it with her into the van."

"There's a splotch of dried mud on it," Klein pointed out. "Here's another scenario. She felt threatened by someone she talked to, dropped it when she was running away, and the guy who lived in the van picked it up."

The marshals had reached out to the detective in charge of the Gordon murder, Detective John Cruse, to inform him of their discovery. Cruse had decided immediately that the finding of the notebook would not yet be revealed to either Jamie Gordon's family or the media. "It will have to come out at some point," he had said. But they all had agreed it would be potentially harmful to both investigations to start a media circus now. They knew that any clue to Jamie Gordon's disappearance would remain on the front pages of the tabloids for weeks.

"A description of all the homeless people Jamie spoke to or described in her notebook will be sent out to every precinct in New York," Cruse said. "The local cops get to know the street people in their area."

Even though it was already early evening, Ramsey and Klein decided to go directly from the crime lab to interview Jack Worth at his home in Forest Hills, Queens. Ramsey's first question had been, "Mr. Worth, in light of the fact that it is now evident that that wrecked van had become the shelter of a vagrant, how is it possible that its presence was never noticed?"

Jack Worth's answer had been both surly and defensive. "Before I answer that, let me give you some background. I've been working there since I was twenty-five. That's over thirty years ago. I worked my way up until I was second in command to Russ Link. He was the manager ever since Mr. Doug Connelly's father died, a couple of years before the bad accident. After that, Doug Connelly barely bothered with the business, except to show up a few times a week. When a major client was coming in, he would do the grand tour of the museum with them, then take them to dinner and the theater. Or he'd travel to their company headquarters in Rome, or London, or who knows where else. It was right after Russ retired and I took over five years ago that the books were showing the deep slide in sales. At that point Doug Connelly became more involved."

He shrugged his shoulders. "That was when one of our new drivers had the accident with the van. He had made a delivery in Pennsylvania and then apparently he had stopped at a bar on the way back. He was just a few miles from here, in Jersey, when he dozed off and hit a tree on someone's lawn. The van was badly damaged, but he was able to drive it back to the lot. Lucky for us, nobody saw the accident, and lucky for him, he didn't end up with a DWI.

"Mr. Connelly didn't want to have it on record that the van had been involved in an accident with a drunken employee. He fired the guy and told me to cancel the insurance coverage. Then he just let the van sit in the back."

"Mr. Connelly seems to be very insurance conscious," Marshal Klein had observed. "Did it occur to him that the homeowner where the tree had been hit should have been notified?" It was basically a rhetorical question. Then Klein added, "Didn't any of the other employees comment on the condition of the van?"

"I think that it was pretty well known among the guys that every-one should keep their mouths shut."

"What is the name of the employee who had the accident?"

"Gary Hughes. He went on to work for a limo service, from what I heard. Good luck to the people who are in the car when he gets behind the wheel." Jack Worth got up and retrieved an address book from the desk in the room and then jotted down the driver's full name and home address. "If he still lives there and if he still works for that company," he commented as he handed Klein the sheet of paper.

"We'll find him," Ramsey said quietly.

Clearly nervous, Jack Worth moistened his lips before he an-swered. "Like I told you, Mr. Connelly knew the business was on the way down. He has been waiting for a bigger offer than the one that's been on the table. He's right about that. The property is worth more than the offer he has. He leases yachts, but he wasn't wasting five cents in these last five years on anything to fix up the complex."

Worth stood up. "Look, it's been a long day. There's nothing more I can tell you. Let's call it quits."

"All right," Klein replied. "We'll stop now, but we'll be calling you again."

"I'm sure you will," Jack Worth replied caustically.

44

Kate's fever was 101.5. Her throat dry with fear, Hannah sat by her bedside. She could only whisper, "Please, dear God, please." She knew that she should call Doug but she didn't want to. *I don't want him blubbering in here,* she thought. *Anyway, Dr. Patel may have phoned him on his own.*

At least that can be my excuse why I didn't call, she thought.

Kate, Katey, please don't die. Please don't die.

At 7:30 P.M. Jessie came in with an overnight bag. Hannah met her in the ICU waiting room. "I brought jeans and a sweater and sneakers, besides your toothbrush and toothpaste," she said. "I figured you'd be a lot more comfortable in these than sitting around dressed up and in heels."

Hannah whispered, "Thanks."

"How is she?" Jessie knew she had to ask the question even though she could see the answer in Hannah's eyes.

"If they can break the fever in the next few hours, it should be okay. If it keeps going up, it will probably mean that there's a secondary infection starting and . . ." Hannah did not finish the sentence. But then she bit her lip and said, "Jess, I'll get changed and go back inside to Kate. I don't want you sitting here if this turns out to be an all-nighter. I'll only worry about you and, I promise you, if the fever breaks I'll go home." She tried to smile. "If that happens, Dr. Patel will throw me out."

Jessie realized that Hannah needed her own space. "Just remember, I'm a phone call away."

"I know."

"What about Doug? Is he coming over?"

"Dr. Patel told me that he had talked to him. He's on his way." Then Hannah burst out, "I just wish that he'd stay away. I swear the only thing that really concerns him is putting the blame for the fire on Gus and making sure that Kate comes up with a story to match that scenario. If there's one thing that's foremost on Dad's mind, it's getting his hands on that insurance money. If he ever collects it all, forget about leasing a yacht. He'll buy one!"

The door to the waiting room was opening. It was Dr. Patel. "Kate is beginning to respond to the medication," he said. "Her fever dropped one full degree. I'm not promising anything but it's certainly a good sign." With an encouraging smile, he added, "I'll be around, Hannah. Get yourself a cup of coffee and something to eat." With a quick nod of his head, he stepped back into the corridor.

"You have just heard good news and splendid advice," Jessie said briskly. "Why don't you go into the ladies' room and get changed? I'll get some sandwiches and coffee from the cafeteria and bring them up. We'll have them here, and then I'll get out of your way." Before she could hear a protest from Hannah, she said, "It's nearly eight o'clock. Dinnertime among the elite."

"Thanks. That would be great," Hannah agreed, even while she thought, Kate's temperature is dropping but I'm grasping at straws if I try to think she's out of the woods. I know that any fever, even if it has come down, is still dangerous.

Jessie went to the elevator while Hannah went to the ladies' room, which was in the other direction. Carrying her bag, Hannah went in and saw that no one was there. With a quick motion, she kicked off her heels and peeled off her jacket, blouse, and dress slacks. I'm taking a chance on someone walking in by doing a quick strip here, she thought, but trying to change in one of those narrow stalls would take twice as long.

She was back in the waiting room just in time to see her father disappear into the ICU. I'll leave him alone with Kate, she thought. Knowing him, fifteen minutes is about as long as he'll stay. Within five minutes Jessie was back with the coffee and sandwiches. As they unwrapped them, Hannah jerked her head in the direction of the ICU. "Doug is here. He didn't see me. Let's see how long he lasts."

Fifteen minutes later, they were finished eating. They were putting the wrappings and the empty Styrofoam cups in the wastebasket as Doug came into the room.

Jessie's first thought was one that she often had when she came face-to-face with Douglas Connelly. He was a stunningly handsome man with sculpted features. His charcoal-brown hair was flecked with gray on the sides and at the temples. His midnight-blue eyes were wide apart and framed by long lashes. His smile revealed perfect teeth, and if they were capped, it was not obvious. He was impeccably dressed in a striped shirt, tie, and cardigan. Hannah had told her that she understood that his new designer of choice was Armani.

With all his good looks and impeccable style, Doug still gave the impression of being the kind of man who was also an athlete. Jessie knew that was an accurate take. She had been with him and the girls on a number of occasions when he was accepting a country club championship trophy for golf or tennis. And she knew that when he was younger he had also played polo.

"Hannah, I just spoke to Dr. Patel inside there," he said. "He's very encouraged that Kate's fever is dropping."

"Yes, I know," Hannah replied.

"I'd stay longer, but I think those fire marshals want to talk to me tonight. I can't imagine what the rush is, why it won't hold till morning. Have you heard from them?"

"No, I haven't. Not since Thursday night."

"I imagine they're with Jack Worth now."

Doug looks worried, Jessie thought, and I don't think it's all about Kate's condition.

Doug kissed Hannah tentatively on the cheek and said, "I am sure our prayers are being answered. The fever seems to be under control."

"Yes. And I've been away from Kate too long," Hannah said. "Good-bye, Dad. Jess, a thousand thanks."

She was gone, on her way back to the ICU. Jessie was glad to have the chance to have a few minutes alone with Doug as they made their way down the elevator and out to the hospital entrance where Doug's car was waiting. "I'd offer to drive you home," he said, "but those marshals are coming and the crosstown traffic is always heavy."

"That's fine," Jessie said. "I see a cab coming." She raised her hand to hail it. "But Doug," she added quickly, "don't forget I'm representing Kate. Anything I can find out to help her, if she's charged with being involved in the explosion, is very important. I'd really like to know what the marshals are up to."

"I'll call you in the morning if there's anything to report," he promised as he got into the car. The minute he was inside, with the door closed, he pulled out his cell phone and called Jack Worth. "Have you spoken to those guys yet?"

"Yes. You know that wrecked van that was in the back parking lot?"

"What about it?"

"Some vagrant has been making it home-sweet-home for the last couple of years."

"For the last couple of years?" Doug repeated in a nervous whisper.

"Yes. They're wondering if he might have started the fire. That's good. At least it's one more angle that might take any suspicion off Kate."

"I can see that and I agree that's good. How often do they think he's been there?"

"From the newspapers they found, he was there pretty regularly and almost definitely the night of the explosion."

"So if he didn't set it, he could be a witness."

Douglas Connelly did not want to consider what that could mean. He broke the connection.

45

Frank Ramsey and Nathan Klein had left Jack Worth and driven over the 59th Street Bridge into Manhattan. When they arrived at the upscale apartment building of Douglas Connelly, they were told by the doorman that he had just returned home. They went upstairs to find the same scenario they had witnessed a few nights earlier. Sandra answered the door and walked them back to the library, where Connelly was sitting, a drink in his hand.

"I just wanted you to know that Kate is running a fever and, as you can see, Douglas is very distraught," Sandra said. "I hope that you make this very short because he needs to relax and have something to eat. The poor man is at the end of his rope."

"We are both very sorry if Ms. Connelly's condition has worsened," Frank Ramsey said sincerely. "If Mr. Connelly intends to go back to the hospital tonight, we certainly understand that, and we can make an appointment to see him tomorrow."

"No. His other daughter is playing the martyr. She wants to be alone with her sister."

"That's enough, Sandra." Still holding his glass, Connelly stood up. "What is this I hear about a vagrant who might have been living in the van?"

"*Was* living in the van, Mr. Connelly," Frank Ramsey corrected.

"And I understand that he may have been there over a period of years?"

"At least two. There are newspapers going back that far."

Douglas Connelly took a long sip from the glass of vodka. "Incredible as it sounds, I can understand how that could have happened. You've seen the shed where the vans are housed. It's open at the front but the sides and back are enclosed. That van was parked behind all the others. In these last few years usually two of the four in the front were in constant service. The other two formed a natural obstruction of any view of the wrecked van.

"Sometimes, when we had a long-range delivery, the driver would leave in the late evening or the very early morning. But certainly no driver would have had any reason to look into that old van. If the person in it got out before people began to arrive in the morning, he wouldn't have been noticed. If he stayed inside the van all day, the vagrant wouldn't have been noticed, either. But, since he would have obviously needed food and at least occasionally some kind of sanitation, I would imagine that he left by early morning, when no one was around, and came back late at night."

"I think you're right," Nathan Klein agreed. "Our people have been canvassing the neighborhood. A derelict dragging a cart has been observed by some in the early-morning hours, but that area, with all the warehouses surrounding your complex, has a number of homeless taking shelter at night."

"There is another possibility, Mr. Connelly," Frank Ramsey said. "We believe that the vagrant may have been there at the time of the explosion. He may have been a witness to what happened that night." With narrowed eyes he watched for Connelly's reaction.

"We know that my daughter Kate and Gus Schmidt were on the premises. But even if by any chance the vagrant happened to see them there together, he would have no way of knowing that Kate had been lured there by Gus Schmidt."

"And that's going to be the official party line," Ramsey sarcastically commented to Klein as they drove back to Fort Totten to file an updated report. When they were finished, they got into their own cars and, weary to the bone, went their separate ways home.

46

At 10:30 P.M. on Monday, Kate's fever shot up alarmingly to 104 degrees. Dr. Patel stayed through the night in the hospital. The nurse told Hannah that he was catching some sleep in a room down the hall but could be back in an instant. Beyond tears and beyond ability to think coherently, Hannah sat in numbed silence in the ICU cubicle beside Kate. Sometimes Kate restlessly stirred, setting off an alarm and causing the nurse to rush in to be sure that she did not pull out any of the tubes that were dripping medications into her arms.

By seven o'clock the next morning, Kate's fever broke. With a broad smile, the nurse asked Hannah to go into the waiting room while they changed Kate's gown and the sheets, which were now drenched with perspiration.

When Hannah, weak with relief, entered the waiting room, she found a priest waiting to speak to her. He stood up and greeted her warmly. He was a tall, thin man who appeared to be in his early sixties, with hazel eyes that crinkled as he greeted her. When he took her hand, his grip was firm and reassuring. "Hello, Hannah. I'm Father Dan Martin. The doctor just stopped by," he said. "So I know Kate is doing better. You have no reason to remember me, but when you were young, your family were parishioners at St. Ignatius Loyola."

"Yes, we were," Hannah agreed, thinking with guilt that since Kate had gotten her apartment on the West Side and she herself had moved to the Village, neither one of them had been much for going to church except at the major holidays.

"I wasn't at St. Ignatius in those years," he said, "but I was on the altar at the funeral mass for your mother and uncle. I was just ordained then and since the accident I've thought so often of your family. You were just a baby but your sister was there. She was only three years old and holding your father's hand. I've attended many sad funerals but that one has always stood out in my mind. I've been praying for Kate since the accident and I just wanted to stop in and see if you wanted me to visit her."

For a moment he paused, then added, "Kate was such a beautiful little girl with that long blond hair and those exquisite blue eyes. The two caskets were in the aisle and she kept trying to pull the cloth covering off the first one as though she knew that was where her mother's body was resting."

"There were a lot of reporters outside the church and at the grave," Hannah said. "I've seen the television clips. It was such a horrible accident. The other two couples who died were well-known in the financial markets."

Father Martin nodded. "I made it my business to call on your father afterward and we became a bit friendly. He was in a terrible state over losing your mother and, of course, his brother and friends as well. The poor man couldn't stop crying. He was absolutely distraught. He told me that if it weren't for his little girls, he'd give anything to have died in the accident, too."

He certainly got over that, Hannah thought, and then she was ashamed of herself. "I know how much he loved my mother," she said. "When I was about thirteen, I asked him why he hadn't remarried. He told me that Robert Browning was asked the same question after Elizabeth Barrett Browning died. His answer was that it would be an insult to her memory to marry again."

"A few months after the funeral, I was assigned to Rome to attend the Gregorian College, and I lost touch with your father. I'd like to give him a call now. Would you mind giving me his number?"

"Of course." She recited Doug's cell and home numbers and, for a moment, almost added the business number of the complex but stopped herself. Father Martin jotted them down.

Hannah hesitated, then said, "After twelve years as a student at Sacred Heart Academy, it would seem as though I should have called to have Kate receive the Sacrament of the Sick."

"I am prepared to offer that now," Father Martin said quietly. "So often, even to this day, people are afraid that to receive it is a sure sign that someone is about to die, which simply isn't the case. It is also a prayer that the patient will return to health."

When the nurse came back to invite them back to Kate's bedside, they found her lying quietly, now seemingly in a deep, restful sleep.

"She's under heavy sedation but sometimes she'll say something," Hannah whispered. "The doctor said that whatever she says is probably meaningless."

"I have seen many instances where the person who appears to be in a coma actually is aware of almost everything that is going on around them," Father Martin said, as he opened the black leather case that he had carried with him into the room.

Father Martin took out his folded stole from the case, kissed it, and placed it around his neck. Then he opened a small jar of sacred oil. "This is pure olive oil blessed by the bishop," he told Hannah. "Olive oil was specially chosen by the Church because of the healing and strengthening effects that are its characteristics in everyday life."

Hannah watched as he dipped his finger in the oil and then made the sign of the Cross on Kate's forehead and hands. Healing and strengthening, she thought as she listened to the words of the prayers Father Martin was offering over Kate. A sense of peace came over her and for the first time she began to believe that Kate might recover fully and be able to explain why she was in the complex with Gus that night.

Maybe I'm being too hard on Dad, she thought. From the beginning he's been afraid that Kate set that fire. Maybe it isn't just the insurance he's worried about. Maybe he's frantic at the thought that if Kate gets better and is found guilty of setting the fire, she faces many years in prison. Maybe I should give him a break.

When she and Father Martin left Kate a few minutes later, she stopped at the desk of the intensive care unit. The nurse, who by now was on a first-name basis with her, said, "Hannah, tell me you're going home."

"Yes, I am," Hannah said. "To shower and change. The fashion business is fast-moving, and so I can't stay away from the office for too long. But looking at Kate now, I'm not afraid to leave her."

Father Martin waited while she retrieved her suitcase and coat from the closet and they left the hospital together. At the door, she said, "I'm going to be honest. I haven't been very nice to my father since all this happened. It's a long story but you've given me some things to think about and I do hope you get together with him soon. It will make all the difference to him, I know."

47

Tim Fleming was the supervising fire marshal to whom Frank Ramsey and Nathan Klein reported. Over the past five days since the explosion at the Connelly complex, they had been submitting daily detailed updates to him regarding the investigation. On Tuesday morning, both refreshed by a good night's sleep, they were in his office at Fort Totten.

Fleming, a solidly built man in his late fifties with iron-gray hair and a poker face, had thoroughly examined the reports and went straight to the salient facts of the case. His well-modulated voice was deep and resonant. "This Connelly guy and his plant manager let a wrecked van sit in their parking lot for five years? Be interesting to see if their drunken driver really did hit only a tree and not some poor guy on a bicycle."

"The exterior of the van was thoroughly checked for any sign of blood or human tissue," Klein reassured his boss. "He did hit a tree. It was an elm and from what they can tell, it was already dead."

"So the drunk driver saved the homeowner from maybe having the tree crash on his house in a storm," Fleming observed. "What a nice guy."

Ramsey and Klein smiled. Their boss was known for that kind of comment. But immediately Fleming was all business again. "Jamie

Gordon's notebook was found in the van, but that doesn't mean that she brought it there herself."

"No, it doesn't."

"And the vagrant who was squatting there doesn't have a record?"

"None that we can find. The fingerprints in the van didn't match up to anybody with a criminal history."

"Okay. We'll call a press conference for noon to give out the new information that a vagrant may have been on the premises at the time of the explosion. I understand that the descriptions of the homeless people listed in the notebook are already being circulated to all the precincts in the city."

Klein and Ramsey nodded.

"The cops know the local street people. I wouldn't be surprised if they don't round up a few of them for us pretty fast. The commissioner has decided that we'll pass out copies of that family picture to the media. But will continue to say nothing to the press about Jamie Gordon's notebook. The guys at the crime lab know that her name is not even to be whispered."

"Absolutely," Ramsey confirmed.

"Telling the media about the vagrant will give them enough to chew on," Fleming said. "They've all but convicted the Connelly daughter who was injured as having set the explosion with her buddy, the Schmidt guy."

He stood up, indicating that the meeting was over. "Twelve o'clock sharp," he said, then added, "You guys are doing a good job, which, incidentally, does not surprise me."

Three hours later the media conference became hot breaking news when the information about a vagrant possibly being present at the time of the explosion was announced. Copies of the picture of the young couple and baby were handed out. After nearly a week of speculation that Kate Connelly and Gus Schmidt were arsonists, the new angle was fresh meat for reporters to keep the story on the front pages.

By two o'clock, the picture taken more than forty years ago in a modest ranch-style home on Staten Island was all over the Internet.

Frank Ramsey was more optimistic than Nathan Klein that the picture would be tied to the vagrant. "My bet is that it got thrown in the garbage when somebody's house was cleaned out," Nathan predicted. "I mean, when a friend of my wife, Sarah, Kat LeBlanc, recently lost her grandmother, there were drawers full of old pictures. Most of them were snapshots, some eighty and ninety years old, of her grandmother's cousins, people Kat couldn't even identify. Sarah asked her if she was going to bring all that stuff home and drag it up to the attic so that her kids could have the job of throwing it out in thirty or forty years."

"What did her friend do?" Frank asked, remembering that his own mother still had boxes of pictures of long-departed relatives.

"Kat kept some of the ones that had her grandmother in them. Then she picked out a few more where she could tell who the people were, and tore up the rest."

"I still say the picture in the van is going to give us a lead," Frank told him, "and I'm itching to pay Lottie Schmidt another visit. The report from the New York IRS should be in sometime today. If Gus Schmidt did pay taxes on a winning lottery ticket, then, as my father used to say, 'I'll eat my hat.' "

"Your hat is safe," Klein assured him. "I'll give the tax guys another call and tell them that, this time, 'urgent' means urgent."

48

Shirley Mercer, an attractive black woman in her early fifties, was the social worker who was assigned to visit Clyde in the hospital. She arrived at his bedside in a ward in Bellevue late Tuesday afternoon. He had been bathed and shaved and his hair had been trimmed. He was suffering from severe bronchitis but in the nineteen hours he had been there, his temperature had returned to normal and he had eaten well. He was about to be discharged and Shirley had arranged for him to be taken to a room in one of the city-run hotels.

Shirley had studied Clyde's file before she went in to visit him. The staff at the shelter where he had collapsed knew very little about him. He had only stayed there occasionally and each time had given a different last name. They believed that his first name was correct. He always said he was Clyde. But the last names always varied. Clyde Hunt, Clyde Hunter, Clyde Holling, Clyde Hastings. Hastings was the name he had given at the shelter last night when he had regained consciousness and was waiting for the ambulance.

Some of the other regulars at the shelter had told the director that they had seen him around for years. "He comes and goes by himself. He doesn't want to talk to anyone. He gets mad if someone bunks near him on the street. You almost never saw him at night for the past couple of years. Everyone figured that he had found a place to hole up."

Another street person had claimed that on Saturday night, Clyde had punched out Sammy when Sammy tried to sleep in the same driveway.

But he has no police record, Shirley noted, and apparently has been homeless for many years. He had told the nurse that he was sixty-eight years old, which seemed about right. But one thing that is certain, Shirley thought, is that if he stays on the streets he'll die of pneumonia.

Armed with that information, she had gone to Clyde's bedside. His eyes were closed. Although the skin on his face was blotched, and the lines between his nostrils and his lips were deep, she could see that when he was younger he must have been a good-looking man.

She touched his hand. His eyes flew open and his head sprang up from the pillow. "I'm so sorry, Mr. Hastings," she said, her voice gentle. "I didn't mean to startle you. How are you feeling?"

Clyde sank back as he looked at the kindly expression in the eyes of the woman who was standing beside his bed. Then he began to cough, a deep, rasping cough that shook his chest and his back. Finally he was able to again sink back into the pillow.

"Not so hot," he said.

"It's a good thing you were brought here last night," Shirley said. "Otherwise, by today, you'd be having a full-blown case of pneumonia."

Clyde vaguely remembered that he had fainted just as he got to the shelter. And then another thought rushed into his mind. "My cart! My stuff! Where is it?"

"They have it for you," Shirley said quickly. "Clyde, is Hastings your last name?"

"Yeah. Why?"

"Sometimes you have given other names."

"Sometimes I get confused."

"I see. Clyde, do you have any family?"

"No."

"No one? A brother or sister?"

Clyde thought of the picture of Peggy and Skippy and him. For a moment his eyes glistened with tears.

"You do have someone, don't you?" Shirley asked, sympathetically.

"That was a long time ago."

Shirley Mercer could see that there was no use talking to Clyde about a possible family connection. "Were you ever in the military?" she asked. "According to your medical report, you have scars on your chest and back. You are about the age of a Vietnam veteran."

She was getting too close. "I was never in the service," Clyde said, then added, "I was what they used to call a conscientious objector when they had the draft back then."

Joey Kelly. *Tell Mama how much I loved her . . .* I never did visit his mother, Clyde thought. I couldn't tell her that he was trying to hold his guts together when he said that. And his blood was soaking through me like I was dying, too . . .

"Shut up," he snapped angrily at Shirley Mercer. "*Shut up.* And tell them to give me back my clothes. I'm out of here."

Shirley drew back, afraid that he was about to strike her. "Clyde," she protested, "you are going to leave now. I'm arranging for you to have your own room in a hotel that the city runs. You'll have your medicine with you and you must remember to take it all. You'll be warm and dry and will have food. You need that to get better."

Be careful, Clyde warned himself. He knew he had been about to hit her. If I do that I'll get arrested and I'll be in one of those hellholes they call jail. "I'm sorry," he said. "I'm real sorry. I shouldn't have gotten mad at you. It's not your fault. You're a nice lady."

He knew what the hotel would be like. A dump. A real dump. I'll clear out as soon as she leaves me there, he thought. I'll find another place like my van where I can stay every night. Then his eyes widened. The television set on the wall behind the social worker was on. He saw some news guy showing the picture of him and Peggy and Skippy. They'll blame everything on me, he thought. The explosion. The girl who came into the van that night.

Trying not to show his panic, he said, "I'll be glad to go to the hotel with you. I figured it out. I can't be on the streets anymore."

"No, you can't," Shirley Mercer said firmly, even as she knew she was reading Clyde's mind. We'll go through the motions of getting him settled and then he'll take off, she thought. I wonder what the truth is about his past, but my guess is we'll never know. She stood up. "I'll get someone to help you dress," she said. "They've got some nice warm clothes for you."

Behind her on the wall the news anchor was saying, "If anyone recognizes the family in this picture, please contact this number immediately. . . ."

49

⸙

Forty-two-year-old Skip Hotchkiss owned five delicatessens in Irvington and Tarrytown, New York. Both towns were suburbs in Westchester County, located less than an hour's drive from Manhattan. From the time he had been a child, he had often gone after school to the delicatessen on Staten Island where his mother had worked after his father disappeared.

The understanding owner, a kindly German immigrant, Hans Schaeffer, had made the young boy welcome. Skip had done his homework in the back office of the deli and, as he got older, he began to stock the shelves and make deliveries.

The homemade salads and cold cuts and apple strudel that the Schaeffers prepared were delicious and often Skip would sit with Mrs. Schaeffer as she did the cooking and baking. Soon he was helping her to make the food. He had plenty of friends at school and was an excellent student but he was never much for sports. The delicatessen was where he wanted to be.

At six o'clock, he and his mother would walk home together. She had never left the small house she had shared with his father. "Never think he abandoned us, Skip," she would say. "He loved both of us so much but he came back from the war damaged and frightened. Something happened that I'm sure he never talked about, even when the doctors tried to help him. Look at all the medals he earned in Vietnam. He paid a great price for them."

"Too great a price?" Skip remembered asking.

He had never forgotten his mother's wistful smile. "I guess it was."

After high school, Skip went on a scholarship to Virginia Tech, where he enrolled in the culinary school. For two years after graduation, he worked as a sous-chef in a restaurant in New York. By then, old Mr. Schaeffer was ready to retire and he turned over the deli to Skip. He sold it to him without requiring a down payment, only a ten-year payout. "People tell me I'm crazy," he said at that time. "I'm not crazy. I know you. You'll have the whole thing paid off in five years."

Which was exactly the way it turned out to be. At that point, Skip, married with two small sons, decided that he wanted to move to Westchester County. He sold the deli and opened the first new one in Irvington. Now, fifteen years later, he was a prosperous, well-liked member of the community. None of his four sons was named Clyde. He often thought that his father had nicknamed him Skip because he didn't like the name, either.

His mother, Peggy, had remained on Staten Island. "All my friends are here," she had told him. "It's not that far so you'll see plenty enough of me." Now in her late sixties, she was an active volunteer in her parish and in local charities. Donald Scanlon, a widower and longtime neighbor who had been a New York City detective, would have given anything to marry Peggy but Skip knew it wouldn't happen. Peggy had never stopped believing that her husband was still alive.

On Tuesday evening, Skip finished making the rounds of his stores and got home at quarter of six. With his four sons now ranging in age from ten to sixteen, he had never allowed his flourishing businesses to distract him from his roles as husband and father.

Sometimes you learn by lack of example, was the rueful thought that occasionally crossed his mind.

When he opened his front door, it was to hear his two middle sons in a heated argument. One look from him settled it quickly. "I suggest you both need a little time in your rooms to cool off," he said, his voice level but unmistakably firm.

"But, Dad . . ." The protests ended and the boys went upstairs, heavy footsteps indicating their displeasure at the banishment. When they were gone, his wife, Lisa, sighed, "I don't know how any woman raises kids alone." She kissed him. "Welcome to the battlefield."

"What was it about this time?"

"Ryan dropped Billy's cell phone in the toilet."

"By mistake, I hope," Skip said quickly.

"Yes, I do believe that. And it even seems to be working okay now. Dinner will be ready in about an hour. Let's have a glass of wine and watch the news."

"Sounds good to me. What time are Jerry and Luke getting home?"

"The usual. Practice will be over pretty soon."

As she walked ahead of him into the family room, Skip Hotchkiss reflected on what a lucky man he was. He and Lisa had met at Virginia Tech. There had never been anyone else for either one of them.

Like my mother felt about my father, was his unexpected thought as he poured the wine from the bar in the family room, touched Lisa's glass with his, and settled down next to her on the sofa.

The CBS news was on. "Stunning new development in the explosion at the Connelly furniture complex that took one life and gravely injured Kate Connelly, the daughter of the owner," Dana Tyler, the coanchor, was saying. "It has been learned that a homeless person had been living in a wrecked van on the property and may have been there the night of the explosion. A picture found in the van may help the police to trace that person. Take a look at it now."

Skip had only been mildly interested in the story, more concerned with the fact that his thirteen- and fourteen-year-old sons were always arguing about something. But then he inhaled sharply. "Oh my God," he said. "Oh my God."

"Skip, what is it?" Lisa's voice was panicky.

"That picture. Look at it. Where have you seen it before?"

Lisa stared. "It's the one your mother has on the mantel. Oh, Skip, is it possible that the homeless man is your father?"

50

On Tuesday morning, the cleanup process to remove the rubble of the Connelly complex began. After intensive investigation, the origin and cause of the explosion and the ensuing fire had been determined beyond any doubt. The gas line, which had been partially unscrewed, a clear sign of tampering, had sent gas flowing into the museum until it was ignited by an exposed wire in the Fontainebleau suite there.

The insurance investigators had found burned and broken claws that had once graced stately antique chairs and tables, as well as bits of material that had been woven three centuries ago. Some of the exhibits had been found as far as a block away in the driveways of warehouses. But now it was time to remove the shattered and potentially dangerous debris.

The forklifts were hauled in on carriers. Dumpsters were lowered from other trucks and placed in the area where the cleanup began. The workers started with the museum, which for years had housed the exquisite antique furniture that Dennis Francis Connelly had been so proud to copy. "It looks like a war zone," Jose Fernandez, one of the young workers, commented to the supervisor. "Whoever set this off meant business."

"It is a war zone," the supervisor agreed. "And whoever set it off did mean business. We've got to watch out for sinkholes. I don't want anybody to get hurt and I don't want to lose any equipment here."

All day, pausing only at noon for a lunch break, the large cleanup crew set about clearing the smoke-charred ruins and knocking over the broken stone walls that were now jagged and listing.

At five o'clock, as they were wrapping up, a sinkhole appeared in the pavement near the area where the vans had been parked. "No harm done," the supervisor said. "Put some yellow tape around it in case some dope decides to come scavenger hunting here tonight."

Grateful for the decision not to do any work on the sinkhole now, they quickly placed four stanchions around the crumbling pavement; bright orange-yellow tape, bearing the word DANGER, was looped from one to the other of them.

Sufficient unto the day, Jose thought as, stretching to relieve his aching shoulders, he got behind the wheel of one of the trucks. With a master's degree in ancient history, and more than one hundred thousand dollars in college loans, he had been grateful to get this job, promising himself that it was just a temporary tide-over until the economy got better. Raised in a housing project in Brooklyn by his parents, who were hardworking immigrants from Guatemala, he was fond of looking for a quotation that might fit the particular circumstance he was in.

Sufficient unto the day, he reflected. What's the rest of that one? I've got it, he thought as he turned on the engine. *Take therefore no thought for the morrow: for the morrow shall take thought for the things of itself. Sufficient unto the day is the evil thereof.* Pleased with himself, Jose put his foot on the gas.

In the distance behind the departing trucks, the evening shadows had already begun to cover the figure that was almost fully concealed under the broken slabs of pavement. It was a skeletal form, still wearing a grimy, tarnished chain with the name TRACEY engraved on the medallion.

51

Justin Kramer spent a good part of both Monday and Tuesday thinking about Hannah Connelly.

He had been touched by Kate Connelly's obvious concern for him when at the closing she had realized that he had been forced to sell the condo because he had lost his job. He had tried even then to assure her that it wasn't that big a deal. Yes, he had enjoyed living there. No, he didn't want to live beyond his means. Two thousand monthly maintenance on top of a mortgage payment wasn't in his budget when he was unemployed.

Giving Kate a bromeliad plant had actually been an afterthought. He had happened to be in the apartment when the real estate agent was showing it to Kate, the prospective buyer. She had admired it and clearly was knowledgeable about plants, and that's how his housewarming gift came about. He liked Kate.

But when he had gone up to the apartment on Sunday afternoon and met Hannah Connelly, something had happened. Her midnight-blue eyes, framed by long lashes, were enhanced by her ivory complexion and cap of shining dark brown hair. She was wearing running shoes and barely came up to his chest. At five feet ten, Justin had always longed for at least two more inches.

Justin remembered how, when he complained about his height,

his father had suggested wryly, "Then stand up straight. There's nothing like a military carriage to make you look taller."

He and Hannah had stood together for a moment before they had gone into the kitchen and he had collected the plant. Then, on the way down in the elevator, Justin had been trying to decide if it would be too much to ask Hannah if she'd had lunch yet.

But he had asked her, and she hadn't had lunch yet, and she did go out with him. And it had been fun. After lunch, Hannah had gone back to the hospital to check on Kate. All day Monday, Justin debated calling her, but decided that he wouldn't want her to feel crowded. He told himself that watering a plant was not necessarily an open channel to developing the friendship that he very much wanted to develop.

On Tuesday, he had a late-afternoon meeting with a prospective client, a man in his late thirties who had inherited some money and was anxious to invest it properly. After it was over, Justin had elected to walk home from his new office. That decision meant that he would pass by Kate Connelly's apartment.

As he did, he glanced sideways at the door, half hoping that Hannah might have stopped there again. Instead, he recognized the man who was coming out. He had seen enough pictures of Douglas Connelly in the newspapers in the last few days to be sure that he was right. Justin stopped. "Mr. Connelly," he said.

Surprised, Douglas Connelly stopped and took Justin's measure, noting his clean-cut appearance, including the fact that he was well dressed in business attire. Connelly forced a smile.

"Mr. Connelly, I know your daughters. How is Kate doing today?"

"She doing better, thank you. How do you know her?"

Briefly, Justin explained the connection, finishing with, "Then I met Hannah here on Sunday afternoon and picked up the plant I had given to Kate."

"That was Sunday afternoon?"

"Yes."

"And you met Hannah here?"

"Yes, sir, I did."

"She didn't mention to me that she was here. That explains it," Connelly said more to himself than to Justin. "Well, nice to meet you." With a brief nod, he stepped into his car.

It was a Bentley. Justin, a car aficionado, admired the stately vehicle as the driver pulled away from the curb. Then he thought that maybe this would be a good reason to call Hannah, to tell her that he had happened to run into her father.

Standing on the street, he pulled out his cell phone. Her number was already on his contacts list.

She answered on the first ring. When he asked about Kate, she told him about going back to the hospital late Sunday afternoon and then finding that Kate had developed a fever Monday night.

The exhaustion in Hannah's voice was obvious.

"How is she now?" Justin asked.

"Better. The fever broke this morning. I had to go to work today but I just stopped in and she's really as good as she can be."

"I was going to suggest having a quick dinner, but I have a feeling you're ready to pack it in."

"Trust me, I am. I never did get to bed last night, but thanks."

Belatedly, Justin remembered that his excuse for calling Hannah was to tell her that he had run into her father. As he did, he realized that nothing Douglas Connelly had told him suggested that Kate had been in a crisis situation in the hospital.

"You just ran into my father coming out of Kate's building?" Hannah asked, astonished.

"Yes. In fact he just got into his car."

"He didn't tell me that he was planning to go over there, but that's not important." Hannah tried to keep the anger out of her voice as she asked herself why her father had gone to Kate's apartment. It certainly wasn't because he was worried that some food might spoil, she thought. He was after the jewelry and probably wanted to go through Kate's desk to find out what he could about her affairs.

It was obvious to Justin that Hannah was distressed by what he had just told her. "Hannah, are you okay?"

It seemed to Hannah that the question was coming from some remote corner of the earth. "Oh, I am," she said quickly. "Justin, I'm sorry. I was just . . . surprised. Thanks again for calling."

Justin Kramer hoped that before she clicked off, Hannah had heard him say, "I'll give you a call in a day or two."

52

Mark Sloane was enjoying his new job. He realized that every morning he was looking forward to getting to work with a vigor that he had not felt for the last several years in his old firm in Chicago.

He liked his condo and had spent Monday evening unpacking paintings and artifacts that he had gathered on his annual overseas vacations.

Then he had grouped them on the floor below the walls where he intended to hang them. The ones that belonged on the shelves of the second bedroom, which he had turned into a den, were already in place. The room had its own full bath and the most comfortable pullout couch he could buy. He had purchased it hoping that his mother would visit him several times a year.

After running into Jessie on Monday evening, Mark had been aware all day Tuesday that Kate Connelly had had a setback and had been running a fever. He realized that his concern for a new neighbor he had never really met was tied in with his visit with Nick Greco and their discussion about Tracey's disappearance. It was as though all the emotional scar tissue that he had formed over the years had suddenly been sliced open.

It was the minute-to-minute waiting, and hoping, and praying that he knew was going on in the lives of Hannah Connelly and her closest friend, Jessie Carlson. There was something about their shared heartsick concern for Hannah's sister, Kate, that reminded him of the day his mother had received the call about Tracey.

The exact moment when that call came was etched in his mind even though he had been only ten years old. He had stayed home from school because he had a heavy cold, and he had been sitting at the kitchen table with his mother. She had just made a cup of tea and a bacon sandwich for him when the phone had rung.

"Missing!" That was the word he had heard his mother utter, her voice quivering, and he had known right away that it had to be about Tracey.

And then the waiting had begun. The waiting that was still going on.

On Tuesday evening Mark did go to the gym. He signed up as a member and did a solid hour-and-a-half workout that relieved the tension in his back and neck. After he had showered and changed, he shoved his exercise clothes into a duffel bag and dropped it off at home. Then, not feeling like grilling the steak that was in the refrigerator, he instead opened his iPhone and did a Web search. Tommy's Bistro was still listed as a pub, located only four blocks from his apartment.

They've probably just kept the name of the place, he thought, as he put on his windbreaker. I can't believe the same owner would still be there after nearly thirty years.

He had not reached his front door before his cell phone rang. It was Nick Greco. "You'll never guess where I'm headed," Mark told him. "Tommy's Bistro, the place where Tracey worked, is just four blocks from here. I'm going there for dinner and maybe if, by any chance, the old owner is still around, I'll try to talk to him. He was the one who was so worried about Tracey that he went looking for her when she didn't show up for work."

"Then I've caught you just in time," Greco said. "I just received a call from one of my friends in the department. They'll be announcing in the next few minutes that they've made an arrest in the murder of another twenty-three-year-old actress who disappeared last month and was found dead. She was strangled."

"I don't understand," Mark said. "Nick, what are you telling me?"

"The alleged killer's name is Harry Simon. He's fifty-three years old and—can you believe it—he works in the kitchen at Tommy's Bistro. And he's been there for thirty years! Like all the other employees, he was questioned when Tracey disappeared but he seemed to have an airtight alibi at the time. Now maybe we'll find out if that so-called airtight alibi still holds up all these years later."

53

Shirley Mercer had escorted Clyde to his room at the city-run An-
sler Hotel. With its gilded ceilings and exquisite candelabra, it had
once housed one of the great dining rooms in New York City. But
that was ninety years ago. In the 1950s, it had fallen out of favor with
sophisticated New Yorkers and eventually was closed. Located near
Macy's department store on Thirty-third Street, for many years it
had been boarded up, and then several years ago had been reopened
as city housing for the homeless.

Shirley had been pleased to see that the room assigned to Clyde
was a single with a cot, a small dresser, and a chair. The bathroom
was down the hall. In the corridor she could see scraps of takeout
food casually dropped on the floor. She knew that the cleaning staff
did the best it could but was always dealing with some people who
had long ago lost any sense of hygiene. Someone in the adjacent
room was playing music so loud that it threatened to shatter her
eardrums.

She observed the expression on Clyde's face as he pulled his cart
into the room. It was impassive, noncaring. I won't be gone fifteen
minutes before he's out the door behind me, she thought.

Clyde began to cough, the deep, rumbling cough she had observed in the hospital. "Clyde, I have a couple of bottles of water
here. You must be sure to take your medicine."

"Yes. Thanks. This is real nice. Homey."

"I see you have a sense of humor," Shirley said. "Good luck, Clyde. I'll look in on you in a day or two."

"That would be nice."

What kind of man was he? Shirley wondered, as she walked down the four flights to the lobby. It was either that way out or trust herself to the elevator that broke down frequently. She had been trapped in it for an hour a few months ago.

When she reached the sidewalk, she stood there long enough to fasten the top button of her coat, then tried to decide if she should stop at Macy's and pick up a present for the baby shower she was going to attend on Saturday. But then the thought of her snug apartment in Brooklyn and the fact that it was her husband's day off and he had promised to cook dinner for them was too inviting. She went to the corner and down the steps to the subway, grateful to be going home to an atmosphere of warmth and love.

If only I could really help people like Clyde, she thought. But I guess the best I can do is to keep him from dying of pneumonia in an alleyway somewhere.

54

❧

Peggy Hotchkiss was in her Staten Island home, settled down in front of the television and watching the same newscast as her son and daughter-in-law. A gasp, followed by a sound that was both moan and sigh, escaped her as she clenched the arms of the club chair where she was sitting.

Her eyes flew to the picture on the mantel over the fireplace of her and Clyde and Skip. It had been taken only a few weeks before she had returned from the pre-Christmas visit to her parents in Florida and found the note and money from Clyde, surrounded by his Vietnam service medals, on the dining room table. She had replaced the picture of them that Clyde took with him with a copy of the one she had given to her mother and father.

Shocked though she had been then, she had also been sure that he would be found quickly and would get help. But he had vanished. For months she had gone to the morgue each time a man of his general height and weight and appearance was found dead without identification. And each time she had stared down as an attendant had lifted the sheet covering the face of the body, then had shaken her head and turned away.

Clyde had vanished without leaving a hint of where he might have gone. After twelve years and no new information, her father had finally persuaded her to have him declared legally dead in court so that she could collect his life insurance. She had been twenty-seven years old when he disappeared. She had worked as a secretary when Clyde was in the service but then, with a baby, she had decided that it made more sense to get a job at the delicatessen only two blocks away rather than commute into Manhattan again.

Now, forty-one years later, Peggy, still pretty at age sixty-eight, a size twelve where once she had been a size eight, was content with her life. Skip had always been the child any parent would dream of raising. Now the income from the annuity he had purchased to supplement her Social Security allowed her to live comfortably. The home that she had never left had been renovated with every convenience from a steam shower in the upstairs bathroom to a new kitchen and thermal windows. "And heaven knows what else he'll want me to have," she would joke to her friends.

Peggy, whose faith was her rock and her strength, was an ecumenical minister in her parish and a regular volunteer at the neighborhood homeless shelter. Years working at the deli had turned her into a superb cook and baker, and the regulars at the shelter always knew when Peggy Hotchkiss had been in the kitchen.

Donald Scanlon and his wife, Joan, had been lifelong neighbors and fast friends of Peggy's since the day they moved into the neighborhood all those years ago. Joan had been dead for five years and, to his friends, Donald made no secret of the fact that he would love to marry Peggy, but he knew better than to ask. Incredibly to him, Peggy was sure that Clyde was still alive and one day would come back.

In her heart, Peggy knew that even if the door suddenly opened and Clyde came in, they would be strangers. But he had needed her all those years ago and somehow she had failed him. She was so wrapped up in little Skip that she had made excuses for Clyde's heavy drinking. She had found the hidden wine bottles and decided not to upset him, that it was just a phase. When she had left for the pre-Christmas visit to her parents in Florida, something had warned her not to go.

"If you recognize any of the people in this photo . . . ," news anchor Dana Tyler was saying as she pointed it out to the viewing audience.

"Recognize . . . recognize . . ." Peggy heard herself sobbing. Desperately she repeated the phone number to call but knew it was jumbled in her mind.

The phone was ringing. She grabbed it. "Hello."

"Mom, it's Skip."

"I have it on, too. I saw it. Skip, what is that number? I didn't get it straight."

"Mom, why don't you let me make the call?"

"They said the picture was found in a van where a homeless man was staying, that he may have been there at the time of that explosion in Long Island City."

"Mom, I know. And the homeless guy who had it may have found it somewhere years ago."

Peggy Hotchkiss suddenly became calm. "No, Skip," she said. "I don't believe that. I have always suspected that if we ever found your dad, it would be because he was in that kind of condition. Oh, Skip, maybe we have found him or will find him. I knew God would answer my prayers. The waiting has been so long."

55

On Tuesday evening, Doug Connelly returned home in a foul mood. He had gone to Kate's apartment on the Upper West Side earlier. When he had arrived there, he asked the desk clerk if he would let him in; he told the clerk he had to check on a few things for Kate. Once upstairs and alone inside, he systematically had gone through Kate's desk. There was nothing interesting in it, he decided.

He knew the combination of her safe. He had overheard her give it to Hannah shortly after it was installed. "Your birthday, three-thirty; my birthday, six-three; and Mom's birthday, seven-nineteen."

Doug had never forgotten that. Mom's birthday, he had thought. How about me? But the information was useful, and if Kate didn't pull through, he believed the jewelry that had been Susan's belonged to him. After all, even though Susan inherited some of it, the rest of it I bought for her, he had told himself. It doesn't matter what Susan stated in her will.

But when he opened the safe, it was empty. Hannah already took the contents, he thought, angrily.

On the way out, he bumped into an acquaintance of Kate's. Justin Kramer, if that was his name. Decent-looking fellow, he thought, and then dismissed him from his mind.

He had gotten back in the car. As usual, when he was waiting for him, Bernard, his driver, had been listening to the news. "Mr. Connelly, they were just talking about that guy who was squatting in the van at the complex."

"What about him?"

"I guess on television they were showing a family picture he had in the van."

"I should hope that if he has any family and they happen to see it, that they're smart enough not to claim him," Doug snapped, clenching his hand involuntarily.

Bernard could see that his boss was in one of his black moods and that the best thing he could do was to keep his head down and his mouth shut. "Are you still planning to stop in at the hospital, Mr. Connelly?" he asked.

"No, I don't think so. Dr. Patel has assured me that Kate's fever is broken and that she is stable. I'm very tired. Let's go home. I won't be going out again tonight."

"Yes, sir."

Sandra had told him that she was going to go to dinner with some of her friends, then to her own apartment for the night. "I want to be here for you, Doug," she had said, "but I do have to look at the mail and do a few errands in the morning."

Doug wondered if any of her girlfriends were named Majestic, but it didn't matter. He could use a rest from Sandra's constant presence of the last several days. He decided to eat at the private restaurant in his apartment building, and then go to bed early. He needed to be calm and quiet and collect himself.

Jack Worth had called him earlier in the day. "I drove by the complex. The cleanup crew is there. That means the insurance investigators have taken what they want and they're finished."

"Well, now that they know there was someone else on the lot, maybe they won't try to hold up on okaying the payout."

I need the money, Doug thought. I'll run out of cash in less than a month if I don't get it . . . What was Kate doing with Gus at that hour of the morning in the museum? . . . By any chance did that homeless guy see anything that might jeopardize the settlement? . . . If I had found Kate's jewelry, I could have pawned it until I got the insurance money, Doug thought. Hannah had one hell of a nerve to clean out Kate's safe.

It was in this frame of mind that he arrived home at seven o'clock on Tuesday evening. He had no sooner walked in when the phone in the foyer rang. Let it ring, he thought. Almost everyone I know calls me on my cell phone.

But then he remembered that he had given both his cell and landline numbers to the insurance company. It was after office hours but . . . With two quick steps he was across the foyer and picking up the receiver. "Douglas Connelly," he said.

"Douglas," an unfamiliar voice said, "this is Father Dan Martin. You might not remember me, but at the time of the tragedy in your family, I was assisting at St. Ignatius Loyola and was present at the funeral mass. We got together a number of times after that but then I was transferred to Rome."

"I do remember you very well," Doug said, trying to put warmth in his voice. "You were very kind and I was in a pretty bad way."

"It was a terrible time for you. I am so sorry about what is happening now. I stopped at the hospital today to see Kate and I administered the Sacrament of the Sick to her. I saw Hannah there and spoke with her, and now I'd very much like to connect with you again."

There is no way I want to connect with you, Doug thought. I don't need anyone to tell me that he'll pray for me and for Kate. I don't think I've been inside a church since the funeral. Rosie Masse always took the girls when they were growing up.

And I really don't want this priest around here when Sandra's on the scene. But if he's free tonight, maybe I can get rid of him fast. "Father, are you calling from St. Ignatius?"

"Yes, I'm living here at the rectory."

"Then you're in the neighborhood. Have you eaten dinner yet?"

"Actually, I'm just on my way out to meet an old friend for dinner tonight. Maybe another night? I'm so glad I happened to catch you."

"Sure. I'll check in with you later in the week, then," Doug said.

"Perfect."

With a sigh, Doug replaced the receiver on the cradle. He'd call the priest back when hell froze over, he thought, then walked into the library. He went straight for the bar and poured a strong double scotch for himself. Sip it slowly, he warned himself. Get the edge off. But before you get too relaxed, call the hospital and ask about Kate. It would be just like Hannah to ask if I visited Kate tonight.

The nurse in ICU was reassuring. "I'm just going off my shift, Mr. Connelly. As you know, Kate's fever broke this morning. She's had a very good day."

"That's great to hear. Thank you for the update," Doug said.

A thought was nagging in his subconscious. Was Kate awake when the priest was with her? He had administered the Sacrament of the Sick. Did that mean Kate had possibly been aware enough to talk to him?

And if she had, what had she told him?

56

On Tuesday evening, Father Dan Martin picked up his former pastor, eighty-seven-year-old Father Michael Ferris, at the Jesuit retirement home in Riverdale, the upper west section of the Bronx. He had offered Father Ferris his choice of places to dine, knowing full well that he would elect to go to Neary's restaurant, the iconic Irish pub on East Fifty-seventh Street in Manhattan.

Opened on St. Patrick's Day, March 17, more than forty-five years ago, it had been Father Mike's favorite dining place when he was pastor of St. Ignatius Loyola and he still loved to go there.

Father Dan had made an eight o'clock reservation and at eight ten they were settled at their table, enjoying a cocktail.

Father Mike was the first one to refer to what was happening to the Connellys. "I knew them all," he said. "Old Dennis and his wife, Bridget. They were parishioners. Then Douglas and Susan were married at St. Ignatius and moved into an apartment just off Fifth Avenue. Doug still lives there."

It was exactly the subject that Father Dan Martin wanted to discuss. He had deliberately not brought it up at first but now the subject was on the table. "If you remember, I was helping out at St. Ignatius at the time of the accident. I was on the altar at the funeral mass. I phoned Douglas the next day. I'd just been ordained. I wanted to help him if that was possible."

"I don't think any of us could have helped him much. He was crazy about Susan. I never saw a couple more in love. And I know he was crushed with guilt about losing not only her, but his brother and four close friends. He was at the helm of the boat but the investigation showed it just plain wasn't his fault. There was no carelessness and certainly no drinking involved. When they would go on a tuna fishing expedition at night, they never had liquor on the boat."

Liz, a waitress who had worked at Neary's since the day it opened, was standing at the table. "Let me guess," she said. "Father Mike, you'll have the Irish salmon appetizer, and the corned beef and cabbage."

"Right you are, Liz," Father Mike confirmed.

"Father Dan, you'll have the shrimp cocktail and salmon as a main course."

"I didn't know I was so predictable, but there you are." Father Martin then smiled and resumed the conversation with his former pastor. "Mike, we've both seen a lot of heartbreak in our day but seeing Douglas Connelly at the funeral of his wife and brother and holding three-year-old Kate's hand has never left me. When I visited him at home afterward, it was like talking to someone who was walking in his sleep."

"I agree. He was riddled with guilt but, on the other hand, so is anyone who survives a tragedy that kills someone they love. In this case, it was two people he loved and four close friends. They had radar on the boat but that was nearly thirty years ago. You would think that leaving a Brooklyn pier at eleven at night, you would have the Atlantic Ocean to yourself, but there was plenty of traffic on it. As you know, they were planning to arrive at the tuna feeding grounds at daybreak, a distance of about seventy miles away."

Father Ferris paused to butter a salted roll, took a bite, and shook his head. "Doug could see the tugboat and they had plenty of room between it and their boat. But what he didn't see, and didn't notice on the radar, was that it was towing a barge. The chains were so long and the night so dark that when Doug, at a safe distance, steered his boat behind the tugboat, the chain literally cut the bottom out of their boat. A life jacket and life raft were stored near the helm. He managed to throw the raft overboard and pull on the life jacket. The others were in the cabin and never had a chance because it sank so quickly."

"No one on the tugboat realized what had happened," Dan Martin remembered.

"No. Tugboats didn't carry much of a crew and, at that hour, who knows who was awake? Of course the next day, after no one could get them on the ship's radio, a search-and-rescue crew went out and found Doug, half dead, lying on the raft. He had been slammed by some of the debris and had deep cuts and bruises from his skull down to his feet. He was in the hospital for three weeks. The bodies of all the others were found, and they delayed the funeral of Susan and Connor until Doug could attend. It's incredible that now his daughter is suffering from a brain injury because that's what happened to him. He had memory lapses and times when he referred to Susan as though she were in the apartment. He was never the same after that—at least while I knew him."

The old priest looked past his companion and sighed. "Old Dennis Francis Connelly used to come here regularly. What a character *he* was."

"He was before my time at St. Ignatius."

"Maybe you were lucky. He was the crabbiest, most superstitious, stiff-necked old Irishman I ever had the hard luck to meet. His background was interesting. He was a street kid from Dublin with a good brain. He was smart enough to know that he needed an education and managed to get a scholarship to Trinity College. As soon as he graduated, he sailed for the United States and got a job as a messenger at the stock exchange. At twenty-two years of age, he had already figured out that was the place to learn how to make money and he sure did."

The appetizers arrived. Michael Ferris looked around the dining room as he picked up his fork. "I remember when Hugh Carey was governor. He was here a lot. He said that the good Lord had changed water into wine but that Jimmy Neary had reversed the process. Jimmy loved that line and always quotes it."

"I never heard that one," Dan Martin said. "But I like it, too."

"So Dennis got rich but it was always under his skin that he didn't come from the kind of family that lived in a castle and rode to hounds. His solution was to create his own background. He made a ton of money, sold his investment company, and opened the Connelly Fine Antique Reproductions firm. That museum was his castle and he loved to show people the antiques in it. He knew the history of every piece of furniture, and let me tell you, before you finished the tour, you knew it, too."

"I read that he didn't marry until he was in his fifties."

"Fifty-five, I think. Bridget O'Connor was twenty years younger. Then the two boys were born."

"They were a year apart, weren't they?"

"Try four minutes apart. Douglas was born one minute before midnight, on December thirty-first, Connor three minutes after midnight on January first. They hadn't expected twins and for Dennis it was a terrible worry. Two generations of twins in his family had died violently and he was sure that his own sons would be cursed. He always referred to them as brothers, even though as I understood it, they were identical. Bridget was forbidden to call them twins. Even as babies, they were always dressed in different clothing and had different kinds of haircuts. If Douglas had bangs, Connor had a crew cut. As they got older, Dennis would tell people who didn't know the family well that his sons were a year apart. They attended different schools from kindergarten through college, but even with all that, they were very close.

Jimmy Neary stopped at the table. "How's everything so far?" he asked.

"Great," they said in unison. "Jimmy, I was just talking about Dennis Francis Connelly," Father Mike said. "You knew him well."

"Saints preserve us. He could always find something that wasn't hot enough or cold enough, God rest him," Jimmy said. "I'm glad that neither he nor Bridget lived to see one of their sons dead and now one of his granddaughters fighting for her life, and that business he was so proud of destroyed."

"I agree," Father Mike said.

Liz cleared their appetizer plates. Both priests decided on a glass of chardonnay.

Father Dan said, "Mike, I brought up the Connellys because, after I read about the accident, I decided to visit Kate Connelly in the hospital. I saw her there this morning and met Hannah. Kate had been running a fever. If it had been caused by a serious infection, the fever could have been fatal but, thank God, it had just broken. I told Hannah that, nearly thirty years ago, I had contacted her father after the boating accident. I thought at that time that maybe I could be of help to him."

"I did, too, back then," Father Mike replied. "But he made it clear that he didn't need any help from me and he didn't need any help from the God who took his wife, his brother, and his friends. When I saw him, it was just a week after the funeral. He had broken his hand and was in terrible pain. The doctor had insisted that he have a nurse with him. I think they were afraid that he was suicidal. He broke his hand by punching the mirror over Susan's dressing table."

Michael Ferris, S.J., observed, "I just hope that the curse his father worried about doesn't land on him. Maybe we should be grateful that Kate and Hannah aren't twins."

57

At seven o'clock on Tuesday evening, Frank Ramsey turned off the television in the family room. He and Celia had watched the CBS local news at six o'clock and seen the anchor, Dana Tyler, show the viewers the picture that had been found in the van. Then Celia had gone into the kitchen to finish preparing dinner. She was taking a roast chicken from the oven when Frank joined her there. He sniffed appreciatively. "I'm hungry and it looks as though we're actually going to sit down quietly tonight," he said.

"I hope so. It certainly hasn't been that way since the fire." She glanced at him. "I don't think you have too much faith that the picture that was found in the van will be useful."

Frank sampled the mashed potatoes. "Excellent," he judged. "To be honest, I think I'm trying not to get my hopes up. That picture is the only thing we have that may lead us to whoever was in the van." It did not even cross his mind to tell Celia about Jamie Gordon's notebook. That information could not be shared on the outside, not even with her.

But Frank realized that ever since the notebook had been found, Jamie Gordon, the murdered student, had been constantly in his thoughts. He knew the hell that her parents had been living in since she first went missing and then when her body was found a year and a half ago. If this homeless guy was the one who did it to her, he wanted him to pay for it.

Ten years ago they had enlarged the kitchen to include a rounded dining alcove, which had become the place where they ate most of their meals. It had an Amish antique barn door that had been sanded, put on legs, and now served as their table. The built-in cushioned bench against one wall and high-backed chairs on the other side were inviting and comfortable and added to the sense of peace and relaxation at the end of the day. Early on in their marriage, they had both agreed that dinner was for conversation, not for watching television.

Together they put the serving dishes on the table and sat down. In the hope of getting some response to the picture, Frank laid his cell phone beside his plate. Less than a minute later, a call came in. He clicked it on. "Frank Ramsey," he said.

"Marshal, this is Officer Carlita Cortez. I just answered a call about the family picture that has been distributed and I think it may be the real thing. I think you might want to speak to this woman."

"Who is she?" Frank laid down the fork that had been halfway to his mouth.

"The caller is Mrs. Peggy Hotchkiss and she lives on Staten Island. She said that the picture she saw on the news is of her and her husband and their son. It was taken forty-one years ago. Her husband walked out on them a short time later. He was a Vietnam vet with serious psychological problems. She never could trace him but has always believed that he might have become a homeless man."

Frank forgot that the dinner he had been so ready to eat was in front of him. "Put her through."

Celia watched as her husband listened and his expression became increasingly intense. Finally, he said, "Mrs. Hotchkiss, I can't tell you how important it is that you called. I can be at your house in less than an hour. You say you have all your husband's military records there. Can you have them available for me to examine? Let me confirm your address."

Frank Ramsey disconnected the call and looked at Celia. "If the picture was still in the possession of this woman's husband, he is Clyde Hotchkiss, a Vietnam vet with a chestful of medals who came home badly damaged emotionally. She told me she's been praying for forty years that she would find him. I just hope that, if it is the same guy, he doesn't turn out to be an arsonist or worse."

Having said that, Frank realized he had almost talked about Jamie Gordon's notebook.

"Frank, you are going to wait ten minutes and eat the dinner I prepared for you," Celia said firmly.

"I'm sorry, Ceil, I will," he said, apologetically. "And, as I said before, the guy who was in the van might have come across this picture years ago. It might have nothing to do with him. But if it does, as a Vietnam vet, his fingerprints are on file with the military. We'll be able to check them."

Frank made a quick call to Nathan Klein and they agreed to meet in about an hour in the Staten Island home of Peggy Hotchkiss. Then, knowing how important it was to Celia, Frank began to eat the dinner that he had so looked forward to and now could not taste. He was already measuring in his mind how bad it would be for the anxious woman he had just spoken to about her long-missing husband, if this highly decorated Vietnam vet was both her husband and a killer.

To say nothing of the reaction of Jamie Gordon's family. The closure that comes from an arrest also brings its own special heartbreak.

It was not the first time in his long career that Marshal Frank Ramsey had reflected on that fact.

58

The red satin shoes. Mommy was dancing in them. Around and around the room. Then Mommy was bending over her, kissing her cheek.

No, it was Hannah.

I'm the one who looks like Mommy, Kate thought, still deep in the abyss of her coma. Hannah looks like Daddy. Daddy, in a small package. I hurt so much. Everything hurts . . .

"The fever is a serious problem." A man's voice, nearby . . .

I can hear you, Kate thought. You just don't understand but I can hear you. Hannah, little sister, don't worry. Something happened to me but I'm going to get better . . .

Daddy was singing to her. "Bye Baby Bunting" . . .

And they were kissing her good-bye . . .

Someone was touching her forehead. "I forgive you . . ."

Someone was praying over her.

I am going to be all right, Kate thought. If only I could tell Hannah . . . and then she felt herself slipping deeper and deeper into sleep . . .

And Mommy stopped dancing and Daddy stopped singing and . . . he never . . .

Her fever finally diminished, she slipped into a deep, restful sleep before she was able to complete her thought.

59

Jack Worth did not sleep well on Tuesday night. The combination of suddenly having time on his hands, coupled with the skeptical attitude of the fire marshals when he'd tried to explain the lack of security on the plant and the presence of the wrecked van, had made him both irritable and nervous.

What am I supposed to do now? he asked himself as the first sign of the dawn became visible in the bedroom windows. Jump every time the phone rings in case it's those marshals wanting to drop in again?

At 5:30 A.M., Wednesday morning, he threw back the covers and got up. I wonder how much that cleanup crew got done yesterday? he asked himself. If the insurance guys gave them the go-ahead, they must be satisfied they don't have anything more to find. And that crew arriving means that the security that the cops and the firemen were providing is finished. I'm going to take a ride and see what's going on over there before anyone shows up.

The decision made, Jack got dressed, rapidly pulling on a running suit, heavy socks, and sneakers. If I take time to shower and shave, I might run into someone getting there early, he thought. I don't need that.

What I need, he decided, is to go down to Florida and hang out there for the winter. And I need to get back in shape. I'm a good ten pounds more than I should be.

Really more like twenty pounds. He pushed back that thought.

Lately he had been seeing the dismissive expression in the eyes of some of the women he'd started to chat up at the bars. He'd never let his barber, Dom, touch up his hair but maybe it was time. Dom had been pushing him to do it. "Jack, I know the ladies love to run their fingers through your strawberry-blond hair. You told me. Well, it's still thick but it's not so strawberry-blond anymore."

Nothing is what it was anymore, Jack Worth thought.

He turned on the light over the staircase, went downstairs, and walked through the living room and kitchen, barely noticing his surroundings. For Jack Worth, the home that he had once shared with his wife was, for the most part, the place where he slept. His job at the Connelly complex had paid him well. His housekeeper came in once a week, which was enough. He was basically neat in his daily routine.

In the summer, an off-the-books landscaper did the mowing and trimming of the outside property, and the same guy shoveled the snow off the sidewalk and driveway in the winter.

Jack Worth valued his freedom. There wouldn't be another "Mrs. Jack Worth." And there would never be another child to put through college.

When Jack got into that kind of thinking, he always got angry. His kid didn't even have his name anymore. And when they did that name change in court, his ex had told him that her husband, the big-shot doctor, would be happy to pay for Johnny's college when he graduated from high school.

I told them that no one else is paying for my kid to go to college, Jack thought, as he slammed the door between the kitchen and garage and opened the driver's door of his BMW. I knew that they just wanted me out of their lives. Stupid. And now I'll be stuck with the tuition next year.

But who knows? Maybe knowing what is going on and that he was out of a job, Doctor Big Shot would say, "I insist . . ."

Insist, Jack Worth thought sarcastically, as he pressed the button that opened the garage door and backed the car out. Yeah. Maybe.

It was only a few minutes past six and the early-morning traffic was just beginning to appear on the road. Give it another hour and every block turns into a parking lot, Jack thought. Welcome to the city.

Even though the explosion had been not even a week ago, the familiar drive to the complex seemed odd and even frightening to him. Something else was going to happen. Something more than what had already happened.

If it had been an ordinary workday, he would have driven to what had been the front entrance of the complex. Jack chose not to do that. His BMW was a familiar sight to watchmen and security cameras in the nearby warehouses, and he did not want it to be noticed that he had made an early-morning visit. Instead, he decided to get in through the service delivery entrance. A temporary fence had been erected since the explosion to keep out intruders. Jack parked his car and easily hopped over it. And they talk to me about security, he fumed.

He turned to walk over to the car park where the delivery vans had been kept and where someone had been staying in the van that had been wrecked. That was when he saw the orange DANGER signs and realized that a section of the pavement had collapsed into a sinkhole. Breaking into a run, he rushed to see how deep it was.

He stepped over the strip of orange tape and looked down. It was the eastern section of the property and by now the early sun was

strong and bright, penetrating the secret of what had been long concealed under the broken pavement.

"No!" Jack Worth whispered. "No!"

He was staring down at the medallion on the grimy chain around
the neck of the skeleton of the young woman who had once been
Tracey Sloane. The medallion that inextricably tied her to him.

60

Clyde woke up early Wednesday morning, blinking against the glare of the sun that was blinding his eyes. He felt awful, hot and cold at the same time, but mostly hot.

Where am I? Sometimes when he hadn't had too much wine, he would ask himself another question: Where am I going?

Clyde shook his head and began to piece together everything that had been happening to him. The shelter. The hospital. His picture on the television in the room there.

Suppose Peggy and Skippy saw it? By now Peggy had probably married someone else, and Skippy had grown up thinking that guy was his father. And all those Vietnam medals were probably buried in a box in the attic. That's if they hadn't already been thrown out.

He forced himself to think even though his head was splitting. If they could trace that picture to him and find out who he was, then even if Peggy and Skippy decided to run for the hills, the cops would still be looking for him. What if they decided that he had set off that explosion?

That Shirley woman. Nice lady. She really was worried about him. But she thought I'd stay in that dump. Clyde pulled himself up on one elbow. He began to laugh, a raspy laugh that turned into a racking cough. Where were those pills she gave me? One hand, then the other, fumbled into the pockets of the poncho he had been given in the hospital. It had deep pockets and he guessed that was good. He could put stuff in them. But the jacket they hadn't given back to him was the one he really wanted.

When the tourists saw that crummy old jacket, they felt sorry for him. The dollars they would drop in his cap added up. He had to get rid of the poncho and cut holes in those new warm, heavy pants. He felt like a baby seal in them, a nice, warm, contented baby seal. People liked baby seals but they didn't feel sorry for them.

I need a drink, Clyde thought. And where did I sleep?

He looked around and grunted in surprise. Somehow he had made his way to Chelsea Piers, right off the Hudson River, close to the Village. He began to have a little more memory about yesterday. Shirley-do-good had said good-bye at the hotel.

He had waited fifteen or twenty minutes or something like that.

The woman at the desk in that excuse for a lobby had asked if he'd be coming back. And he said that he would come back for sure.

When he had coughed so hard on the street, someone had dropped ten bucks in his cap and someone else had dropped a couple of bucks and he had gotten a couple of bottles of wine. So it had been a good night. The trouble was that he couldn't keep up the coughing so that more people would feel sorry for him. He needed to look cold and hungry and not like a baby seal.

Clyde dropped his head back onto the newspapers. Last night had worked out. He had slept with no one around him, with the good sounds of New York filling his ears. The traffic on the West Side Highway, and now and then a plane flying overhead, and the early-morning ferries beginning to cross the Hudson. He had settled down here with his newspapers around him, and the warm clothes he didn't want had made him feel like a baby in his mama's arms when he was falling asleep.

But now he was scared. The picture. The girl. He knew he had hurt her. He had punched her real hard. But he didn't know what happened after that.

I started to go after her. I was mad. I was afraid she'd tell on me and I wouldn't be able to come back to my van. And then . . .

He began to cough again. He pulled himself up as his body shook and trembled with the force of the deep, rattling protest from his lungs. It was harder and harder to breathe. He couldn't breathe and he couldn't stop coughing.

"Are you all right? Do you need help?"

Clyde tried to say, "Go away. Leave me alone." He swung his fist up but it didn't hit anything. He fell back on the newspapers and couldn't pull himself up again even though he was clawing for breath.

Three minutes later, he did not hear the screech of the siren as a patrol car pulled off the West Side Drive to answer a 911 call from a young woman jogger pleading for help.

She pointed to the crumpled figure on the ground. "Be careful, Officer. I think that man is dying but when I asked if I could help him he tried to punch me."

"All right, ma'am. Please stand back. I'll send for an ambulance." The young police officer walked over to look at Clyde. Observing his deep, frantic efforts to breathe, the officer's first thought was that this guy would be lucky to still be alive when the ambulance arrived.

61

Sal Damiano, the foreman of the cleanup crew, made an early decision on Wednesday morning that fixing the sinkhole in the pavement would wait until the job of hauling off the rubble of the complex was completed.

Once again, broken slabs that had once formed walls, chunks of machines that had fashioned fine-grained mahogany and maple into furniture, battered cans of oil that had been used to keep the museum antiques from drying out, were systematically lifted by forklifts and dropped into Dumpsters.

When Jose Fernandez had arrived home the evening before, he had opened his computer and looked up the Connelly complex on the Internet. Sitting in the kitchen of the four-room apartment in the housing development near the Brooklyn Bridge, he had told his mother about what he was researching.

"Mom, take a look at the pictures of that museum, the way it was until the explosion. That furniture must have been worth a fortune. They called that room the Fontainebleau bedroom. The real Fontainebleau was where Marie Antoinette slept before the French Revolution."

Jose's mother, Carmen, turned from the stove and looked over his shoulder. "Too fancy. Too much trouble keeping it clean. Who's Marie Anter—"

"Antoinette. She was a French queen."

"Good for her. One hundred thousand dollars in student loans and you're clearing trash that used to be expensive furniture."

Jose sighed. It was a familiar refrain. He knew it would have been smarter to get a business degree, but there was something in his DNA that had made him want to know everything he could about ancient history. I'm still glad I studied it, he thought. I just wish I didn't have all these loans. But I'll get a teaching job someday. He was already going to City College on weekends to get a master's degree to teach Spanish. He knew he'd make it. And his student loans were a fact of life. He'd pay them the same way he'd pay off a mortgage or a car.

The only problem was that he didn't have a house or a car.

But for some reason, all day Wednesday, as he shoveled and hauled debris at the Connelly complex site, the sinkhole kept capturing his imagination. In ancient times, new cities were built on top of the ruins of the old ones that had been devastated by warfare or floods or fire.

During the summers of his junior and senior years in college, he had walked and hitched his way through the Middle East and Greece. When he was twelve, he had read a book about Damascus and he remembered how excited he'd been when he finally arrived there. At that moment, he had whispered to himself the first words of that book: "Damas, Damascus, oldest city in the world, city upon a city . . ."

Then, the next summer when he was in Athens, he had learned that, even with all the archeological excavations that had already been done, as they had started to widen the streets to prepare for the Olympics, they had uncovered another layer of settlements from ancient times.

I must be losing it, Jose thought, as he hauled and carried and pushed and pulled in his area of the cleanup. I'm comparing a sinkhole in a parking lot in Long Island City with places like Damascus and Athens.

But at five o'clock, as the tired crew gratefully wrapped up for the day, he could no longer resist the impulse to take a closer look at the sinkhole. It was almost dark but there was a flashlight in the truck. He got it and started to walk to the rear of the parking lot.

From behind him, Sal called, "Are you planning to walk home, Jose?"

Jose smiled. Sal was a nice guy. "Just want to take a quick look over there." He pointed to the sinkhole.

"Well, be sure to make it quick if you're riding back with me."

"I will." Breaking into an easy jog, Jose covered the distance in seconds. As Jack Worth had done hours earlier, he stepped over the orange tape and, careful not to get his weight too close to the edge, switched on the flashlight and pointed it down.

It was not the medallion on the necklace that he noticed first. Even through the grime he could still make out the engraving on it.

Tracey.

It was the sight of strands of long hair still attached to the skull of the skeleton that made him too numb to move or even call out. The incongruous memory of a high school biology class flashed through Jose's brain. He remembered the teacher saying, "Even after death, hair and nails continue to grow."

62

As usual, Peggy Hotchkiss attended the daily 8 A.M. mass at St. Rita's, her parish church on Staten Island. Even though she had not closed her eyes all night, it had not occurred to her to break this habit of forty years. Daily Mass was an integral part of her life and St. Rita, the Advocate of the Hopeless and even the Impossible, was her favorite saint. But this morning her usual prayer to her was even more intense. "Let them find him, please. I implore you. Let them find him. I know he needs me."

The fire marshals were so kind, she thought. When they came to the house, they had been so careful to say that it was entirely possible that the homeless person in the van had found, or maybe even stolen, that picture from someone else.

"He didn't," Peggy had told them. "I will stake my life that Clyde kept that picture. I saw what happened to the Connelly complex on television. I can only imagine if Clyde was sleeping in that van right by the explosion. Of course he would have rushed to get away and wouldn't have had time to even grab that picture."

She had observed the skepticism on the faces of the marshals but they had been very polite. She could tell that they did not want to upset her by indicating that the homeless man might have been Clyde, but she had made it easy for them.

"I want to find him," she had told them. "His son wants to find him. We're not ashamed of him. He went to Vietnam and he was proud to serve his country. He didn't give his life there, but because of what happened to him there, he lost the rest of the life he would have enjoyed."

St. Rita's was only five blocks from home. Unless the weather was terrible, Peggy always walked. At quarter of nine, she was turning onto her own street when her cell phone rang. It was Fire Marshal Frank Ramsey.

"Mrs. Hotchkiss," he said, "a homeless man was just brought into Bellevue Hospital in Manhattan. They recognized him in the emergency room there. They had only discharged him yesterday. He gave his name as Clyde Hastings. We think he may be your husband."

Peggy tried to keep her voice steady. "I'll be right there and I'll call my son. I know Bellevue is around Twenty-third Street. Isn't that right?"

"Where are you right now, Mrs. Hotchkiss?" Ramsey asked.

"A block away from my house."

"Mrs. Hotchkiss, go home and wait. I'll have a police car pick you up in five minutes. I am very sorry to tell you that the man in the hospital is dying of pneumonia. If he is your husband, even after all these years, you might be able to persuade him to tell us what he may know about a girl who is missing."

An hour later, Peggy was in the emergency room of Bellevue Hospital. Skip had arrived minutes before her. "Are you okay, Mom?" he asked, quietly.

"Yes, I am."

Frank Ramsey was waiting for her. "They have him in a private room down the hall. The doctor told us that he doesn't have long. We are hoping that we can get him to talk to us about a young college student who may have tried to interview him about living on the street."

Her throat dry, unconsciously moistening her lips, her hand clutching the steady arm of her son, Peggy followed the tall figure of the fire marshal until he stepped aside to let her precede him into the small room.

Even before she took a second look, Peggy knew that it was Clyde. The high forehead, the slight widow's peak, the almost invisible scar on the side of his nose. His eyes were closed, his harsh, belabored breathing the only sound in the room. Peggy took his hand. "Clyde, Clyde, dear, I'm here."

From far away, Clyde heard a remembered voice, soft and gentle, and opened his eyes. Sometimes he had seen Peggy in his dreams but now he knew he wasn't dreaming. The woman looking down at him with tears slipping down her cheeks was Peggy. He pulled in a breath. He had to talk to her. He managed a smile. "Do I have the honor of addressing the beauteous Margaret Monica Farley?" he asked, his voice weak and tired, then added, "Oh, Peggy, I missed you."

"I missed you, too. So very, very much. And Skip is here. We love you. We love you."

Clyde weakly turned his head to see the man standing next to Peggy. Both of their faces were so clear but behind them it was starting to get dark. My son, he thought, and then he heard him say, "Hello, Dad."

"I'm sorry," Clyde murmured. "I'm so sorry."

Frank Ramsey and Nathan Klein stepped forward. Before Peggy arrived at the hospital, they had tried to question Clyde about Jamie Gordon, but Clyde had closed his eyes and refused to answer them. They both could see that his death was imminent. Bending over Clyde, his voice urgent, Ramsey said, "Clyde, tell Peggy about the notebook. Tell her if you saw the girl."

"Clyde, it's all right, dear. You would never mean to hurt anyone," Peggy whispered. "I want you to tell them what happened."

It was so peaceful now. Peggy holding his hand. It felt so good.
"The girl followed me. I told her to go away. She wouldn't."

He began to cough. This time his breath wouldn't come back.

"Clyde, did you kill her? Did you throw her in the river?" Ramsey
demanded.

"No . . . no. She wouldn't go away. I punched her. Then she left.
And I heard her scream . . ."

Clyde closed his eyes. Everything was beginning to go dark.

"Clyde, she started to scream," Frank said. "What happened
then? Answer me," he demanded. "Answer me!"

"She screamed, 'Help me, help me!' "

"You were still in the van?"

"Ye . . ."

He could not finish the word. With a long sigh, he exhaled his
last breath. The tormented life of Clyde Hotchkiss, husband and father, Vietnam veteran, hero and homeless drifter, was over.

63

On Wednesday afternoon, Hannah and Jessie met for a quick lunch at a small restaurant in the Garment District, a block from Hannah's office. Hannah had stopped by the hospital briefly that morning. Now that Kate was no longer in a crisis situation, Jessie knew that she and Hannah needed to talk. They both ordered a sandwich and coffee. This was not going to be like their dinners at Mindoro's, where they would sip wine and eat pasta and catch up with each other.

Jessie looked approvingly across the table at her friend. Hannah's eyes were bright. The shadows under them were gone. She was wearing a high-neck white sweater with a designer scarf in shades of blue around her shoulders. "You look great," Jessie said. "I would guess that you slept well last night."

Hannah smiled and said, "You look great, too. That's another suit I'm glad I talked you into buying. Green tweed is perfect with your red hair. I passed out at eight o'clock last night and woke up at eight o'clock this morning. I didn't even get to the hospital yet but when I phoned they said that Kate was sleeping quietly and her temperature is normal. I know I can't ask for more than that at this point."

Jessie did not waste time engaging in meaningless optimism. "No, I don't think you can, but the fact that the fever is gone is the best possible news."

"Yes, it is. Jess, how does the fact that someone might have been in the van the night of the explosion affect the suspicion that Kate and Gus set it off?"

"It certainly adds a whole new dimension. I gather you didn't see the news last night?"

"No, I didn't."

"They found a family picture in the wrecked van. It's all over the media. They're hoping to use it to identify whoever was there."

The waiter had arrived. "Two ham-and-cheese on rye, lettuce, with mustard. Two black coffees," he verified as he roughly put down the plates on the table, followed by the coffee cups.

Jessie looked at the splatters of coffee in her saucer. "Four-star dining," she murmured. "Oh well. The sandwiches here are always good."

"If they do find out who was in the van, what do you think that means for Kate and Gus?" Hannah demanded.

"I don't know. That van was in the far back end of the lot, a good distance away from the buildings. If some homeless person was in it, he may have been sleeping off a hangover and know absolutely nothing. But it does mean, as far as I can tell, that they have to nail down who was there and what it means. And that is potentially good for Kate."

"It's good unless whoever was there saw something that would be bad for Kate." Hannah took a sip of coffee and picked up her sandwich.

"Knowing you, you'll eat that half and leave the other on the plate," Jessie said matter-of-factly.

"You're right. What can I tell you? It's awfully big. You probably were working out at five A.M. You need to finish yours."

"I was working out at six A.M.," Jessie confirmed. "Hannah, I get the feeling that you are worried that Kate was involved in the explosion. Am I wrong to feel that way?"

She watched as Hannah framed her response. She does think, or know, that Kate was involved, Jessie thought, dismayed.

"All right. Let me tell you exactly what happened. On Thursday afternoon when Dad was alone with Kate, she said something to him. I was just coming into the intensive care unit but I could see his face. He looked scared. That's the only word for it: scared. When I insisted that he tell me what Kate had told him, he said that she was sorry about the fire."

"She was sorry about . . . ," Jessie began to repeat slowly.

"You can imagine what I was thinking, that Kate set the fire. But then a few days later, Dad said that he realized he had been so shocked about everything that he was garbled about what Kate had told him. He claimed that what she said was that she was sorry about the fire, meaning that she knew how much he loved the complex."

"That is one very big difference, to say the least," Jessie snapped. "Which version do you believe?"

"I cannot believe my sister is an arsonist."

"Nor can I," Jessie said emphatically, "but I have to tell you that Doug has been on the phone with me. He's determined to create the scenario that Gus tricked Kate into meeting him at the complex. The way he explains her call to him is that she was always very friendly with Gus and just happened to call to chat with him. The rest of the scenario that Doug wants to put out is that Gus hated him so much for forcing him into retirement that he figured out a good way to punish Doug. He tricked Kate into meeting him at the time he knew the explosion would go off. He probably told Kate that he needed her help. But something went wrong. Gus gets killed and Kate gets badly injured."

Jessie took the last bite of the first half of her sandwich and reached for the other half. "A disgruntled employee blew up the complex. The injured daughter is an innocent victim and the insurance is paid. Get the picture?"

"Suppose, if Kate recovers—make that *when* Kate recovers—and can talk about it, she says that that is not the way it happened?" Hannah asked, quietly.

"I don't know." Jessie did not want to tell Hannah that she was sensing a certain desperation in Douglas Connelly. No matter what, he can always get a lot of money for just the property, she thought. But he's counting on the big prize, millions more in insurance. I wouldn't want to be the one to stand in his way of getting it.

64

Lottie Schmidt could see from the caller identification on her phone that it was Gretchen. It was Wednesday midafternoon, which meant that Gretchen might have canceled yet another appointment with one of her massage clients. After she got back to Minnesota and was inside her beautiful home, it finally got through her thick skull that those fire marshals were so interested in her house because they wanted to know how she was able to pay for it, Lottie thought.

She folded her hands in her lap. She had been sitting at the table of their small dining room going through some photo albums when the phone rang. Then, not wanting to pick it up and wishing she had the courage to walk away, she listened to Gretchen's frantic message. "Mama, I know you're never out at this time so why aren't you picking up? Mama, did Poppa do something funny to get the money to buy my house? If he did, why didn't you tell me? I never would have shown those pictures to those marshals or cops or whoever they are. Why didn't you say it straight? Mama, a lot of things went wrong in my life. You and Poppa were so strict. Never let me have any fun. Always telling me to study harder, that my marks were never good enough. I married Jeff to get out of the house and that was a nightmare. I waited on him hand and foot because that was the way you waited on Poppa. And—"

The thirty-second limit for leaving a message on the answering machine was up. Thank God, Lottie thought, then shrugged. What can you do? Buy the house for her and you're a saint. Now her big mouth might cause her to lose it and it's my fault.

She looked down at the photo album. She and Gus had both been twenty years old when they were married by the minister in her mother's backyard in Baden-Baden, Germany. She was wearing a white blouse and skirt, and Gus a rented blue suit. The next day they had left Germany to go to America.

I was smiling, Lottie thought. I was so happy. Gus looked scared but happy, too. I knew how definite he was, and how rigid, but it didn't matter. It still doesn't matter. He loved me and he took good care of me. He was such a proud man. When we moved here to Little Neck, and our friends were so thrilled to buy new furniture and show it off, I would say to him, "Gus, don't have that look on your face. I know what you're thinking. That they paid too much for it. That it's cheaply made. Let them enjoy it."

He had made their own furniture himself. In all these years, they had only redone the upholstery twice and of course he had done the work in their garage.

For a craftsman like that to have been so insulted, so wounded. It explained everything.

The doorbell rang. Lottie had been so lost in reminiscing that the time had gone by more swiftly than she had realized. It was already three thirty, and Peter Callow, the young lawyer who had grown up in the house next door, was coming to talk to her.

She had called him after the fire marshals were at the house on Monday.

Lottie knew that this was going to be hard. It was embarrassing to put herself in the hands of someone whom she could still see as the kid who broke her living room window playing softball.

She got up, her hands pressing on the table to ease the weight on her knees, walked to the door, and opened it. The self-assured attorney in an overcoat, business suit, and tie still had the same warm smile of the eight-year-old who was so grateful when she had told him that she knew he didn't mean to break her window.

As she took his coat and put it in the hall closet, and then as they walked into the living room, she was assuring Peter that, since Gus had died, she was doing all right, that she would be all right. After he refused coffee or tea or even water, they sat down. "How can I help you, Mrs. Schmidt?" he asked.

Lottie had decided that she would not beat around the bush. "Five years ago, Gus told me that he had won a lottery. That was all he said. He used the money to buy a house for Gretchen in Minnesota and an annuity so she could pay the overhead."

Peter Callow did not say how wonderful that was. He knew immediately that there was more to the story.

"They're trying to blame the Connelly explosion on Gus. The fire marshals were at the wake and came here Monday. They were asking about Gretchen's house."

"How did they know about it?"

"Because she couldn't wait to talk about it," Lottie snapped, bitterly.

"If Mr. Schmidt won a lottery and paid whatever taxes he owed, there shouldn't be a problem," Peter said. "The marshals will be able to check that out very easily."

"I'm not sure Gus won a lottery," Lottie said.

"Then where did he get the money for the house and annuity?"

"I don't know. He never told me."

Peter Callow could see, from the deep crimson blush that was enveloping the cheeks of the elderly woman who had been his former neighbor, that she was lying. "Mrs. Schmidt," he said gently, "if they can't find any record of Mr. Schmidt winning a lottery and paying his taxes, they'll be back here questioning you. And I would have to assume that they'll even go out to Minnesota and talk to Gretchen."

"Gretchen hasn't any idea where her father got the money to buy her house."

"And Mr. Schmidt never gave you a hint?"

Lottie looked away. "No."

"Mrs. Schmidt, I want to help you. But you know that the media is going as far as it can, without risking a lawsuit for libel, to speculate that Mr. Schmidt conspired with Kate Connelly to set off the explosion. How long has Gretchen had the house?"

"Five years."

"Wasn't that about the time that Mr. Schmidt was asked to retire?"

"Yes, it was." Lottie hesitated. "Peter, will you be my lawyer? I mean, can you be with me when they are talking to me?"

"Yes, of course I can, Mrs. Schmidt." Peter Callow got up. The way this seems to be going, he thought, my new client may soon have to invoke the Fifth Amendment and say nothing further to anybody.

65

Frank Ramsey and Nathan Klein stayed in the hospital with Peggy and Skip as they made arrangements with the funeral home in Staten Island to come for Clyde's body.

Then, composed and calm, Peggy called her pastor at St. Rita's to tell him that she had seen her husband just before he died, and that she wanted to have a funeral mass on Friday morning.

They were sitting in a small office where they had been invited to wait while the doctor signed the death certificate and she made the calls. Skip was standing protectively behind Peggy, but when she laid down her cell phone, she suddenly turned in the swivel chair and asked, "What are they going to put down as the cause of death?" Without waiting for an answer, she said, "Because if they put acute alcoholism, I want the death certificate torn up. Clyde died of pneumonia."

As she spoke, the doctor, who had hurried to Clyde's bedside when the alarms on the machines that monitored his breathing had gone off, tapped on the partially open door of the room and came in. He had obviously overheard Peggy, because he said, in a gentle and understanding tone, "You are absolutely right, Mrs. Hotchkiss. Your husband died of pneumonia and I assure you that is what is on this certificate."

Peggy's hand began to tremble as she reached for the envelope he was holding out to her.

"I'll take it, Mom," Skip said.

Peggy dropped her hand. Then looking past everyone, she asked, "You know what crazy thought went through my head just now?" It was a rhetorical question. Skip and the doctor and the fire marshals waited.

"A *Tree Grows in Brooklyn* is one of my all-time favorite books," Peggy told them, the tone of her voice reminiscent. "When the character Johnny, who was an alcoholic, dies, his wife pleads with the doctor to make the cause of death 'pneumonia' because he really did have pneumonia. She tells him that she has nice kids and doesn't want them to ever have to say that their father died of alcoholism. Well, I've got a nice son and four nice grandchildren and my husband was a war hero and I won't have anyone forget that."

"Mom, you heard what the doctor said. It's okay." Skip put his hands on his mother's shoulders.

Peggy brushed back the tears that were beginning to slip down her cheeks. "Yes, of course and thank you. Thank you very much."

"My sympathy, Mrs. Hotchkiss." With a brief nod, the doctor was gone.

Steadied by Skip, Peggy stood up. "I guess there's nothing more I can do here. The funeral director said he would take care of clothing for Clyde." She looked at Frank Ramsey and Nathan Klein. "You've been so kind. If I had been too late to see Clyde before he died, it would have been terrible for me. I wouldn't have been on time if the police car hadn't picked me up and rushed me to the hospital. I needed to have him go, knowing that we were with him and that we loved him. But now you have to tell me: Who was the girl you asked Clyde about?"

"Mrs. Hotchkiss, we can't give you details but we're eternally grateful that you were there to urge your husband to answer our questions," Frank Ramsey said.

"I never knew Clyde to tell a lie or even shade the truth," Peggy said firmly. "He told you that he punched the girl and she got out of the van and then he heard her scream, 'Help me, help me.' What happened to that girl?"

"I can tell you that she never made it home that night," Frank Ramsey said.

"Did you believe Clyde?" Peggy demanded.

Frank wanted to say "yes" to comfort her, but looking into the now-blazing eyes of the widow of Clyde Hotchkiss, he said, "What he told us opens a whole new avenue as we try to solve the death of this young woman. It may turn out to be incredibly valuable information and we thank you for persuading him to share it."

Twenty minutes later Frank and Nathan were having lunch in a sandwich shop near the hospital. When they were seated and had ordered, Frank asked the first question. "What do you think?"

"I don't know. Maybe Clyde couldn't bring himself to tell his wife and son that he was a killer," Nathan suggested.

"He admitted punching her and that accounts for the black-and-blue mark on Jamie's chin." Like Nathan, Frank was thinking aloud.

"He was probably pretty drunk when he hit her. She got out of the van. I remember reading that she was a good athlete. I think she was on the track team in high school. That means she was both young and fast. Once she was out of the van, I bet he couldn't have caught up with her," Nathan pointed out.

It was the kind of investigative analysis that was second nature to both of them.

"Or maybe the punch knocked her unconscious and he had all

the time in the world to tie her up, strangle her, put her in the cart, and dump her in the river."

"Assuming, of course, that he happened to have twine with him in the van. That would have come in handy," Klein said, sardonically.

"If she was already dead, he could have left her there and come back with the twine," Ramsey shot back.

The sandwiches arrived. Unlike the ones that, unbeknownst to them, Jessie Carlson and Hannah Connelly were enjoying ten blocks away, these looked as though they might have been made yesterday. Nathan shared that possibility with Frank Ramsey.

"Or maybe the day before yesterday," Frank said as he signaled for the waiter to ask the chef to try again.

When the new sandwiches arrived, they ate in silence, each busy with his own thoughts. The silence was broken when Ramsey said, "The more I think, the more improbable it is that someone happened to be outside that van at what was probably sometime between midnight and six in the morning. And if there was someone else there, why would he attack Jamie Gordon? Doesn't make sense. I think Clyde Hotchkiss couldn't admit in front of his wife and son that he killed a college girl because she annoyed him. I just doubt that, when he meets or has met his Maker, he can talk his way out of that one."

"Do we tell the boss and Cruse that we think it's time to let the Gordon family know that we believe we have found Jamie's killer?"

"We'll tell him what we have, but I'm going to recommend that for now they say absolutely nothing about the notebook or Clyde Hotchkiss. My gut tells me that we haven't got all the facts yet. But one thing I do know is that the next thing we have to do is find out where Gus Schmidt got that money to buy his daughter's home. We both know he never won a lottery, and soon we should have confirmation of it. That's when we really begin to lean on Lottie Schmidt. She may be seventy-five years old and not weigh more than ninety pounds but don't let that fool you. She's a tough old bird and I'd bet the ranch that she knows exactly how and where Gus got that money. Our job is to get her to talk."

66

The fact that a kitchen worker named Harry Simon at Tommy's Bistro had been arrested for the murder of another young actress had jolted Nick Greco to the core of his being. He spent all Wednesday afternoon examining and reexamining every inch of the file containing the investigation into the disappearance of Tracey Sloane.

Over and over he read the statement of Harry Simon, taken nearly twenty-eight years ago, and tried to find anything that he might have overlooked. He remembered Harry very well. He was then in his early twenties, thin but wiry build, average height, a sallow complexion, and small eyes. His subservient, eager-to-please manner as he had answered the questions had been off-putting but he had certainly given the impression of being so very, very shocked about Tracey's disappearance.

Disgusted, Greco reread Simon's statement. "We got off at eleven. Some of the waiters and waitresses and busboys were going to Bobbie's Joint for some drinks. Tracey said that she had an early-morning audition and was going home. I started to walk to my apartment, too."

His apartment was in the opposite direction from the way Tracey would have gone, Nick Greco noted.

"Then I thought, What am I going home for? I was pretty broke but I thought, well, so I'll nurse a couple of beers. We all pay our own checks. So I just went back and joined up with them," Harry had said.

Every one of the other employees had vouched for the fact that Harry arrived there just about eleven thirty. They had all agreed they were all at Bobbie's by about ten after eleven. Not more than twenty minutes later, Harry was with them.

It was a pretty strong alibi, Nick Greco remembered. Unless Harry and maybe an accomplice had dragged Tracey off the street and into a hallway or some kind of vehicle.

Very unlikely in that short a time.

We asked the others if there was anything about Harry that suggested he was excited or nervous when he got to Bobbie's, Greco thought, as he pored through the reports containing the statements of the other people who had been at that bar. They had all said he had seemed to be in good spirits.

But now we know that he's an alleged killer who may have managed to stay under the radar for almost thirty years. The homicide squad will be going back through their unsolved cases, particularly involving young women, to see who else might have been Harry's victim.

The young actress he had killed two weeks ago had been on her way home from her waitress job in the Lower East Side at midnight when he had accosted her on the deserted sidewalk. He had dragged her into the rear courtyard of a boarded-up apartment building, where he had molested and killed her. Then he had carried her body to his truck, which was parked around the corner on a dark dead-end street. Harry didn't allow for the adjacent building's security camera that had captured him committing the crime.

Frustrated and angry at himself, convinced that he must have missed something about Simon when Tracey went missing, Nick Greco decided to call Mark Sloane to ask him to have dinner. He

knew that Mark had to be on a roller coaster of emotions. Harry
Simon had worked with Tracey. Harry Simon was an alleged murderer. Had he been the one who had abducted and killed Tracey,
and then somehow managed to show up twenty minutes later to
have a beer with his friends?

From the tone of Mark's voice, Nick Greco knew that the
younger man welcomed the chance to talk to him again. Mark said
he had a late-afternoon office conference and seven o'clock would
be the best time for him.

They met at Marea, an upscale restaurant on Central Park South.
When extending the invitation, Nick had decided that the last thing
Mark Sloane needed was to have dinner in a restaurant that would
remind him of Tommy's Bistro.

Both men were prompt and were seated at the corner table that
Nick had requested. It was obvious to Nick that the arrest of the
kitchen worker had hit Mark Sloane hard. He seemed tense and
even defensive, as though he expected to hear more bad news and
had to prepare for it.

They both ordered red wine, looked at the menu immediately,
and ordered their dinner. Then Mark opened the conversation. "I
wasn't much good at the office today," he admitted. "I kept thinking
that the guy they arrested had to be responsible for Tracey's disappearance, too."

"If he was, he almost certainly had an accomplice," Greco said
flatly. "And yet every instinct I have tells me that this guy is a loner."
Compassionately, he looked across the table at the troubled face of
the brother of Tracey Sloane. He could guess what he was thinking.
The arrest of Harry Simon had been breaking news in the media.
This morning the fact that Simon worked in the same bistro where
Tracey Sloane was working before she vanished nearly twenty-eight
years ago had been blazed across the headlines. The Sloane case

would again be hashed and rehashed even though Simon's alibi seemed to be so strong.

After they placed their orders, Mark suddenly asked, "Didn't this restaurant used to be San Domenico?"

"Yes, it was." Nick Greco had the continuing feeling that Mark was afraid of what Nick might tell him tonight.

"I thought the address sounded familiar. I was in New York about eight years ago. There was a law firm interested in me. The offer I received wasn't good enough. I came here to dinner one night. It was very good then and from the fact that every table is taken, I guess it's still very good."

"It is," Greco replied.

The waiter brought their wine. "The salads will be arriving shortly," he promised.

"Have you told your mother about the arrest yet?" Greco asked.

Mark took a sip from his glass. "Yes, I did. I knew that I couldn't wait to get any more information. I was afraid that the news about Simon's arrest and his connection to Tracey would be on television in Illinois. When she disappeared in New York, it was major news there. I didn't want my mother to find out about it from anyone else. She needed to hear it from me."

He took another sip and added, grimly, "My mother remembered that when she met and spoke to the people at Tommy's to thank them for doing everything they could to help the police find Tracey, that guy was slobbering all over my mother and telling her how much everybody all loved my sister."

"The word I hear from my guys is that the homicide squad questioned Simon up and down and sideways for hours last night. He admitted killing the girl in the Lower East Side but swears he had nothing to do with Tracey disappearing."

Greco felt the vibration of his cell phone in the pocket of his suit jacket. The call was coming in from the detective who had taken over the Tracey Sloane file. His hand cupping the phone, he leaned his elbow on the table, hoping to conceal the fact that he was answering it in the no-cell-phone restaurant. "Greco," he said.

"Nick, it's Matt Stevens."

"What's up? Anything more with the Simon guy?"

"No, not yet, but it looks as though the remains of Tracey Sloane have been found."

It was obvious to Nick that Mark had overheard, because his face went deadly pale.

"Where?" Greco asked.

"You're not going to believe this, but she was in a sinkhole of the parking lot of the Connelly furniture complex, where they had the explosion last week."

67

Little fragments of thoughts were floating through Kate's mind. Gus. She had called him.

And she knew right away that she had upset him. Why?

He had agreed to meet her.

Why did he sound scared on the phone?

There was no reason . . .

Kate felt herself falling back into a warm darkness. *To sleep, but not to dream.* She tried to whisper. Her dreams scared her . . .

She felt her eyelids fluttering . . . But they felt so heavy. Sighing, she closed them again. Why was she so afraid? She remembered. She was little and she was running in her flowered nightgown and she had reached the end of the hallway. But someone grabbed her before she could get down the stairs . . .

And she tried to scream but . . .

Kate drifted back into a healing sleep.

68

Shaking and trembling, Jack Worth had driven home early Wednesday morning. It was only when he arrived there that he realized how absolutely stupid it had been to bolt from the complex after he looked into the sinkhole.

A normal reaction would have been to dial 911. Sure, when the cops arrived, they'd have asked him what he was doing there in the first place. His answer would have been, "I just came to check on the progress of the rubble removal. I have every right to be here. I worked at this plant for thirty years and I was the manager for the last five years until the fire last week."

He had to calm down and figure out what he would tell the cops if by any chance his car had been spotted this morning.

Tracey Sloane. He had been one of the many people questioned when she disappeared. He was in his late twenties then, working as a junior accountant for the Connelly complex. He used to hang out at Bobbie's Joint in the Village at night. That was when it began to fill up with the would-be actors and actresses who worked as waiters in the local pubs and bistros. Bobbie's was a gathering spot for guys his age to hook up with pretty girls.

Tracey Sloane had been the pick of the litter. She brushed me off, Jack thought, carefully rehearsing what he would tell the cops. Then, one day, I was passing one of those little jewelry shops they used to have in the Village and a guy was carving names on fake blue sapphire medallions. He had a bunch of them hanging on chains in the window with names already on them. I saw one with the name TRACEY on it. It cost eight bucks. A couple of nights later I saw Tracey at Bobbie's Joint and tried to give it to her. "No strings," I said. "When I saw it, I couldn't pass it up. The medallion is the color of your eyes."

I tried to give it to her in front of her buddies from Tommy's, Jack reminded himself. One of the guys at the bar said, "It won't do you any good." And we all laughed.

Then she bought it from me.

That was about six months before she disappeared, Jack remembered.

He told the police at the time that he had been a little disappointed because he had never seen her wearing the necklace whenever they had bumped into each other at Bobbie's.

By three o'clock Wednesday afternoon, and after two beers and a sandwich, Jack Worth was continuing to rehearse the story he knew he would have to give, trying to make it the same as the version he had given nearly twenty-eight years ago.

The night Tracey disappeared, I worked at the plant until about quarter of six. I went straight home from work. That's what I told the detectives when I was questioned. I lived in Long Island City, about a mile from the plant. I wasn't feeling good and went to bed early. I wasn't married yet.

How could he explain how Tracey Sloane ended up buried on the parking lot? They were paving over the parking lot at that time, Jack thought. I'll tell the cops that I had mentioned that to the guys at Bobbie's only a few nights before Tracey disappeared. The guys had been joking about taking a tour of the fancy furniture in the museum. I told them that they'd have to wait. We'd had a lot of snow in the past couple of winters and the parking lot was all cracked and was being repaved.

I did tell some of them that. I know I did. Let the cops start questioning all the rest of them again.

It was the best story he could come up with, and it was near enough to the truth that maybe it would sound convincing. A flash of anger still went through him when he remembered offering Tracey the necklace all those years ago. She had said, "Blue is my favorite color and sapphire my favorite stone. Look, I love it, Jack, but I want to pay for it. Even I can afford eight dollars."

When I wouldn't let her pay for it, she took it off and tried to hand it back to me. I said, "Okay, you say you like it, I'll let you pay for it. And if you don't believe it was only eight dollars, walk down MacDougal Street and you'll see these little things hanging in the window."

Feeling deep resentment even after all these years, Jack remembered the wise guy who had heard the two of them talking, and who had watched as Tracey handed him the money. He'd had the nerve to tell him later that evening, "Jack, face it. Tracey has class. You're not her type."

When would someone in that cleanup crew look down into the sinkhole and blow the whistle? Jack Worth waited in dismal anticipation.

Jack had the television on, flipping from one news channel to another. They were all wringing out the story of the derelict who had been positively identified as the person squatting in the van of the Connelly complex. He was Clyde Hotchkiss, a decorated Vietnam War vet who had returned home deeply emotionally wounded and who, after a troubled period of trying to recover, had abandoned his wife and baby more than forty years ago. Incredibly, Hotchkiss had been finally reunited with his still caring wife and son only minutes before he had died in Bellevue Hospital this morning.

The media had caught up with Peggy and Skip as they got out of Skip's car at Peggy's home in Staten Island. Neither of them would comment as they hurried inside to get away from the cameras and microphones.

By the time the five-thirty local news came on, the media had additional details. After he had returned from Vietnam, Clyde Hotchkiss had worked as the foreman at a large construction company. An electrician who had worked with him was interviewed. "There was nothing Clyde didn't know about the job. Plumbing, heating, you name it."

The reporter asked, "Do you think he would have been capable of setting off that explosion?"

"In his right mind, no. Years ago he was a good man. But if you're really asking if he had the technical know-how to set it off, the answer is yes. When you're building a house and you're running a gas line into it, like he did all the time, you have to know what you're doing."

That kind of talk should make Doug feel good, Jack thought. And this guy, Hotchkiss, has been living on the streets for forty years. Maybe he really was hanging around the complex twenty-eight years ago. Maybe they really can pin Tracey's murder on him.

Frank realized he had not called Doug to warn him that, at any moment, somebody was going to sound the alarm about Tracey Sloane's remains being found on the property.

Finally, Jack summoned up the courage to make the call. But it was actually a relief when Doug did not answer. Jack knew that the discovery would be bound to upset him on more than one level. He won't want to be reminded that his brother, Connor, who died in the boating accident, had also been one of the guys who knew Tracey Sloane, he thought, grimly.

69

Justin Kramer did not hesitate to admit to himself that he was enormously drawn to Hannah Connelly.

From the minute she opened the door of her sister Kate's apartment and stood in its door frame, something had happened to him.

She had been wearing a running suit that outlined her slender body and tiny waistline. Her eyes were a deeper shade of blue than her sister's and were shaded with long dark lashes. Justin didn't know what kind of person he had expected to meet. Probably a look-alike for Kate, who was tall and blond, he had thought.

But even in his brief encounter with Douglas Connelly, Justin had seen that Hannah resembled her father, who was a very good-looking guy.

He certainly gave me a quick brush-off, Justin thought, and there's no question that he looked upset about something. Then when I phoned Hannah, she didn't sound happy to know that her father was in her sister's apartment.

I wonder why.

On Wednesday evening when Justin got home from work, he decided to satisfy his curiosity about the Connelly family.

An expert at seeking and locating information, he began his computer search with the most recent material, which consisted primarily of the articles about the explosion.

The fact that Kate and a former workman who was known to be disgruntled were under suspicion for setting off the explosion was old news. From the beginning, Justin hadn't believed that Kate was involved in any wrongdoing and he still didn't believe it. Having met Kate Connelly that one time at the closing, he was totally convinced of that fact.

The newspaper articles referred to the tragedy twenty-eight years ago when Kate and Hannah's mother and uncle and four other people were drowned in a boating accident. Their father had been the only survivor.

Justin continued to search until he found pictures of the funeral of Susan Connelly and her brother-in-law, Connor. Even though it was so many years ago, he felt emotionally stirred when he saw pictures of three-year-old Kate, holding her father's hand, going in and out of St. Ignatius Loyola Church, and then at the family grave in Gate of Heaven Cemetery in Westchester County.

Under the name CONNELLY on the large, ornate headstone, he could make out the names of the people already buried in the plot at that time, DENNIS FRANCIS CONNELLY and BRIDGET O'CONNOR CONNELLY. Probably the grandparents, he thought.

He took a final look at the picture of Kate and her father placing a long-stemmed rose on each of the coffins and then looked up Dennis Francis Connelly. What he learned about the founder of the Connelly complex was both surprising and unsettling.

"That guy was weird," he said aloud. "I wouldn't have wanted him as a father."

Shaking his head, Justin turned off the computer. It was seven o'clock. Would Hannah be at the hospital with her sister? Or maybe out to dinner with someone?

Justin felt a twinge of pure jealousy at that possibility. I hope not, he thought. It can't hurt to phone her. He was already reaching for his cell phone. Hannah answered on the first ring.

"I'm just getting out of a cab at my apartment," she told him. "Kate had a good day except she seemed restless. The doctor says that's a good sign. She may be trying to wake up."

"That's great," Justin replied, hesitated, and then asked, "Have you had dinner yet?"

"No, but I honestly couldn't face sitting in a restaurant."

"Do you like Chinese?"

"Yes."

"Shun Lee West is a few blocks away. The best Chinese restaurant in the city. Let me pick up whatever you'd like and bring it down. I'll set the table, heat it up, serve it, and clean up. You don't have to do anything."

He held his breath.

Hannah began to laugh. "It's the best offer I've had all night. I like wonton soup and sesame chicken. Do you have my address?"

70

After realizing that Hannah must have taken Kate's jewelry, Douglas Connelly slept very poorly on Tuesday night and awoke on Wednesday morning with a headache. Sandra had slipped into his apartment early, and her presence was both annoying and convenient. She talked too much. She kept flipping her long platinum blond hair from behind her shoulders to the front of her shoulders. Then she dropped her head forward so that it covered her face. Then she lifted her face so that her hair parted like the Red Sea, and batted her eyes at him seductively.

They must have had a charm school in North Dakota or wherever the hell she came from, Doug thought, and this was one of their lessons about how to flirt discreetly. As discreetly as a Mack truck plowing through Central Park.

But amazingly, Sandra could cook. She said he needed a solid breakfast and that she was going to fix it. Other mornings when she'd stayed over, they'd had room service sent up from the restaurant in the building. The poached eggs were barely warm by the time they arrived, and the toast was brittle, and for all the money the place charged, they could never manage to deliver the coffee piping hot.

Wednesday morning with the almost Miss Universe in the kitchen, the orange juice was cold, the eggs perfectly poached, the bacon strips just crisp enough, and the toast an even shade of brown.

Sandra had also cut up the grapefruit and oranges and pears she'd found in the refrigerator and put together an appetizing fruit platter.

The daily maid service handled the cleaning of the apartment. They came in at one o'clock so that if Doug slept late, or had a visitor, they weren't annoying him by scurrying around with the whine of the vacuum in his ears. Bernard, the driver, took care of filling the refrigerator with essentials and stocking the bar. If Doug planned a cocktail or dinner party, one call to Glorious Foods, the upscale caterer, took care of everything.

But after breakfast and, by a near miracle, Sandra had cleaned up the kitchen, Doug wished she'd get out. He needed to think. Instead it was she who asked, "Doug, did you visit Kate yesterday?"

"No, I heard she was resting after the fever broke."

"I think you should go there this morning and I'll go with you. Don't forget I met her and I'd like to say a prayer over her."

That will start World War III with Hannah, Doug had thought as he pushed himself away from the breakfast table.

But an hour later he and Sandra were speaking with Dr. Patel. "Kate is restless," the doctor said. "I take that as a very good sign. I like to think that she is fighting her way back, that she doesn't want to be sedated anymore. The brain swelling is down. I must caution you that until she is fully out of sedation, we won't know if or how much brain damage she may have suffered. I will also tell you that it would not be unusual for her to have absolutely no memory of anything immediately preceding the accident."

"Can we look in on her now, Doctor?" Sandra asked.

Doug was uncomfortably aware that Sandra had taken on a certain attitude, almost as though she were the authorized voice of the Connelly family. He put a restraining hand on her arm. "I am very anxious to see my daughter," he said, with the emphasis on *I*.

"You're not going to refuse to let me say a prayer for her, Doug?"

Doug was not happy that Dr. Patel was a witness to the exchange.

He hated that, after she slipped off her coat, Sandra was wearing a tight low-cut sweater that would have been more suitable in a night-club in the Meatpacking District. He'd been too engrossed in his own thoughts to notice it before.

But thankfully, Dr. Patel had told him that Hannah had already been there this morning. She almost certainly wouldn't be back in the next ten minutes. He wouldn't have to tell her that he had let Sandra go in to visit Kate. "Come along," he said brusquely to Sandra.

Kate was stirring but her eyes were closed. Doug took her hand. "Baby, it's Daddy. I love you so much. You've got to get well for me and Hannah. You can do it. We need you."

Easy tears slipped from his eyes.

On the other side of the bed, Sandra smoothed her hand softly over Kate's bandaged forehead. "Kate, it's Sandra. We had dinner to-gether the night of the accident. I thought you were so beautiful and so smart and you are. And you're going to be again. And I want to be-come your best friend. And if you're in trouble, I'll be there for you."

"That's enough, Sandra," Doug interrupted, his voice an angry whisper.

"Well, I am going to say a prayer." Sandra closed her eyes and looked upward. "Beautiful Kate, may you be blessed and healed. Amen."

Kate, who could not communicate with them, had heard every-thing. As she slipped back into sleep, she had one thought that was clear in her mind. *Bimbo.*

Doug had hoped that Sandra might want to check her mail or have dinner with her girlfriends again tonight, but she climbed back into the Bentley and told Bernard, "We're going home, Bernard. But I'm making reservations for tonight at SoHo North, so we'll need you to pick us up at eight thirty. Our boy needs to get out. He has far too much on his plate and it's not fair."

Doug had been about to tell Sandra that he could feel the beginning of a splitting headache and needed to lie down in a dark room and be quiet. He wanted to insist that Bernard drop her off home now. But then again, the prospect of being completely alone tonight was not appealing, either. Dinner with some good wine in the same dining room as the celebrities who were always at SoHo North was more to his liking. "Sounds good to me," he said, trying to sound cheerful.

At twenty minutes of six, the telephone rang. Sandra had just prepared a scotch for him and an apple martini for herself. She ran to the phone and looked at the caller ID. "It's Jack Worth," she told Doug.

"Let it ring. I'm not in the mood to talk to him."

Ten minutes later the phone rang again. "The number doesn't show," Sandra reported, as, holding the martini, she ran across the library again to glance at the landline phone on the desk.

"Forget it. No, wait, I'll take it." Doug had suddenly remembered who might be calling.

"Connelly residence," Sandra answered, in a voice that was her concept of the proper way for a housekeeper or secretary to answer the phone.

"Put Doug Connelly on," a low, angry voice told her.

"Who is calling, please?"

"I said to put him on."

Sandra covered the speaker with her hand. "I think it's some kind of nut. He won't give his name and he sounds as though he's furious about something."

Not knowing what to expect but suddenly fearful, Doug got up and hurried across the room. "Douglas Connelly," he said when he picked up the receiver.

"Did you know who you were messing with when you pulled that switch?"

Doug recognized the voice but was bewildered at the question.

"You thought you could get away with a dumb trick like that, you stupid idiot? You can't. I want four million dollars deposited in my account by Friday morning or you won't live to see Saturday. That's the three million five hundred thousand you owe me plus interest for pain and suffering."

"I don't know what you're talking about!"

"Then think about our last transaction and maybe you'll get it. But tell you what? Maybe you need a little more time to put together that kind of money. So you have until next Monday. But if it goes that long, make it four million two hundred thousand dollars. The extra two hundred grand is for making me look like a fool."

Doug heard the click of the receiver in his ears. His hand clenching, he replaced the phone in the cradle.

"Dougie, Dougie, what is it? You look like you're going to faint. Who was that? What did he say?" Sandra was beside him, steadying the hand that was holding the drink that was now spilling down his sleeve.

"Oh my God," Doug moaned. "Oh my God. What am I going to do?"

71

At five o'clock on Wednesday evening, Frank Ramsey and Nathan Klein rang the bell of Lottie Schmidt's home. Now that they had received confirmation that Gus had not won a lottery within the United States, they had agreed that this time there would be a harder edge to their questioning, with Frank playing the more sympathetic role and Nathan expressing disbelief at Lottie's lottery claim.

Lottie opened the door on the second ring of the bell, but if she was surprised to see them, she did not indicate it. Something in her attitude was also different. They both noticed that right away. She seemed less frightened and more sure of herself. "I would have appreciated a phone call," she said as she stepped aside to let them in. "And you might have saved yourself a useless trip. I'm leaving in the next few minutes to go to my neighbor's house. She was kind enough to invite me for an early dinner."

"Then I'm very glad we caught you, Mrs. Schmidt," Frank said, pleasantly. "We'll only be a few minutes." He started to turn from the foyer into the living room.

Lottie stopped him. "I think it would be more to the point if we sat at the dining room table. I have some photo albums there that I think might interest you."

She did not tell them that after her neighbor Peter Callow left the other day, she had sat at that table, thinking long and hard. It was obvious to her that while Peter would defend her, he did not believe that she was ignorant of where Gus had gotten the money for Gretchen's house. If he doesn't believe me, no one else will, she had reasoned. Well, I'll find a story that might hold up.

With that thought in mind, she had pulled down the folding stairs to the attic, climbed up, and retrieved a now-dusty photo album and several framed pictures of severe-looking people in formal dress or military uniform. The items were from a box that had not been disturbed since the first day they moved into the house.

Carefully wiped off, the album and the pictures were now spread out on the dining room table. She invited the detectives to sit down there. Unlike the other time they had come into her home, she did not offer them water or coffee.

"You have heard my husband described as a master craftsman who was forced into retirement by Douglas Connelly and his minion, Jack Worth," she said, her voice level. "Gus was that. He was all of that. But he was also part of one of the finest families in Germany." She turned the album around. "In World War I, his grandfather was an aide to the kaiser. His name was Field Marshal Augustus Wilhelm von Mueller. That is his picture with the kaiser."

Stunned, the two detectives stared at the album.

"And this is a picture of his grandfather's home. Gus's father was the second son in the family. Gus's father and mother died in an accident when he was a baby. Gus was their only child. The horse-drawn carriage they were riding in overturned on a rainy night. After they died, Gus was brought here and was raised with his cousins." Lottie pointed and continued: "It was a castle on the Rhine and it was filled with furniture and paintings that were priceless antiques. My husband did not learn to love and appreciate beautiful furniture and art in a public museum. He lived for the first eight years of his life in what was in essence a museum, and he never forgot it."

Lottie turned the page. "There is Gus with his cousins when he was six years old. You will notice that they were all girls. Gus was the only male grandchild and would eventually have inherited the castle and everything in it."

Her voice becoming more emotional, she said, "Gus's grandfather regarded Hitler with contempt and disdain. The family was not Jewish, but like many others of their rank they disappeared and died when Hitler came to power. Their homes and property were confiscated. Gus was in the hospital because of a burst appendix when his family was arrested and taken from their home.

"The Gestapo came to the hospital. The nurse hid Gus and showed them the body of a boy that age who had just died and told them that he was the von Mueller child. They accepted what she said and left. The nurse, whose last name was Schmidt, took Gus home that night. That is how he survived."

"He was raised as the child of the nurse?" Ramsey asked.

"Yes. She moved to a different city and enrolled him in school. She told him that he must never talk about his former life because he, too, would be taken away. He was terrified by the cruelty of what happened on Kristallnacht and by the fact that his Jewish friends at school had to wear yellow armbands. That was, of course, before they, too, disappeared."

"Then he was the only survivor of the family?"

"Absolutely. Everyone died in the camps. His grandfather's castle was taken over by the Nazis and later bombed during the war. So no one was really sure if there was anything belonging to the family that was left. Gus never wanted to talk even to me about the past. After the war, the German people suffered terribly. Gus had quit school when he was sixteen, after the nurse who had adopted him became ill and died. He was completely on his own and found a job in a furniture repair shop. We were both twenty years old when we were married. He was wearing a rented suit."

She smiled reminiscently, then said, "You see, that was why people found Gus unyielding, even autocratic. He came by it naturally. He was the offspring of a noble family."

"Mrs. Schmidt, this is absolutely fascinating," Frank Ramsey said, "but how does it fit in with the fact that Gus was able to give Gretchen enough money to buy a very expensive home five years ago and an annuity to help support it?"

"As you must be aware, there are organizations that track down property that was stolen by the Nazis. I knew years ago that Gus had been in touch with them. More than that I don't know. He hated to refer to the life that existed before his family disappeared. His pain was too deep. His heart was broken. What he did tell me five years ago was that he had finally heard from one of the search organizations and they had negotiated a deal with the present owner of one of the paintings that was proven to have been in the castle. The new owner offered to pay a fair price for it, provided his name never was revealed. Gus accepted the offer. He never told me more than that but that was the money he used to buy Gretchen's house. He received payment for a painting that rightfully belonged to him, and that is why, gentlemen, I ask you to leave my home and stop trying to make Augustus Wilhelm von Mueller II into a thief.

"I know, even though he is dead, you are convinced he is an arsonist," Lottie said bitterly as she stood up and pushed back her chair. "Isn't that good enough for you?"

Silently, they followed her to the door. After they went out she closed it behind them and then they heard the decisive click of the lock turning.

As they looked at each other in the gathering darkness, Frank's cell phone rang. It was a detective from the precinct near the complex. "Frank, we just got a call from the Connelly place. They have a sinkhole in the parking lot and there's a skeleton in it. It's pretty obvious it's been there a long time. It looks like a woman. She's wearing some kind of necklace with the name Tracey on it. They think it's

Tracey Sloane, a young actress who disappeared about twenty-eight years ago."

"We'll be right there," Frank said. He turned off the phone, looked at Nathan, and tersely told him of the incredible find at the complex. They both rushed to the car. As Frank turned on the engine, Nathan asked, "Frank, Hotchkiss had been missing for nearly forty years. Do you think he might have been hanging around the Connelly plant when Tracey Sloane disappeared?"

"I don't know," Frank said. "But if he was, it's going to be damn hard to prove it."

72

Justin and Hannah were seated at the table in her small dining room. They had just finished the excellent selection of the Chinese food that Justin had brought in and were reading their fortune cookies. Justin unfolded the small slip of paper in his cookie and read it aloud. "The Year of the Snake will bring you much happiness."

He checked the search mechanism on his phone and learned that the Year of the Snake was starting in less than two months.

Hannah's fortune was not as straightforward. "Wisdom comes to those whose minds are open to the truth . . . That's a big nothing," she said laughing. "I wish I'd picked yours."

"There are more of them. Want to try again? Or I'll share mine with you."

They smiled at each other. Each was comfortably aware that something was beginning between them and they both liked it. Over dinner, Justin had told her about himself. "My mother was from the Bronx. My father from Brooklyn. They met at Columbia. After they got married, they moved to Princeton. My mother teaches English lit and my father is chair of the Philosophy Department. I have a younger sister. She's a medical resident at Hackensack Hospital."

As he spoke, Hannah could see the animation in his face and could sense that Justin had enjoyed a normal, happy childhood. Wistfully, she reviewed her own growing-up years. Dad always on his way out. Rosemary Masse telling him he should remarry, that his little girls needed a mother. Hannah thought of how she used to pretend her mother was alive and would talk to her. Her mother would tell her that it was wonderful that she got an A on her spelling test.

She did that because her best friend in the first grade, Nancy, would tell her that her mother said she was so proud of her because she got an A. And then they went out for ice cream. I told her that my mommy took me out for ice cream, too, Hannah remembered. And Nancy said, "But you don't have a mommy. Your mommy is dead."

I didn't speak to Nancy for days and Kate kept asking me what was wrong. She was nine years old then. Finally I told her. She said that I shouldn't be mad at Nancy, that I should tell her that my mommy is in heaven but I do have a big sister and she doesn't, so I'm lucky. Then Kate and Rosie took me out for ice cream because I had gotten an A, too.

Hannah realized that she hadn't just been thinking about that but was actually telling it to Justin. She laughed self-consciously. "Hey, you're a good listener."

"I hope so. On the other hand, my sister says that I talk too much."

The phone in the kitchen began to ring. Justin saw the panic in Hannah's eyes as she jumped to answer it. "Hannah, take it easy," he counseled but he followed her into the kitchen, hoping against hope that it would not be bad news about Kate's condition.

The caller was Hannah's father. His loud, overwrought voice made it easy for Justin to overhear. "I just got a call from those fire marshals. All the water from the hoses caused a sinkhole in the back parking lot. They found the skeleton of a young woman there. They think they know her identity but they didn't give me a name."

"A skeleton!" Hannah exclaimed. "Do they know how long it's been there?"

"They didn't say. Hannah, this is so bizarre. I don't know what to think."

"Dad, are you alone?"

He did not answer for the moment but then said, "No, Sandra is with me. We were just going out when the phone rang."

"Do the police want to talk to you?"

"Yes, they're on their way here. I think it's detectives from New York, not those fire marshals."

"Then, obviously, you have to wait for them. Send for dinner from the restaurant in your building. The marshals may be there for a long time."

"Of course. That's what I should do. Hannah, I don't know what to think. Between what happened to Kate and Gus and the explosion and that tramp living in the van and the insurance company refusing to discuss payment with me . . ." Douglas Connelly began to sob.

"Dad, hang on. None of this is your fault."

"I know it isn't, but that doesn't mean . . ." At the other end of the phone Douglas Connelly realized that he was babbling. He had been about to say that he had to put his hands on $4 million in the next five days. He had been counting on the insurance money for the antiques in the museum and the value of the buildings, but now he might need to talk to the broker who had people interested in buying the property. Maybe he could make a quick deal with one of them and get a $4 million deposit even if he had to let it go at a bargain price.

If they blamed the fire on Gus and Gus alone, the insurance company would have to pay at some point, but I need the money now, he said to himself.

"Dad, are you all right? Are you all right?" Hannah realized that her voice was rising.

"Yes, yes. Just terribly shocked."

"Call me after the police talk to you no matter what time it is."

"All right. Good-bye."

Justin and Hannah looked at each other as she replaced the phone. Silently they went back to the table and sat down. Then Hannah poured tea into each of their cups. "Can you imagine tomorrow's headlines?" she asked.

"I can," Justin told her. "Your father used the word *skeleton*. That could mean that the body was there a long time, maybe even before your grandfather bought the property sixty years ago."

At the surprised look on Hannah's face, he explained, somewhat sheepishly, "I looked up everything I could find about it. Haven't you ever done that?"

"No, I haven't. I mean Dad told us that his father, our grandfather, made his money on Wall Street, cashed in, and bought the property. He had already started collecting antiques. He built the factory and showroom and museum and bought many more antiques. Dad was just starting college then. He's fifty-eight now. I don't think Dad likes the idea of having daughters our age. He wants us to call him Doug instead of Dad. But we always missed having a mother, so turning him into a pal rubbed us both the wrong way."

Justin got up. "I don't blame you. All right, I know I promised you that I wouldn't stay late but after that call from your father, do you want me to hang around until you hear from him again?"

Hannah did not hesitate. She smiled weakly and said, "I'd really like that."

"Good. And I also promised you I'd clean up the kitchen. So you have that cup of tea and let me do that."

Hannah again attempted a smile. "I won't stop you."

As she sipped the tea, it occurred to her that if Doug had been told about the discovery of the skeleton, the odds were that Jack Worth knew about it, too. After the explosion, she had put the number of his cell phone on her contact list. Since Kate had been in the hospital, her phone was never more than the reach of her hand away. She had changed into a sweater and slacks when she got home from work. Now she pulled the phone out of her pocket, opened it, found Jack's number, and called him.

If her father's voice sounded frightened, Jack Worth sounded as though he were facing a firing squad. "Hannah, I know about it. I can't talk. The detectives are here. They're taking me to police headquarters to question me. Hannah, no matter what you may hear, I did not kill Tracey Sloane."

73

From the moment he was arrested by the detectives in the kitchen of Tommy's Bistro on Tuesday evening, Harry Simon had been defiant. After he had been read his Miranda rights, they took him to police headquarters. He had agreed to talk to them, insisting he had done nothing wrong. But there was no way he could ever refute the evidence on the security cameras. Harry Simon was, unmistakably, the man who had dragged Betsy Trainer, the young waitress and aspiring actress, through the alleyway and into the courtyard where he had molested and strangled her.

Only a part of the actual crime was on camera, but it was clear from the view of the assailant's face and the dragon on the back of his jacket that Harry Simon was the man who was leaning over the helpless figure on the ground. The cameras had captured Betsy's terrified expression as he forced her into the courtyard. Twenty minutes later, they again registered her face, her unseeing eyes now staring straight ahead, as he carried her lifeless body to his car.

Obviously stunned as the detectives ran the tape for him, his only response was, "Yeah, it looks like me. But I don't remember doing nothing to nobody. If that was me, and I'm not saying it was, I was out of my mind. I'm bipolar. Sometimes I forget to take my medicine."

"Do you need medicine to recognize your own face on the tape or that cheap jacket with the dragon on it that you were wearing then and that you were wearing when we picked you up?" one of the detectives shouted sarcastically. "Do you need medicine to understand what you did to that girl?"

Harry did not budge an inch from his insistence that he did not remember anything about the murder, even though he continued to be grilled all Wednesday morning and afternoon.

The detectives had switched their questioning midstream to the disappearance of Tracey Sloane. "You worked with her years ago. Did you ever go out with her?"

"Nah, she never gave me a glance."

"Did you like her?"

"Everybody liked Tracey. She was fun to be around. She wasn't like some of the other waitresses, who'd start chewing out the kitchen people if their orders weren't ready."

"You're sure you never went out with her? Someone told us they saw you in a movie together."

"That's a lie. Tell 'someone' to get new glasses."

"Maybe you forgot that you made Tracey Sloane disappear, the way you forgot you killed Betsy Trainer last week. Maybe you had a buddy grab Tracey the way you grabbed Betsy and then you met him later after you established your alibi at Bobbie's Joint. Maybe Tracey was still alive when you met him later."

"That's a really good 'maybe' story," Harry Simon replied, obviously enjoying himself. He had always known that someday he would be caught, but there was no death penalty in New York, so he considered himself lucky. He figured that if he'd been arrested in Texas after that barfly disappeared, or in California after the model he met on the beach disappeared, or in Colorado when that hitchhiker he picked up disappeared, he'd probably have ended up on death row.

Even as the detectives pounded their questions at him, he let his thoughts drift. He'd met all of them when he was on vacation. He never told anyone the truth about where he was going on vacation. He'd tell the guys in the kitchen at Tommy's that he was going some-where else, and when he came back, he'd show them pictures of himself on a beach and say he'd been to the Jersey shore or Nan-tucket or Cape Cod. Not that anyone cared but it was a good way to cover his tracks. Just in case.

The anger and frustration he saw on the faces of the detectives had actually invigorated and amused Harry Simon.

"Like I say, it's a good 'maybe' story," he repeated. "Even twenty-eight years ago, the blocks between Tommy's Bistro and Tracey's apartment were always crowded. How do you think I could drag Tracey off the street without nobody seeing me?"

Harry knew he had said too much.

"So you did follow her?"

"I knew where she lived. I knew which way she had to walk home. So did everybody else. And, remember, I was at Bobbie's eighteen minutes after the others got there."

At three o'clock Wednesday afternoon, Harry finally indicated that he had had enough of their garbage and that he wanted to talk to the lawyer who had gotten him out of a speeding ticket last year. "The cop's radar gun wasn't working right," he said, smiling. "The judge threw it out."

The detectives knew that they had to stop the questioning, but they couldn't resist the sarcastic comment that there was a big difference between beating a speeding ticket because of a de-fective radar gun and beating a homicide that was recorded on camera.

When attorney Noah Green arrived an hour and a half later, the detectives led him to the small holding cell where Harry Simon was waiting. When the detective left the enclosure, Harry Simon said, "Hi. Glad you came. This is the first time I've been in big trouble."

"Very big trouble," Noah Green corrected. "The police told me that they have you on camera killing the woman on the Lower East Side."

"I've told them that I've been off my medicine and don't remember anything about her," Harry replied, dismissively. "Maybe you can get me off on insanity."

Noah Green grimaced. "I'll do my best but don't count on it."

Harry decided to test the waters. "Suppose I can tell them something about Tracey Sloane."

"Her name has been all over the news since you got arrested. You worked with her and the cops questioned you when she first disappeared. What are you talking about now?"

"I mean, like, maybe I began to follow her that night to see if maybe she'd have a drink with me but then I saw her get in a vehicle."

"They said on the news that you have always denied having any idea what happened to her. Now you're saying you saw her get in a vehicle. You'd better be careful or you'll end up convicting yourself on that one, too. On the other hand, if you weren't involved and really do have some important information that helps them to solve Sloane's disappearance, I would say that maybe we can cut some kind of deal that wouldn't keep you in prison for the rest of your life."

"Let me think it over."

"You can't just tell them she got in a car. They won't believe you and even if they did, it doesn't help them."

"I didn't say a car. I can describe it. I can get specific."

"Harry, have you got something to tell me or not? I'm your lawyer. This is confidential. It doesn't go any farther than me unless we decide that it should."

"Okay. This is what happened. I was following her the night she disappeared. Like I said, I thought if I ended up on her door-step, well, maybe she'd invite me in. Probably not but I . . ." Harry hesitated. "I couldn't help myself. I was about half a block behind her. But then there was a red traffic light at the corner. Somebody who was stopped at the light called out to her. A minute later, the passenger door opens and she hops in like she couldn't wait to get in."

"She must have known the person," Green commented, as he studied Harry's sly expression. Somehow he had the gut feeling that Harry was telling the truth. "Why didn't you tell that to the police when Tracey disappeared?" he asked.

"Because I had followed her and that didn't look good. Because I had gotten together with the others at Bobbie's and I had a good alibi. So I let it go. I didn't want them looking too deep into my background. I had a few minor problems when I was in high school. I was scared they'd pin her disappearing act on me if I opened my mouth."

Noah Green thoroughly disliked his client and was ready to go home. "I doubt very much if telling the detectives that you saw Tracey Sloane get in a car that night will do you much good in your current situation. In fact, I agree they'll probably end up pinning her disappearance on you."

"I didn't say I saw her get into just any car. I just told you I can describe it. It was a midsize black furniture van with gold lettering that had the word 'antique' on the side. Now, if we give them that, can you get a plea deal for me?"

"Are you absolutely sure you want to reveal this?"

"Yeah."

"I can't make any promises to you that it will help at all. Let me think about how I approach the detectives with this information. I'll see you tomorrow morning at your arraignment. Remember, don't talk to anybody, and I mean anybody, about anything."

A weary Noah Green left his client at five minutes past five on Wednesday evening. It was precisely at that moment that, in Long Island City, Jose Fernandez walked across the parking lot of the Connelly complex and looked down into the sinkhole and saw Tracey Sloane's remains.

74

When Frank Ramsey and Nathan Klein drove into the Connelly property Wednesday evening, they learned that the detectives who had finished questioning Harry Simon were on their way to the site. I'd be rushing to get here, too, if I had been working a cold case that's been around for over twenty-eight years, Frank thought.

Now officially a crime scene, the parking lot was already swarming with activity.

The cleanup crew had been ordered to stay, and Jose Fernandez, the young worker who had found the skeletal remains, was being questioned in a police mobile unit. His story was straightforward and backed up by his boss. "Last night, it was pretty dark when we set up the poles around the sinkhole. We couldn't see into it and anyhow it had been a long day. This morning, Sal, the boss, decided that we'd worry about the sinkhole later because our job was to get rid of as much debris as possible."

At that point, Jose decided to throw in a brief history of his interest in archeological finds. You never know if one of the detectives has a sister who is a principal in a school and could use a substitute teacher, he thought. He cited his master's degree, then said, "So, I was curious to take a look. Sal told me to make it quick because he was driving me back to the garage. I jogged across the parking lot to the sinkhole and looked down and . . ."

Then he shrugged. The vivid memory of the curled-up skeleton with the long auburn hair sticking to the skull would haunt him for a long time to come.

Jose and everyone else in the cleanup crew were soon cleared as potential suspects. Their IDs were checked, their names, addresses, and phone numbers taken, and they were permitted to leave.

Frank and Nathan knew that they would not be part of the investigation that would follow the finding of the remains of Tracey Sloane. While, of course, there would be an autopsy, they had zero doubt that it was her. The investigation would be purely within the jurisdiction of the Manhattan district attorney's office, where the case had remained cold for all these years. But they stayed until their own boss, Marshal Tim Fleming, arrived and conferred with them and the DA's detectives.

At a grim conference in the police mobile unit, they all agreed that it was now appropriate to publicly release the fact that Jamie Gordon's notebook had also been found in the wrecked van, and that the deceased vagrant Clyde Hotchkiss had admitted punching her, but not killing her.

The same thought was on all of their minds. Hotchkiss had been living on the streets for forty years. Was it possible that he had been hanging around the complex twenty-eight years ago, and, if so, could he be responsible for killing both Jamie and Tracey?

It was already a matter of record from the questioning of Jack Worth twenty-eight years ago that he had tried to give Tracey the necklace as a gift, but that she had refused him and had actually paid him for it months before she died. Jack had admitted then that he was hurt and disappointed. But he swore he had not killed her. And he was being brought in for questioning again now.

"So we have the plant manager who was working here when

Tracey disappeared and who may have been insulted when she refused to let him give her a gift that cost eight dollars. We have a
dead vagrant who admits that Jamie Gordon was in the van with him
and who may very well have been hanging around here twenty-eight
years ago. And we have a murderer who worked with Tracey and
who can't account for eighteen minutes the night she vanished," one
of the detectives said in summing up.

Frank Ramsey and Nathan Klein could have gone home then,
but by silent agreement they waited and soberly watched as the sinkhole was photographed and searched for any clue that might deter-
mine if it was the actual location where Tracey died.

It was nearly 10 P.M. when, with searchlights illuminating the
grim scene, the skeletal remains were carefully lifted onto the medical examiner's stretcher.

Pieces of dark blue cloth that had once been slacks and the ivory-
colored remnants of wool that had once been a sweater dropped
onto the jagged base of the sinkhole as Tracey Sloane was moved
from the place where she had been hidden for longer than she had
lived.

75

Mark Sloane left the Marea restaurant, his dinner untouched, after telling Nick Greco that he needed to go home and call his mother. From the description of the necklace, he had no doubt that the remains found in Long Island City were those of his sister.

In one of the last pictures she had sent home, Tracey had been wearing the blue medallion with her name on it. She had written, "Dear Mom and Mark. How do you like my sapphire necklace? A bargain for eight dollars, don't you think? When my name is in lights on Broadway, maybe I can buy the real thing. Wouldn't that be great!"

Why and how did Tracey's body end up in Long Island City? It might never have been discovered if the Connelly complex had not exploded. It was also totally bizarre that one of the young women he happened to run into in the lobby of his new apartment building was the daughter of the owner of the complex where Tracey's body was found.

Mark looked at his watch. It was only eight o'clock. He knew that he also wanted very much to talk to Hannah Connelly. Maybe she could help him find out quickly if Harry Simon had ever worked at Connelly's, or maybe had a relative who had worked there. By now the records of nearly thirty years ago are probably gone, he tried to warn himself. The IRS doesn't require you to keep them for more than seven years.

He found himself reaching for his cell phone. This is crazy, he thought. It's just that I want an answer. Maybe all these years, I still thought that one day Tracey would come back into our lives. I'll be thirty-eight in a couple of months. She was only twenty-two when she vanished. I have to call Mom tonight to tell her that Tracey's been found. I want to be able to also tell her that, maybe very soon, we'll be sure that the creep who worked in the kitchen is the one who did it and that he'll never walk the streets again.

Tracey. Big sister. *Mark, you've got a good pitching arm. Come on, make me miss this pitch . . .*

Tracey taking him to the movies on Friday night. They'd have a hamburger and french fries and a soda first at McDonald's and when they got to the movies she'd ask, *Popcorn or a Hershey bar, Mark? Or both?*

Mark realized that he had his cell phone in his hand and was dialing 411 for information. He was relieved that Hannah Connelly's apartment phone number was listed. As he was connected to her number, he thought that if she doesn't want to see me, she can just say so.

The phone was answered on the second ring. Hannah Connelly's "Hello" was breathless, almost as though she were frightened to answer the call.

"Hannah, I'm Mark Sloane. I live one floor below you in apartment 5C. We met in the lobby last Thursday night."

"Yes, I remember." Now her voice was cordial. "You rode up in the elevator with Jessie and me. I'm afraid I was pretty upset."

"Have they told you yet that skeletal remains were found on your family's property in Long Island City?"

"How do you know that?" Now her tone was wary.

"Tracey Sloane was my sister." Mark did not wait for a response. "I just heard about it. I'm on my way home. I'll be there soon. May I come up and see you?"

"Yes, of course. Mark, I am so sorry."

Fifteen minutes later, Hannah was opening the door of her apartment for Mark Sloane. When she had met him last Thursday evening, she had been so conscious of the fact that she was openly crying and embarrassed to be seen that she had hardly noticed the tall, attractive man who was standing in front of her. But now what she noticed first was the expression of pain in his eyes so visible that it hurt to witness it.

"Come in, Mark," she said. "Please, come in."

He followed her into the apartment, noticing that the floor plan seemed to be an exact duplicate of his own, one floor below. Unlike in his apartment, though, there were no pictures set out on the floor and waiting to be hung. This apartment had the comfortable feeling of a lived-in home.

Even as he observed that, Mark realized how absolutely irrelevant it was to be thinking about wall decorations.

He had somehow expected that Hannah Connelly might be alone, but there were two other people in the room. One was Jessie, the tall redhead lawyer he had met the other night. The other was a guy who was probably a few years younger than he, but who was obviously aware of what was going on. His handshake was firm. "I'm Justin. You must be going through a lot," Justin Kramer said quietly.

Mark didn't want to become emotional in front of these people who were strangers. His knees suddenly felt weak and he sat down on the couch.

His voice sounding hollow to his own ears, Mark heard himself saying, "I was with the detective who investigated my sister's disappearance nearly twenty-eight years ago. He's retired now but has always kept a copy of the case file. We were at dinner when he got the call that Tracey's remains may have been found.

"Or, almost certainly, have been found," Mark corrected himself.

"I guess the reason I'm here is that I need to have answers. When Tracey disappeared, someone who worked with her in the restaurant was questioned but his alibi was too good. It checked out. But maybe he had an accomplice, I mean maybe someone who worked at the Connelly complex."

Mark could feel the burning in his throat. "I know the detectives will be asking the same questions, but I have to call my mother now, to let her know Tracey has been found. She already knows that the guy who worked with Tracey and who was slobbering about how wonderful Tracey was has been arrested for allegedly killing another young actress. I know that no matter what she's ever said, my mother still hoped Tracey would come home someday. I know how I feel. I need to have answers. If there are any records of employees from around that time available somewhere, could I possibly get my hands on them? I need answers. My mother needs answers . . ."

Mark's troubled voice trailed off. He stood up. "I'm sorry," he said. "I'm not usually like this."

It was Jessie who answered him. "Mark, we're all stunned at the discovery of your sister's remains. Maybe there will be an answer. The plant manager who has worked for Hannah's family for thirty years, and who gave Tracey the necklace, is being questioned by the police right now. He was also questioned when Tracey first disappeared."

Then, studying Mark's drawn expression and knowing he was

about to break down, Jessie said, "I think you should call your mother before she hears it from someone else."

Jessie had not intended to say anything more than that but then added, "Why don't I go downstairs with you? I think you could use a cup of tea or coffee. I'll make it while you call your mother."

76

Martha Sloane had been shattered by the phone call that night from her son, Mark, telling her that Harry Simon, the kitchen worker at Tommy's Bistro, had just been arrested the night before for allegedly murdering another young actress. The victim had been a girl so much like Tracey, waiting on tables and trying to achieve her dream of becoming an actress.

It's not so much for me, Martha thought, as she tried to keep herself busy with the kind of tasks that she would always assign herself on one of those days when her mind would be filled with anguish at the possibility that Tracey might still be alive out there somewhere and needing her.

But her house was already immaculate, the closets already in pristine order. It was not her day to volunteer at the nursing home and her book group meeting was not scheduled for another week.

Harry Simon. Odd that with all the people she had met at Tommy's Bistro when she had gone to help find Tracey, and whose faces were now a blur to her, his was very clear in her mind. He had been a thoroughly unattractive human being, with his narrow eyes and pinched face and obsequious manner. He was crying when he spoke to me, Martha remembered, and he tried to hug me. I pulled back and that Nick Greco, who was in charge of the investigation, said something like, "Take it easy, Harry." And he stepped between us.

But I thought Simon's alibi was supposed to be so good.

I hate the word *closure*, Martha thought. I hear the word and I almost go crazy. Doesn't anyone understand that there's no such thing? Unless closure means that the person who took your child's life away will never have the chance to take another life. That is a sort of closure.

The rest of it is that you finally have your child's body back and it's in a grave that you can visit and plant flowers there. That's a form of closure, too. You don't have to worry anymore that your child is lying in a swamp or being kept prisoner.

Somehow, Martha Sloane had the feeling that soon she would know. Mark had told her that if Harry Simon confessed, or there was anything else new to report, he would call back. Otherwise, he'd talk to her again in the morning.

That was why when her phone rang that evening, after she had wrapped up the dinner she could not force herself to swallow, Martha knew that Mark had something important to tell her.

She could hear that his voice was breaking and he was on the verge of tears when he said, "Mom, they found Tracey."

"Where?"

Steeling herself, the mother of Tracey Sloane listened to her son's halting voice. A sinkhole in a parking lot in a furniture factory. She was heartsick. "Was Tracey alive when she was left there, Mark?" she asked.

"I don't know yet but I don't think so."

"Mark, you didn't believe me, but I told you that in my heart I had given up hope that Tracey was still alive. I think you are the one who still held out some measure of hope. But now we know. Well, I didn't expect to be coming to New York so soon, but I think I'd like to come tomorrow and stay with you for a few days."

Martha Sloane did not add that she knew that Mark needed her as much as she needed him.

"I'd like that, Mom. I'll make a plane reservation for you for the late afternoon. I'll call you first thing in the morning. Try to get some sleep. I love you."

"I love you, too, dear." Martha Sloane replaced the receiver and with slow, measured steps walked out to the foyer and reached for the light switch. For the first time in nearly twenty-eight years, the overhead light on the porch went off.

77

When Doug received the call Wednesday night that skeletal remains had been found in a sinkhole in the parking lot of the complex, and that the fire marshals were on their way to question him, he
told Sandra to go home. "You've been a big help but I need to be by
myself now. Call one of your friends for dinner. Get your hair done
or something in the morning. Then come back. I don't want—"

He stopped himself. What he had been about to say was that he
didn't want Sandra acting like the lady of the house, or butting in
when he was talking to the marshals, or leaping to answer his phone
whenever it rang.

Sandra had pelted him with questions when she answered the
call from, as she described him, "the guy who sounded as though he
was furious about something." He had explained his distress over the
call. "It's from an investment advisor who lost a lot of money. I encouraged him to have his clients invest in a new hedge fund, but the
guy who runs it turned out to be a disaster. His clients lost everything
they put in and now he's blaming me."

"That doesn't sound right to me, Dougie," Sandra had said in-
dignantly. "I mean you may have suggested that guy invest in something, but investing is always a gamble. My father told me that. He
said that if you put a few dollars a week in the bank, you'd be sur-

prised how it will grow and you'll always feel secure knowing you have something behind you."

"Your father is a very wise man," Doug Connelly said bitterly, as he finally eased her out and escorted her to the door. Bernard, who had expected to drive them to dinner at SoHo North, was instead chauffeuring her to her own apartment.

Doug went straight to the library and poured himself a double scotch, then realized that the fire marshals had undoubtedly called Jack Worth as well. He picked up the phone to call Jack, but Jack did not answer his cell phone.

Then he remembered that Jack had called him a couple of hours ago, but he had decided to ignore the call.

Thirty-five minutes later, the fire marshals Ramsey and Klein arrived. On the way, they had discussed their strategy for talking to Douglas Connelly. They fully expected that he would absolutely disclaim any knowledge of knowing Tracey Sloane and any knowledge of how her body ended up underneath the pavement in the parking lot.

They had also agreed that Jack Worth was more than a mere person of interest. He was now being questioned in the Manhattan district attorney's office. "I think we're going nowhere with Douglas Connelly," Ramsey said as he parked the car in a no-parking spot and flipped down the visor to display their "Fire Department Official Business" status.

The doorman told them that Mr. Connelly was expecting them and that he would let him know that they had arrived. On the way up in the elevator, Klein asked, "What are the odds that his lady friend is still around?"

"Fifty-fifty," Ramsey replied. "She would drive me nuts but my guess is that he's the kind of guy who likes having someone thirty-five years younger hovering over him."

Douglas Connelly was waiting for them, the door of his apartment open behind him. They could detect the smell of liquor on his breath and see the glazed expression in his eyes. As they had expected, he directed them straight to the library, where a half-filled glass of whiskey was on the table next to his chair.

As they both declined his offer of a glass of water, or something stronger, Frank glanced at the bookshelves that covered the walls. He had the fleeting thought that the books on display looked like matched sets, the kind of rare first-edition volumes that are finished with gilt-edged pages and illustrations. He wondered if Connelly had ever taken the time to open one of them. And then he wondered if the books, like everything else in this apartment, were copies of the real thing.

As he motioned for them to sit down, Connelly opened the conversation. "I cannot begin to tell you how absolutely shocked I was to receive your phone call. Do you have any idea whose remains were found or how long he might have been there?"

"We think we know the identity of the person and in fact it was a young woman," Ramsey said. "Does the name Tracey Sloane mean anything to you, Mr. Connelly?"

The fire marshals watched as he frowned in concentration.

"I'm afraid not," he said firmly. "Who was she?"

"A twenty-two-year-old young woman, aspiring to a theatrical career, who disappeared on her way home from work nearly twenty-eight years ago."

"Nearly twenty-eight years ago? You think she was buried in our parking lot for that long?"

"We don't know," Frank answered. "But you do not recall ever having met her?"

"Twenty-eight years ago, I was a very happily married man and the father of two young children." Douglas Connelly's tone became icy. "Are you in any way insinuating that I had any connection to that young woman at that time?"

"No, we are not."

"When exactly did she disappear?"

"It will be twenty-eight years this November thirtieth."

"Wait a minute. The horrible boating accident that took the life of my wife and brother and four close friends was on the third of November that year. I was in the hospital until November twenty-fourth. Are you daring to suggest that a week later, when I was still recovering from terrible injuries, that somehow I was involved in—?"

Ramsey interrupted him. "Mr. Connelly, we are suggesting nothing. We are here because that girl's skeletal remains were found on your property."

"Was Jack Worth working at the complex at that time?" Nathan Klein asked.

"I assume that if you have any interest in Jack Worth, you already know that he has been working for our family for well over thirty years."

"Were you friendly with him back then?" Klein asked.

"Jack started as an assistant bookkeeper. I was the son of the owner and had no reason to fraternize with him. He worked his way up in the company until our longtime manager, Russ Link, retired five years ago. By then Jack had proven himself to be fully capable of taking over the day-to-day running of the business and I put him in charge."

"Then your relationship has always been a business one?" Klein persisted.

"Primarily. In these last five years, outside of office hours, we have had dinner occasionally. Like myself, Jack has been concerned that the forecast of the market for the antique reproductions we manufacture is not healthy. That is a fact of life that we both recognize. The answer is to close shop and sell the property, but not at a bargain price. I have been waiting for an appropriate offer."

"Aside from your business relationship, what do you think of Jack Worth?" Ramsey asked bluntly.

"Both before and after his divorce some years ago, everyone was aware that Jack was a womanizer. In fact, I know that my father, shortly before he died, had blasted Jack about being too attentive to a young secretary in the executive office who was married. She told my father that Jack wouldn't stop insisting on having a drink after work. Apparently, to be rejected, even by someone who was happily married, was a personal insult and challenge to him."

The fire marshals stood up. "Mr. Connelly, you've been very helpful," Frank Ramsey said. "We won't bother you anymore to-night."

"It isn't a bother," Douglas Connelly said as he got to his feet, too. "But may I ask, what is your interest in Jack Worth? Did he know the woman whose remains were found today?"

Neither detective answered the question. With a polite "Good night, sir," they left the apartment. At that point, neither Ramsey nor Klein was about to tell Connelly that Jack Worth was then in the Manhattan DA's office being peppered with questions about Tracey Sloane.

Questions, they were to learn, he answered over and over again with the same sixteen words. "I did not kill Tracey Sloane and I did not bury her in that parking lot."

78

On Thursday morning at seven o'clock, Lawrence Gordon received a call from Detective John Cruse, who explained that two fire marshals who were investigating the explosion at the Connelly complex would like to see him. "Something has come up that we need to talk to you about, sir," Cruse said.

"It's about Jamie, isn't it? Do you know who took her life?"

"Mr. Gordon, we didn't want to contact you sooner because we knew that what we would tell you would be very distressing to you and Mrs. Gordon, and we wanted to have as much information as possible. Fire Marshal Frank Ramsey and Fire Marshal Nathan Klein and I can be at your home in an hour. I'm not sure what your schedule is today, but can you wait for us?"

"Of course, come right over." Lawrence had just finished showering and shaving. His bathroom was on the opposite side of their large bedroom and, with the door closed, Veronica had not heard the ring of his cell phone. That was another habit he had acquired in the nearly two years since Jamie had gone missing. Even after her body was found, he had continued to keep the cell phone close to him, waiting for the call that the police had tracked down her killer.

Now, hating to do it, he sat on the side of the bed and put his hand gently on Veronica's face. She opened her eyes immediately. "Lawrence, is something wrong? Are you all right?"

Veronica often got up by the time he was dressed, put on a robe, and had coffee with him downstairs. But if she was asleep, he never woke her up. Too often, the fact that she was still sleeping meant that she had been awake most of the night.

"Sweetheart, I'm fine but Detective Cruse and two fire marshals are on their way here to talk to us. It's about Jamie."

Lawrence watched as his wife closed her eyes in pain. "You don't have to talk to them," he said. "I can handle it myself if you want."

"No, I want to hear what they have to say. Do you think they've arrested someone?"

"I don't know."

They both dressed quickly. Instead of wearing his usual business suit, shirt, and tie, Lawrence put on casual slacks and a long-sleeved sports shirt. Veronica, her hands shaking, reached for the exercise clothes that were her usual morning choice. She went to the local gym faithfully every morning for a nine o'clock exercise class.

Dottie, their live-in housekeeper of many years, was in the kitchen. The coffee was ready and the table already set in the breakfast room. When she caught a glimpse of their faces, her cheerful "Good morning" died on her lips.

"Three investigators are coming," Lawrence told her. "We think they may have information about Jamie."

"You mean about who killed her?" Dottie asked, her voice quivering.

Dottie had worked for them since before Jamie was born. Her grief when they lost Jamie had been as deep as anyone who had not been the girl's parent could have felt.

"We hope so. We don't know," Lawrence said quietly.

When Cruse, Ramsey, and Klein arrived a half hour later, they accepted the offer to have coffee, then sat across the table from Jamie's parents. Cruse concisely repeated for both of them that Ramsey and Klein were fire marshals and the lead investigators of the explosion and fire at the Connelly complex.

"We have learned that a homeless man had been sleeping at night for probably several years in a van that was parked at the far rear of the Connelly property. It had been in a collision some years ago and left at the back of the parking lot. When the van was discovered to be filled with old newspapers, it was sent to the crime lab. While there, under further examination, Jamie's notebook was found," Cruse explained.

"Jamie's notebook!" Veronica exclaimed.

"Yes. It has her name on it and is clearly the one she was using when she did the interviews of homeless people for the project she was working on. We were able to trace the identity of the homeless man who was living in the van through a family picture we found there. You may have seen it on the news. It showed a young couple with a baby."

"We both saw it," Veronica said numbly. "Did that man kill our daughter, and if so, have you arrested him?"

"His name was Clyde Hotchkiss. I must first tell you that he died yesterday morning at Bellevue Hospital."

Lawrence and Veronica gasped and reached for each other's hand.

Ramsey waited for a moment, then said, "He had been brought to the hospital when a passerby saw him collapsed on the street near the West Side Highway. He was dying of pneumonia and lived only a few more hours. We were notified because hospital personnel recognized him from the newscasts and contacted us. We were able to speak with him briefly."

"What did he say?" Lawrence demanded. "What did he say?"

"We asked him about Jamie. He admitted that she got into the van and kept bothering him with questions. He admitted punching her once but claims she jumped out of the van and then he heard her cry, 'Help me, help me!' "

"Did he try to help her?" Lawrence Gordon's face was pale, his eyes glistening with tears.

"No, he did not. He died admitting only that he had punched her, and swearing that he did not kill her."

"Do you believe him?"

The marshals looked at each other. "I'm not sure," Frank Ramsey said.

"I don't believe him," Nathan Klein said flatly. "His wife and son, who had not seen him since he walked out on them nearly forty years ago, had also been contacted and had come to the hospital. They were there when we talked to him. His wife begged him to answer our questions, but I think he couldn't admit to killing Jamie in front of her and his son. The information that we are giving you will be released at a police press conference at noon today."

"Then he either killed her or ignored her cries for help. God damn his rotten soul to hell!" Lawrence Gordon's face was contorted with grief and rage.

It was Jamie's mother who said quietly, "The other day that psychic told me that we would have an answer about what happened to Jamie soon. Somehow I knew she was right. Well, we have an answer, I guess."

Then, as Lawrence wrapped his arms around her, Veronica began to sob, "Oh, Jamie, Jamie, Jamie!"

79

On Thursday morning, Hannah stopped at the hospital at eight o'clock on her way to work. It had become part of her daily routine to start her day sitting by Kate's bedside and talking to her, hoping and praying that maybe she was getting through to her.

She again thought about the book that she had read that had been written by the neurosurgeon who had supposedly been in a deep coma but had heard everything that was going on around him.

Maybe it's like that for Kate, she thought, as, holding Kate's hand in hers, she told her about Justin Kramer bringing dinner in from Shun Lee West last night, and how he wanted her to know that her bromeliad plant was thriving. "He's kind of special, Kate," she said. "I really like him. Before I met him, he told me how he brought the plant to you as a housewarming gift."

Then, as she spoke, for the first time she felt Kate squeeze her hand for a brief moment.

When Dr. Patel came in to see Kate, and Hannah told him what had happened, he answered, "I'm not surprised. Since that fever broke, Kate is making a remarkable recovery. The brain swelling is completely gone. There is no sign of further bleeding. We will be gradually taking her off heavy sedation starting today. If all goes well, by tomorrow or Saturday at the latest, she'll be in a private room. I have every hope that she will regain consciousness. Even if she does not remember the immediate past, and by that I mean the explosion. I believe she will make a full recovery."

As he spoke, Kate again squeezed her hand. "Doctor, Kate is trying to let me know that she is aware that I'm here," Hannah exclaimed. "I'm sure she is. I've got to leave her now and get to work but you couldn't have given me better news. Thank you. Thank you so much!"

Kate tried to move her lips. Hannah, stay with me please, she wanted to say. I keep having the nightmare. I don't want to have it anymore. I don't want to be alone.

80

At seven o'clock on Thursday morning, after being questioned all night at the Manhattan district attorney's office, Jack Worth was told he was free to go home. When he had first arrived, he had been read the Miranda warnings. He had originally told the detectives that he didn't need a lawyer and would gladly cooperate with them. After the initial shock of being taken in for questioning, he had decided that he had a straight story, there were no holes in it, and that a rush to get a lawyer might make him look guilty.

Over and over as the hours passed, he had answered the increasingly scornful questions the detectives had thrown at him. "When you were at the complex, for whatever reason, very early in the morning, and you looked down into that sinkhole and saw that girl wearing your medallion, why did you run away? Why didn't you dial nine-one-one right away?"

"Look, I never forgot the grilling I got twenty-eight years ago just because I bought that damn eight-dollar medallion with Tracey's name on it and tried to give it to her," he said. "She wouldn't take it as a gift, but she liked it and gave me the money for it. I never went out with her alone. I never saw her wear the necklace. I got scared because I knew just what you cops would be thinking. Come on. Give me a lie detector test. I'm not worried."

Jack's attitude had changed when they began to question him

about Jamie Gordon. "I read about that poor kid. You're telling me that two years ago she was in that van in the parking lot sometime between midnight and six in the morning and you're asking me what I know about it! I was the plant manager, not the night watchman. Listen, I've tried to be on the level with you guys, but I'm tired and I want to leave now." He stood up. "Anyone stopping me? Am I under arrest?"

"You are not under arrest and you are free to go, Jack," he was told. "We may want to talk to you again, but now you can go home."

A terrified Jack Worth, knowing that he would undoubtedly hear from them again soon, walked quickly out of the room.

81

Attorney Noah Green was thoroughly repulsed by his new client, Harry Simon. "Well, he's not really new. Do you remember that I got him off on a speeding ticket a couple of years ago?" he asked his wife, Helen, on Thursday morning over their usual breakfast of coffee and a bagel at their small law office in lower Manhattan.

They had met in law school and were married the day after they were sworn in to the New York State Bar twenty-six years ago. Optimistically, they had opened a law office with the money that they had suggested their relatives and friends give to them in lieu of other wedding presents. To their deep disappointment, Helen had had several miscarriages and they had never had children.

They had both developed good reputations in the legal community and their practice had thrived. Helen Green concentrated on family law, and most of her clients were women. Many of them had been victims of domestic violence or were seeking child support from their ex-husbands or boyfriends. Noah's clients were usually people buying or selling their condos, writing their wills, or trying to fight expensive motor vehicle violations. Their private joke was that Helen's practice often ended up being pro bono and that Noah's clients paid the bills.

While Noah and Helen had a standing agreement that they would try hard to avoid discussing their cases at the dinner table,

Noah had told her the night before about his visit to see Harry Simon, and that now he had to decide whether to approach the police with the information that Simon claimed to have about the night Tracey Sloane had disappeared.

Helen had been initially appalled at the idea that her husband was representing a murderer whose crime had been indisputably captured by a security camera. "Noah, I want you to withdraw," she pleaded. "We don't need this. If Simon told you to give this information to the police, then do it and get out."

"Helen, I don't like him any more than you do. I didn't even feel good about getting him off on that speeding ticket. Maybe the radar gun wasn't working properly, but I did believe that young state trooper when he testified that Harry was driving like a bat out of hell that day and almost cut off a family with a bunch of kids in a station wagon. But, you know, Helen, this is a very high-profile case. Simon can't really pay much, but he is entitled to an advocate and the publicity could draw in a lot of new clients for me, especially if I'm able to get him a better deal with the information about Sloane."

Noah and Helen both remembered that they had been students at New York University School of Law when Tracey Sloane vanished. They had occasionally gone to Tommy's Bistro, where Tracey had worked at the time of her disappearance, and had even talked between themselves about whether she had ever been their waitress. They had concluded that, on the few occasions they had been there, their waitress had been an older woman with a strong Italian accent.

"All right, Noah," Helen said, reluctantly. "It's okay with me if you want to represent him." She added wryly, "But I don't have to be thrilled about it."

Noah had spent a restless night, still not sure that it was a good idea to go to the police with Simon's story about Tracey Sloane getting into some kind of furniture van. But then on Thursday morning, as he finished his bagel and coffee, he decided that Simon

really didn't have anything to lose. The Lower East Side case by itself would put him in prison for the rest of his life. Simon's only shot
at doing less than life without parole was the Sloane information.

"Helen, I'm going to call the DA's office this afternoon about
what Simon knows. I just want to finish up a few things here before
I make the call."

At two minutes of twelve, Helen came rushing into Noah's office.
"Noah, turn on the television, quick. There's a police press confer-
ence that you have to see. The lead-in said that it's going to be about
Tracey Sloane."

Noah grabbed the remote and clicked it. The small television on
the wall of his office went on. The press conference was just about
to begin. He heard the solemn voice of the police spokesman announcing it had been confirmed by the medical examiner's office
that the remains of the long-missing Tracey Sloane had been found
at the Connelly furniture complex in Long Island City. "The explosion last week created a deep sinkhole in the back of the property
and a member of the cleanup crew removing the rubble discovered
the remains at five o'clock yesterday evening."

The spokesman continued: "As of this point, we can release the
following limited information. Our investigation has revealed that a
homeless man, Clyde Hotchkiss, who had been a decorated veteran
of the Vietnam War, had been living for a number of years in a dis-
abled van at the rear of the Connelly property. Before his death at
Bellevue Hospital yesterday, which preceded the discovery last night
of Tracey Sloane's remains, Hotchkiss was questioned about the disappearance of Barnard College student Jamie Gordon, whose body
was found in the East River a year and a half ago. A notebook with
her name on it had been discovered in his van following the explosion. Ms. Gordon had been interviewing homeless people as part of
an academic project that she had been working on at the time she
went missing."

"Is there any connection between the two cases?" a reporter shouted.

"Please let me finish," he responded. "Mr. Hotchkiss acknowledged that Ms. Gordon had climbed into the van and tried to talk to him. He admitted that he became very angry and that he punched her in the face. He claimed that she had then fled the van and moments later, he had heard her cry for help. Before his death, he consistently denied that he had followed her or caused her any other injury."

The spokesman looked directly at the reporter who had called out the question. "At this point, we have no idea if Mr. Hotchkiss was involved in the disappearance of Tracey Sloane. We do not know where he was living twenty-eight years ago. The fact that her remains were found only yards from where he had been recently living in the van may or may not be significant. At the present time, we do not know. We can state, however, that Clyde Hotchkiss is strongly suspected to be responsible for the death of Jamie Gordon."

"Helen, they just said that Tracey Sloane's remains were found at the Connelly Fine Antique Reproductions complex!" Noah exclaimed.

"Yes, they did. I can hear. I know what you're thinking."

In his mind, Noah Green was again seeing the furtive expression in Harry Simon's eyes as he told him that Tracey Sloane had willingly gotten into a black furniture van with gold lettering on the side panel that had the word "antique" on it.

That creep was telling the truth, Noah thought. None of this was public information until two minutes ago. Noah took out his cell phone and called Detective Matt Stevens, who had questioned Simon the previous day. "What's up, Noah?" he asked.

"What's up is that I'm on my way in to talk to you. I can represent to you that Harry Simon might have useful information regarding Tracey Sloane's disappearance, and it's not what you're thinking. He didn't do it but he could end up being a valuable witness. When I was with him yesterday, he told me that he can describe the type of vehicle that she willingly got into the night she disappeared. But he won't talk unless he has assurance that it will help him in a plea agreement on the Lower East Side case. He's no fool. He knows the kind of proof that you have with that tape."

"The thought of giving that creep one day less in prison makes me sick," Stevens replied. "And, anyhow, I don't have that kind of authority. That would have to come from the DA himself or one of his top assistants."

"Well, talk to one of them now. But I'm telling you that what Simon told me was before that press conference, so it's legit. And if anyone doubts about the timing of his information, I will withdraw as his attorney and become a witness. He may be a useless piece of garbage but in this case I can swear, as an officer of the court, that he talked to me yesterday. And particularly after watching that press conference, I think that what he said is going to help you. I'll be there in a little while."

Noah Green put his cell phone in his pocket and looked at his wife. "Wish me luck," he said.

An hour later, Noah was seated in the impressive private office of Ted Carlyle, the district attorney of Manhattan. Detective Matt Stevens, his expression inscrutable, was next to Carlyle. After expressing his own repulsion at giving Harry Simon anything, DA Carlyle agreed to offer Simon twenty years without parole on the Lower East Side murder of Betsy Trainer if the information about Tracey Sloane proved to be of substantial value.

"If it doesn't completely pan out, we're back to life without parole," Carlyle stated emphatically. "I'll bury him."

Green responded, "He will certainly understand that."

"All right," Carlyle replied. "Now what are the details that he claims he has?"

"He followed Tracey Sloane from the restaurant the night she disappeared. He saw her get into a furniture van a couple of blocks away."

Noah could not help savoring the look of astonishment on the faces of the two men. "The van was stopped at a light. Somebody inside it called out to her. The door opened and she willingly got into the van. From where he was a short distance behind her, Simon couldn't see the driver, but he could see that it was a black furniture van with gold lettering on the side panel that had the word 'antique' on it."

Noah's voice became firm. "As I said before, I want you to check the time I was with Simon yesterday afternoon. I left him just before five o'clock. It was a few minutes later that Tracey Sloane's remains were discovered in a sinkhole in the parking lot of the esteemed Connelly Fine Antique Reproductions complex."

"Why didn't he tell this to Nick Greco when he was first questioned right after Sloane went missing?" Carlyle demanded.

"I asked him exactly the same question," Noah replied. "He said that he was afraid about something in his background and that he would end up making himself a suspect."

"He's right about that," Carlyle snapped.

82

Sammy was one of the many street people who was questioned by the police as to whether he knew the homeless man who called himself Clyde. At first he had said that he had never heard of him. He didn't want to get in trouble. But when one of his friends tipped him off that it had been on television that maybe Clyde had killed a couple of girls, Sammy was seized with a sense of civic duty.

Tony Bovaro was a young cop in the Chelsea district who would wake him up in the morning if he was squatting outside a building or near a townhouse and say, "Okay, Sammy, you know you're not supposed to be here. Get moving before I have to take you in."

This time, it was Sammy who went looking for the officer. On Thursday afternoon, he caught up with Officer Bovaro, who was seated, with his partner, in a squad car. "I got something to tell you, Officer," he said, trying to conceal the fact that he had a pretty good buzz on.

"Hi, Sammy. Haven't seen you in a couple of days," Bovaro said. "What's up?"

"What's up is that you should take a look at the black-and-blue mark on my chin."

The twenty-four-year-old police officer got out of the squad car and examined Sammy's grime-covered, splotched, and unshaven face. But then he did notice the ugly black and purple swelling on

Sammy's jaw. His interest deepened. "That's pretty nasty, Sammy. How did it happen?"

Sammy could see that the cop was listening to him with respect. "That guy, Clyde, the one they think murdered that college student, he damn near killed me last week. I tried to set up near him and he didn't want me there. And then when I said I wouldn't leave . . ."

Sammy did not mention that he had deliberately knocked over the bottle of wine Clyde had been enjoying. "Anyhow, Clyde punched me so hard I almost had to go to the hospital but I didn't. That guy was mean. He was crazy. Just so you know, I hear that he admitted punching that girl. But I bet he killed her. I don't know about the one thirty or so years ago. But if he was around here and she got in his way, I bet he killed her, too."

"Okay, Sammy, take it easy," Officer Bovaro said, even as his partner grabbed the radio to call in that they had new information about Clyde Hotchkiss.

An hour later, Sammy was in the local police station recounting his story with gusto. As he was speaking he embellished it, claiming that the street guys were all afraid of Clyde Hotchkiss. "We called him Lonesome Clyde," Sammy said, his sly grin revealing several missing teeth. Then, for the benefit of the investigators who had not yet seen a close-up of his jaw, he thrust it forward. "Clyde had a terrible temper. He was a killer. I could be dead right now the way he hit me."

When Sammy left the police station, he was followed by a reporter who had noticed him going in and who was curious as to why he was there. "It was my duty to come forward," Sammy said earnestly. Then, with further embellishment about how he had barely escaped with his life, he retold his story.

83

Nick Greco reflected on the nearly twenty years that he had spent working on the Sloane case before he had retired. His determination to solve it had been well known throughout the office and so had the fact that he had taken a copy of the entire file with him when he had left.

Now, with the discovery of her skeletal remains, Detective Matt Stevens, who had taken over Greco's position, was keeping him informed of whatever developments would occur. Stevens had told him earlier that neither Harry Simon nor Jack Worth had in any way changed their stories. Both absolutely denied having anything to do with Tracey's death.

"Nick, we know Simon didn't have time to abduct her," Stevens had said. "And Worth claimed he went home to bed that night after working at Connelly's. Hotchkiss admitted he punched Jamie Gordon, and we think he killed her. And for all we know, he was hanging around Long Island City twenty-eight years ago. He could have been panhandling in Manhattan the night Tracey Sloane disappeared. By then he'd been missing for over ten years and his wife had given up trying to find him. We'll probably never know if Hotchkiss killed Sloane."

Nick Greco did not believe that the vagrant who admitted punching Jamie Gordon had anything to do with Tracey Sloane's disappearance. His gut feeling was that it had been a person who had somehow been in Tracey's circle of trusted friends. From everything they had learned about her, he did not believe that she had a secret romance going on or that she would have allowed herself to be lured by a complete stranger.

All day Thursday, Nick had once more been going through the list of Tracey's friends, coworkers, and the diners who always requested her table. There were more than one hundred of them on the list he had compiled all those years ago. He had been Googling them, one by one, to see if any of them had ever been in trouble in the past twenty-eight years.

A few of them were already dead. Others had retired and moved to Florida or Arizona. Not one of the people he could trace had led anything other than an ordinary life.

He had watched the press conference at noon and asked himself if a man on his deathbed would concoct a lie that, in a way, was almost as bad as admitting that he had killed Jamie Gordon. Nick didn't think so. If Hotchkiss was going to lie, why would he have admitted knowing Jamie Gordon at all? He could have said that he found her notebook in the street in Manhattan and picked it up.

That would have been a believable story—or at least one that would have been almost impossible to disprove. And it would have exonerated him, at least in the eyes of his wife and son. So why admit punching her and then not trying to help her when she screamed?

Greco concluded that Clyde Hotchkiss had made a truthful deathbed statement.

At three o'clock, Matt Stevens called him with another update. "Nick, I could lose my job telling you this," he began.

"I know you could. But you know you won't because it's just between us. What have you got?"

"Harry Simon's lawyer is working out a deal. Simon claims

through his lawyer that he was following Tracey Sloane that night, but that someone called out to her and she willingly got into a van."

"A van?"

"Yes. Simon said it was a midsize black furniture van with gold lettering on the side, and he could read part of the wording. He swears 'antique' was one of the words. Jack Worth, the plant manager at the time of the explosion, was already working back then at Connelly Fine Antique Reproductions as an assistant bookkeeper. We'll see if he's willing to come back and answer some more questions. We'll really lay into him this time. Let's hope he hasn't lawyered up."

"All right, thanks, Matt. Keep me posted."

After they had finished speaking, Nick Greco sat for a long minute at his desk as his mind made the connection between Connelly Fine Antique Reproductions and the names on his list of people who had been questioned in Tracey Sloane's death.

Then, almost with a jolt, he remembered one of those names. Connor Connelly. Connor had dined at Tommy's Bistro a number of times, Greco recalled. We had been told by some of her coworkers that Connelly had always requested Tracey's table. And he was one of the men in the picture Tracey had on top of her dresser in her bedroom. But his name had been removed from the list of people to question when we learned that he had died in a boating accident weeks before Tracey disappeared. That was what I was trying to remember, Nick thought. I saw his name on the copy of my original list when I looked at it again yesterday.

This time when he opened his computer, Nick began a search for everything he could learn about Connor Connelly and his entire family.

84

On Thursday morning, Douglas Connelly did not wait for the phone call he knew he would get. Instead he called the person "with the angry voice" himself.

"You will get your money, though I am still not convinced that I am guilty of what you accuse me of," Connelly said, trying to sound calm, his hand clenching involuntarily. "Sure, your client can have a bunch of goons work me over, but that won't bring you one cent. You've made plenty in the past on the, shall we say, 'tips' I've given you, so you can afford to wait a few weeks and you'll be paid in full. Paid without a pain-and-suffering bonus, I might add."

He listened, then said, "I am filing suit against the insurance company. Gus Schmidt and Gus Schmidt alone set that fire. When my daughter called him, as she regularly did on a friendly basis, Gus decided that there was another way he could hurt me for firing him. He never planned to get caught in that explosion. But he did plan to leave my daughter there to die. And she was the one who dragged him out even though she was badly injured. Besides that, I have plans to sell the property to a developer. I have insisted on a five-million-dollar deposit, which will be coming shortly."

He listened some more, then added, "By the way, with all your ranting the other day, you didn't mention the last tip I gave you. I would stake my life that that one went over pretty well."

As he ended the conversation, Doug heard the key turn in the door. Sandra was letting herself in. It was only quarter of eight. He wasn't ready to have her back yet. He wanted to go to the hospital to see Kate and he didn't want Sandra trailing along. He took a long breath. Well, as long as she is here, let her cook breakfast again, he thought. And the odds are that Hannah will be at the hospital sometime between eight and quarter of nine. She always stopped there before she went to work.

I don't want to run into her, Doug thought. She's been downright hostile to me and I'm sick of it.

"Dougie . . . ? Dougie . . . ?"

"I'm in here," he called. He heard the click of her heels as she scurried down the hall to the library. When she appeared in the doorway she was wearing her usual morning garb, a tight sweater and tighter jeans. It was a sunny day and even from a distance her heavy black eye makeup looked glaringly inappropriate. Doug had the fleeting thought that the doorman must have been amused at her early arrival. He knew the staff of the building had their gossip chain and suspected that the ladies who visited him were subjects of intense interest.

Sandra was click-clicking across the room, her arms outstretched. "Oh, Dougie, I couldn't sleep last night thinking of how many problems you have." She patted his cheek. "We didn't shave today."

Doug pushed her away. "All right, Sandra. I'm not much in the mood for cutesy."

"That's because you haven't had breakfast. I know where I'm needed." She saluted him. "Your chef at your service. Aye, aye, sir."

Douglas Connelly watched Sandra until she had walked across the library and turned down the hall to the kitchen. Then he went over to the door and closed and locked it behind her. He had to talk to Jack Worth and find out what was going on with him. I should have taken his phone call yesterday, he thought. I didn't leave a message for him when I tried to call him back, but he could have seen that my number was on his unanswered-calls list.

Doug walked over to the landline phone and put his hand on it. I don't care how much technology is advancing in cell phones, he thought. I think the old-fashioned ones like this are clearer and they don't suddenly lose the signal. His mouth felt dry. The bravado he knew he had gotten across when he promised a quick repayment was gone. Six months ago, he had turned down the offer that had been on the table for the property. Maybe that manufacturer had found another place to buy.

And something else. Most of the news last night had been about finding Jamie Gordon's notebook in the van and Tracey Sloane's body in that sinkhole in the parking lot. It looked as though the cops thought that homeless guy, Clyde Hotchkiss, killed both of them. Before Hotchkiss died, he admitted punching the Gordon girl. They even had a construction guy who had worked with Hotchkiss after he came home from the Vietnam War and he had said that Hotchkiss knew everything about gas lines and would certainly have the know-how to set an explosion.

One more argument for the insurance company, Doug thought. They have got to pay me. *They have got to pay me.*

His hand was still on the phone. Should I call Jack? he asked himself. Why hasn't he called me back? The minute he knew that I tried to reach him, he should have picked up the phone and returned the call. He knows better than to ignore me. Doug closed his hand on the receiver and picked it up. Jack answered on the first ring. "Pretty strange stuff going on, isn't there, Doug?" he said, his voice both worried and sarcastic.

"What do you mean?"

"I mean I was at the DA's office all night being questioned."

"Do you have a lawyer?" Doug asked. "Because if you don't, you should have one."

"No, Doug, I don't have a lawyer and I don't need one. As I've told these detectives, I have absolutely nothing to hide and was glad to answer their questions. It was no problem."

"You're a fool," Doug said curtly, then slammed down the phone.

Two hours later, showered and shaven, calmed by the excellent breakfast Sandra had cooked for him and knowing that the designer tweed jacket with leather elbow patches looked good on him, Doug arrived at the hospital with Sandra.

The doctor had already left, but the nurse in charge of the desk in the intensive care unit was bursting with good news for him. "Dr. Patel has decided that we're going to lose our patient," she said. "Tomorrow morning Kate will be switched to a private room. And by then she won't be receiving any more sedation. Isn't that good news?"

"It couldn't be better," Doug said heartily. "Now, I am sure that there are some private rooms that go at considerably higher prices. I want one of them for my daughter."

"I can arrange that, sir. Yes, those rooms are beautiful. It will feel like sleeping in her own bed."

Sandra had tiptoed into Kate's cubicle. "I think she is starting to come out of the coma," she said in a stage whisper. "I think she's remembering the accident. She just mumbled something like, 'Don't . . . please don't . . .' "

Doug bent down and kissed Kate's forehead. "Daddy's here, little girl," he said soothingly. "Daddy will always be here for you."

85

When Doug and Sandra got back to the apartment, the message light was flashing on the phone in the foyer. Sandra said, "I'll check it, Dougie."

He gripped her arm. "I like to check my own phone messages."

"Dougie, you're hurting me. I'll have a black-and-blue mark. I bruise easy. Well, just go answer it yourself." Her heels beating an angry staccato on the marble floor, she flounced down the hallway toward the bedroom. "And I'm getting my stuff together and going home!" she yelled back. "I don't need to put up with your lousy mood anymore today!"

Go and be damned, Doug thought. He pushed the play button on the answering machine. It was from the caller he feared. The voice was ominously friendly. "Doug, about our earlier conversation. I think you went a bit overboard with your remarks. I do expect payment in full on the terms I laid out. I've done some fact-checking. You told me a few months ago that you had an offer on the table for the property and you told me who made it. You did tell me the truth about that, and that's good. You gave me the important details, including the down payment they were willing to make. But there's one problem now. They bought another site in Long Island City last month, so they don't need or want your place anymore."

There was a pause. "Just so you know," the message continued, "I also understand that you may not be able to collect the insurance on the property. That's most unfortunate. I want to be clear: I'm willing to give you one more week to put together what you owe me. All of it. One more week and that's final."

The click in his ear sounded like a gunshot as Doug put down the receiver. He heard Sandra coming back down the hall. This time her attitude was different. "Dougie, I'm sorry. I know how upset you are. Call Bernard and let him drive us up to Westchester and let's have a nice cozy lunch at an inn somewhere."

"I can't do that," Doug said, his voice measured and calm. "As soon as Kate is settled in her private room, I'm going over to the hospital to see her." He looked at Sandra. "And I'm going alone."

86

At ten o'clock on Thursday evening, after saying good night at Clyde's wake to a close group of friends who still remembered her husband from his better days, Peggy and Skip went back to her home. Celia and the boys were driving down in the morning for the funeral. Together mother and son watched a replay of the press conference from earlier that day that was being repeated on the news. It included an update with part of an interview with a vagrant named Sammy.

Choking with rage, Peggy called Frank Ramsey on his cell phone.

"How could you?" she demanded. "How could you? I trusted you. You know I trusted you. Clyde told you as much as he knew about Jamie Gordon. He admitted he punched her." Her voice rising, she shouted, "He told you what he knew! He told you on his deathbed! He said that Jamie jumped out of the van and he heard her scream for help. You know that Clyde was a heavy drinker. All he had wanted to do was sleep, but that Gordon girl kept pestering him. He just wanted to get rid of her. You know he didn't kill her!"

"Mrs. Hotchkiss, I know how upset you are, but we don't know that he didn't kill her."

"I know he didn't kill her! Listen to what that creep had to say. Even he admitted that Clyde did not try to follow him! You betrayed me, Frank Ramsey! You asked me to persuade him to answer your questions on his deathbed. I'm sorry now that I asked Clyde about the Gordon girl. I'm sorry for her and I'm sorry for her parents. But you have practically announced that he was her killer, and without any idea of where Clyde was nearly thirty years ago, you have insinuated that maybe, just maybe, my husband, an injured war hero, was responsible for the Sloane girl's death, too. I hope you're happy, Mr. Ramsey! I hope you're happy! And go to hell!"

Frank Ramsey had put in a very long week. He and Celia were just getting into bed when the call had come in from Peggy Hotchkiss. Celia could not hear what Peggy was saying but she could tell that a very angry woman was screaming at Frank.

When the call ended, she asked, "Frank, what was that all about?"

Frank Ramsey looked every minute of his forty-eight years and more when he answered, "Celia, I'm very much afraid I was listening to the voice of truth. I let Mrs. Clyde Hotchkiss down. I believed Clyde when he said he didn't follow Jamie Gordon out of the van. We all agreed to put his name out as a possible suspect in the Tracey Sloane murder for a very specific reason. But it wasn't a good enough reason and it's my fault."

87

Mark called in to the office on Friday morning at nine o'clock to say that he hoped to be there by noon, but he would certainly be in time for the one o'clock client meeting. He had never told his new employer about Tracey. Now he explained, as briefly as he could, to the senior partner at his law firm that the Tracey Sloane who had been in the television news yesterday and in the headlines of today's papers was his sister.

As quickly as he could without being rude, he managed to cut off the outpouring of condolences he was hearing from his boss. "It's going to be much easier for my mother and for me to know that Tracey's remains will be in the family grave with my father," he said. Then, once again, he declined the sympathetic offer to take the day off and insisted that he would attend the meeting.

He had made the call as he was sitting at the breakfast table with his mother. She had arrived last night on what was supposed to be a five o'clock flight from Chicago but because of the snowy weather there, the flight was delayed. The hour's difference in time between New York and Chicago meant that it was past ten o'clock when she arrived at LaGuardia Airport, and it was almost eleven by the time they had collected her bags and taken a cab to the apartment.

When they arrived, it was to find the table already set and the food Jessie had ordered waiting for them. A few minutes later they were sharing the platter of assorted sandwiches and the sliced pineapple and strawberries, and then choosing from the selection of petite dessert tarts Jessie had prepared. He had told her that the first thing his mother ever did when she returned home, after she had been out, was to make a cup of tea. Last night Mark had found that the kettle had already been filled, and the teapot with teabags in it was on the stove.

Now Martha Sloane, a robe over her long cotton nightgown, said, "I can't believe I slept this late, and I can't believe I slept at all. When I got here last night, I was so afraid that I'd just lie awake thinking and thinking. I didn't even realize how hungry I was. I hadn't had anything yesterday except a piece of toast at breakfast. But after that lovely supper, and then finding the bed all turned down and ready for me, I guess I just relaxed and oh, how I needed to do that."

"You sure did, Mom. You looked exhausted."

Mark was already dressed to go to the office, except that his collar was open and he had not yet put on a tie. He had earlier told his mother about going to Hannah Connelly's apartment before he had phoned her on Wednesday evening to tell her about Tracey, and that one of Hannah's friends, Jessica Carlson, had come down with him while he made the call.

"I guess you know that I was pretty upset, Mom. I hope I didn't make it harder for you," he said now.

"No, and I'm glad that you weren't alone when you called me. It's good that you had a friend with you."

"I had just met Jess a few minutes earlier," he explained. "No, that's not quite true. I met her and Hannah Connelly the night I moved in here last week. We rode up in the elevator together. Do you realize how impossible it would have been to imagine that we, who were perfect strangers, would meet and then find out that Hannah's family owns the property where Tracey's body was found?"

When he spoke of Tracey, he was deliberately using the word

body. He did not want his mother dwelling on the image of what had been found in the sinkhole. A skeleton with a cheap necklace still clasped around its throat.

They sat quietly for a moment, then Martha said, "It does seem impossible, Mark. Do you remember that quote from Byron, 'stranger than fiction'?"

"Yes, of course."

"'Tis strange—but true, for truth is always strange. Stranger than fiction."

"That certainly applies in this case," Mark said, fervently. He sipped his second cup of coffee. He knew that now they were both preparing themselves for what was going to happen. After his mother got dressed, they were going to the medical examiner's office to arrange for Tracey's remains to be shipped to the funeral director in Kewanee. Next week there would be a funeral mass, and Tracey would be buried with their father in the cemetery only a few miles from the house. Tracey would finally be home.

Putting off the moment when he would once again suggest that he go alone to the medical examiner's office, he said, "Mom, Jess is a lawyer. She's very smart and she's very kind."

Martha Sloane's maternal instinct told her that her son liked this lady very much. "I'd love to meet her at some point, Mark. Tell me about her."

"She's about thirty. She's tall, slender, with lovely red hair down to her shoulders." He did not tell his mother that when he had finished speaking with her the other night, after he hung up the phone, he had burst out sobbing and buried his face in his arms at the table. Jessie had leaned over, put her arms around him, and said, "Let it out, Mark. You need to cry."

Later, when Jessie knew he hadn't had dinner, she had scrambled eggs for both of them. Then yesterday, she had phoned to see how he was doing, and when she learned his mother was coming in fairly late, she asked if it would be okay to leave something light to eat in his apartment. "I'm sure she won't want a heavy dinner," she had said, "so if you drop off your key in Hannah's mailbox, I'll get something in for you both. There's a gourmet deli in your neighborhood that you probably don't know about yet. I'll pick up something there. Anyhow, Hannah and I will be going out to dinner nearby, so it's simply no trouble."

Martha Sloane pushed back her chair. "Now, Mark, before you start suggesting again that I wait for you here while you go to make Tracey's arrangements, I'm going to shower and get dressed. We will do this together."

Mark knew better than to argue. He cleared the table and loaded the few breakfast dishes in the dishwasher, then walked into the living room to wait for his mother. He sensed that there was something different about the room. He looked around and then realized what it was. The pictures he had laid on the floor in anticipation of hanging them over the weekend were already on the wall in the exact spots he had marked for them.

Obviously, Jessie had done that, too. I'll invite her to have dinner with Mom and me tonight, Mark thought. I know Mom wants to meet her and thank her for being so thoughtful. And so do I. I'll call her right now.

When he walked into his bedroom to make the call and to get his tie and jacket, Mark had a spring to his step that had not been there since before Tracey left home. Since the time when she used to pitch to him in the backyard or take him to the movies and buy him candy or popcorn. Or both.

88

Nick Greco did not realize when he began his research into the Connelly family on Thursday afternoon that he would find reams of material on Dennis Francis Connelly, the brilliant, powerful, and eccentric grandfather of Kate and Hannah Connelly.

Dozens of articles had been written about him. Many of them began by chronicling his humble beginnings in Dublin, where Dennis had been a street urchin who was arrested several times for stealing. Then, after finally staying in school long enough to finish the eighth grade at age sixteen, he completed high school in only two years, won a scholarship to Trinity College, and graduated summa cum laude in less than three years.

The pictures of him as a teenager and in his early twenties captured a thin, somewhat tall figure, unsmiling, and with eyes that seemed to look at the world with angry resentment.

And if he felt resentment, he had a right to feel it, Greco thought as he read that Connelly's father and uncle, who were twins, had died when they were only twenty-six years old, burned to death when they were trapped in a raging fire that swept through the dismal factory where they both worked seven days a week.

The twenty-four-year-old mother of Dennis had been six months pregnant when his father died. Three months later she gave birth to twin boys, so small and already malnourished that they survived only a few days. Then, at age seven, Dennis had begun to try to support his fragile and heartbroken mother with a combination of begging and working odd jobs. And sometimes by stealing.

When he was ten, a kindly old woman, who could not live alone, had hired his mother as a housekeeper. Giving both of them a home, she soon recognized how smart he was and persuaded Dennis to go back to school.

He was an angry and proud man, Greco thought as he skimmed through the rest of the articles about the early life of the founder of the Connelly complex.

He quickly read through the accounts of Dennis sailing to the United States, getting a job on Wall Street, and beginning to amass his fortune.

At that point in his research, Nick turned off his computer and took his regular train home. On Friday morning he was back at his desk by eight o'clock and resumed his Internet research.

His interest deepened when he read that Connelly had finally married at age fifty-five because, as he had put it, "a man wants to know that his descendants will enjoy the fruits of his labor."

Not the best or most romantic reason to marry, Greco thought as he studied the formal wedding picture of Dennis Connelly and his timid-looking, thirty-five-year-old bride, Bridget O'Connor.

According to the *New York Times* birth announcement, their son Douglas was born on December 31st of that year. A year later, their son Connor's first birthday was celebrated in January at their Manhattan townhouse.

What's that about? Nick asked himself. A year later Douglas would have had a first birthday, too. Was Connor adopted? The answer came when Nick read an article in a small religious magazine in which Dennis Connelly had bared his soul to a sympathetic priest. He had shared with him that his sons were really identical twins, one born on December 31, the other four minutes later, on January 1 of the following year.

He related that he had lived in constant fear of what he regarded to be the family curse, as he put it, that had begun when his father and his father's twin had perished in a factory fire, and then his own twin brothers had died at birth. "My mother never had enough to eat when she was pregnant with them," Dennis Connelly had told the priest.

Then he admitted that because his twin sons were actually born in two different years, he had hoped to avoid the curse that had befallen his father, his uncle, and his siblings. He explained that he never referred to them as twins, nor had he allowed anyone else to do so. "They never wore matching outfits. We never celebrated their birthdays together. And they always went to different schools."

It was clear to Nick Greco from everything he had read about the life of Dennis Connelly that his early traumatic losses had profoundly affected the way he raised his sons. He wanted them to be competitive on every level. He wanted them to be strong. He wanted them to play football on varsity teams at separate colleges. If they were injured, they were expected to play through the pain and recover quickly. Even when they were small children, he had no sympathy if they complained of any ailment. If they fell off their bikes, he made them get right back on.

In an interview when Dennis's son Douglas was twenty-one years old and had just graduated from Brown University with both academic and athletic honors, Douglas had been asked, "Do you feel that you have had a privileged life?"

"Yes and no," he had answered. "I know that by almost any standard, I would be considered privileged. On the other hand, I remember reading that the son of President Calvin Coolidge had a miserable job one summer and his friend asked him why he would take it when his father was president of the United States. His answer was, 'If your father was my father, you'd have taken that job, too. My father thinks the same way. He has never cut us any slack.'"

Greco leaned back in his chair for a long minute, struck with the realization that he had broken through. *The background is the answer,* he thought. *The background has always been the answer.*

To verify what he now believed he knew, Greco returned to his computer search to see if he could find any coverage of the funeral of Connor and Susan Connelly.

89

Hannah did not know why she was feeling so uneasy. Justin phoned her at noon on Friday. "How are your father and sister?"

"I saw Kate this morning. She was restless, but they're moving her to a private room today, so obviously she's getting better, which is wonderful."

"Hannah, you still sound worried. How is your father?"

"He called me about an hour ago. I hate to say it, but I think he's more worried that Kate is going to admit that she and Gus together set the explosion than he is relieved that his daughter, my sister, is going to be all right. With him, it seems it's always been about the money, and it always will be."

"When are you going to see Kate again?"

"I always stop by when I'm leaving work."

After Justin reluctantly said good-bye to her, he debated about sending flowers to Kate, since she would now be in a private room. Then he thought, No, I have a better idea. When she has recovered a little more, I will bring the bromeliad plant to her room. Satisfied, he turned back to the folder on his desk.

It contained documents he had prepared regarding investment strategy for a widow who did not have the faintest idea of how to manage her considerable estate. "I just charged whatever I wanted on my AmEx," she had told Justin, "and my husband, Bob, paid all the bills."

Bob made big money, Justin thought, and he spent a lot of money, too, but it was certainly his to spend.

His thoughts turned back to Hannah. From what she tells me, her father has been living beyond his income for a long time. No wonder he's worried that the insurance claim will be denied. From what she said, the antique furniture in that museum was insured for nearly $20 million. That's an awful lot of money to let slip through your fingers.

90

Frank Ramsey awakened on Friday morning at six o'clock, as usual. He had slept well, despite the unsettling phone call from Peggy Hotchkiss, because he had been weary. But as soon as he woke up, a heavy sense of having let her down came over him. He showered, dressed, and went downstairs. The coffee was on a timer and he poured a cup and began to sip as, with the other hand, he opened the refrigerator and took out a container of orange juice and then a package of blueberries. From there he went to the pantry, viewed his choice of breakfast cereals, and selected one.

"Sit down," Celia told him. "I'll put breakfast out."

He had not heard her come down the stairs, but as always, he was glad she was there. She was wearing satin pajamas with a matching robe that came down to her knees. It was one of his gifts to her on her last birthday. The saleswoman had assured him that his wife would love this set and fortunately she had been right. Ceil did love it. And he loved her in it.

"I'm sorry about that call last night," she said matter-of-factly as she poured orange juice into a glass. "But from what you told me, I can understand why Mrs. Hotchkiss was so upset."

"So can I," Frank agreed. "Ceil, there's no question that her husband admitted punching Jamie. Drunk or not, that was a nasty thing to do, and it certainly proves that he had a hair-trigger temper and was capable of violence."

He gave her a grateful glance as she refilled his coffee cup. "And Ceil, it's entirely possible that Hotchkiss was in the area twenty-eight years ago and somehow crossed paths with Tracey Sloane. Just about every man who was ever on the list as possibly being connected to Tracey was checked and rechecked and it's always come to a dead end. Maybe Clyde is the one who killed her." He paused. "Obviously the fire department is not involved in that investigation," he said.

"It sounds like you're trying to convince yourself that Hotchkiss killed one or both of those girls, but you're just not there," Celia commented.

Frank shrugged. "I think you know me too well. I am trying to convince myself. But I think we're all missing something."

Celia poured herself a cup of coffee and sat across from him. She knew that her husband used her as a sounding board when he was thinking aloud. "So what do you think you're missing?" she asked.

"Well, for example, Lottie Schmidt."

"That poor woman! Come on, Frank."

"That poor woman is a consummate liar and a consummate phony. The fact is that Lottie Schmidt has come up with the most fantastic yarn to explain how Gus was able to buy that house in Minnesota for their daughter. According to her, Gus came from an aristocratic family in Germany and when the Nazis took over, they confiscated all of his family's property. She claims that he got a big reparation payment five years ago. We're having one of our computer experts research her story. He promised a report by noon at the latest."

"My guess is that Gus came by that money honestly, one way or the other, and Lottie is worried she'll be in trouble with the IRS because he didn't pay taxes on whatever money he received."

"There's more to it than that," Frank said firmly. "And somehow I think it has to do with the whole mess surrounding the Connelly fire and the fact that there's no question that it was deliberately set."

Three hours later, the computer expert who had been tracking Lottie's story about Gus's background called Frank as he and Nathan were catching up on their emails in their Fort Totten office. "Frank, I've got the whole Schmidt background for you. I just emailed it. You're going to love it. It's pretty much what you told me you suspected. But she didn't just make the whole thing up. She actually came pretty close to the truth. Close but no cigar."

"I can't wait," Frank Ramsey told him. "Lottie Schmidt put on such a good act of being an aristocratic wife that Nathan and I almost kissed her hand. As she was throwing us out of her house," he added.

91

Attempting to exude an air of confidence, Jack Worth strode into the same room in the Manhattan DA's office on Friday morning where he had been questioned the day before. He had received the call to come back in from Detective Stevens less than an hour before. He took a seat at the table opposite Stevens, cheerfully noting to him that their meetings were getting to be a routine. Then Jack added emphatically that he had absolutely nothing to hide.

The questioning began. And it was the same as yesterday. Why didn't he call 911 when he looked down into the sinkhole and saw the medallion that he had tried to give to Tracey Sloane?

"I told you yesterday and I'll tell you again now and I'll tell you tomorrow, if we're still here, that I panicked. Sure, I should have called nine-one-one. It was the right thing to do. But your guys put me through a meat grinder twenty-eight years ago. Obviously, I should have known there was no way I could avoid going through it again. So here we are."

For two hours Matt Stevens repeated much of the same questioning, then played his trump card. "Jack, we know what happened to Tracey that night," he said. "We have found a reliable eyewitness who saw her get into a vehicle willingly."

Stevens and the other detectives watched closely to see the reaction of the man who they believed had picked up Tracey that night.

But Worth seemed unruffled. "So why didn't your so-called reliable eyewitness come forward when she disappeared?" he asked. Now there was a sneer in his expression. "I guess you thought you'd bowl me over with that crazy story."

"She got into a midsize furniture van. It was black with gold lettering on the side that said FINE ANTIQUE REPRODUCTIONS," Matt Stevens snapped, his voice rising.

"I don't believe you!" Jack Worth shouted. "You're making this up. Look, I told you I'd take a lie detector test. I want it done now. And then I'm going home and you can try out that fairy tale on the next poor slob you pull off the streets."

It was on the tip of Jack's tongue to tell these cops that he wanted to talk to a lawyer, but then his instinct told him it would make him look guilty and stopped him. I'll pass that lie detector test and prove to them once and for all that I don't know what the hell happened to Tracey Sloane, he decided. And I don't care if I ever find out. What a bunch of garbage! How stupid do they think I am?

92

At one o'clock Friday afternoon, Frank Ramsey and Nathan Klein were at the doorstep of Lottie Schmidt's home. They had not warned her that they were coming because they did not want to put her on guard. Neither did they want to find her sitting with a lawyer when they arrived.

When she opened the door, Lottie's face froze into angry disapproval, but beyond that Frank noticed the look of fear that crept into her eyes. "Come in," she said, her voice sounding dull and weary. She held up her hand to show that she was holding a cell phone. "I'm on the phone with my daughter. I'll tell her that I'll call her back."

She led them back to the dining room, where the photo albums and pictures she had shown them on Wednesday were still on the table. Without being invited, the marshals sat down in the same seats where they had previously been.

Lottie did not try to continue the conversation with her daughter in privacy. She spoke into the cell phone. "Gretchen, those fire marshals you met at the wake are here to talk to me again. I'll call you back later."

"Put on the speaker and I'll talk to them! I'll tell them what I think of them for harassing you!" Ramsey and Klein could both hear Gretchen angrily shouting as Lottie broke the connection and turned off her phone. She sat down opposite them and folded her hands on the table. 'Well, what now?" she asked.

"Mrs. Schmidt, in this day and age, I'm afraid that almost any story can be quickly checked," Frank Ramsey said in a conversational tone. He paused. "Including yours. The facts are that your husband did grow up on the von Mueller estate. But he was not a member of the family, nor was he an heir to any fortune. His father was a gardener there, as were his grandfather and great-grandfather. Augustus von Mueller was indeed an aristocrat, but he was an only child and he had five children, all of them girls."

Frank opened the photo album and pointed to one of the pictures that Lottie had already shown to them. "It is indeed your husband in this picture with the von Mueller girls. As a child he played with them. Any facial resemblance is purely coincidental because all of the children were blue-eyed blondes. And it's a real stretch to try to point out a family resemblance between your husband and Field Marshal Augustus von Mueller."

Ramsey paused, then continued: "The entire von Mueller family was arrested and did indeed disappear after Hitler came to power. The castle and the property were confiscated by the Nazis. The servants who took care of the grounds were allowed to leave. Your husband's father died of a heart attack around that time. Your husband was raised by his own mother, not by some kindly nurse who adopted him. Whatever valuables were recovered after the war were claimed by a distant cousin of the von Muellers and were eventually turned over to him."

Lottie Schmidt's expression did not change as she listened.

"Mrs. Schmidt, if your husband had good taste and autocratic manners, it was because as a child he observed them, not because they were in his blood," Klein said. "Don't you think it's time to tell us where Gus got the money to buy that house for Gretchen?"

"I want to call my lawyer," Lottie Schmidt said.

Both marshals got up to leave. When they were almost at the front door, she called out to them. "No. Wait. Come back. What's the use? I'll tell you what I know."

93

Jack Worth continued his attempt to appear confident as he was hooked up to the lie detector machine. "When you see the results, you'll know you've been wasting your time," he told Detective Matt Stevens. "And mine," he added.

"We'll see," Stevens said. He began by asking Jack the usual litany of routine questions about his background that they knew he would answer truthfully.

"What is your name? How old are you? Where do you work? How long have you worked there? Are you married? Do you have any children?"

When the basic questions were completed, Detective Stevens moved on to the areas of inquiry that were pivotal to the investigation. "Did you ever drive a furniture van belonging to the Connelly furniture company?"

"Occasionally," Jack responded promptly. "If my own car was being serviced, they would allow me to take one of the smaller vans home overnight."

Matt Stevens was disgusted to see that Worth looked supremely confident.

"What color are the Connelly vans?"

"Black with gold lettering. Old man Connelly decided that it looked classy and it's always remained the same."

"Were you driving one of those vans the night Tracey disappeared?"

"No. I went home feeling lousy and I went to bed."

Matt Stevens observed that the computer readings on Worth's physical reactions remained fairly constant.

"Anyhow," Worth continued, "if I had been driving a Rolls-Royce, Tracey still wouldn't have gotten into it. She never gave me a second look."

"Do you have any idea who else might have been driving one of the vans the night she disappeared?"

"No, I don't."

Again, Stevens could discern no physiological reaction to the question.

"Do you have any idea if Tracey Sloane knew anyone who worked at the Connelly complex?"

"No, I don't."

"All right. Let's move to a different topic," Stevens said. "Did you ever have any contact with Jamie Gordon?"

The computer registered a significant change. "No, I didn't."

"Do you have any knowledge of what happened to Jamie Gordon?"

"No, I don't," Worth insisted, as the computer continued to indicate a substantial change.

"Did you kill Jamie Gordon?" Detective Stevens demanded.

As the reaction being registered on the computer skyrocketed, Jack Worth ripped the wires from his body and jumped up. "I'm done with you!" he shouted. "I thought this was all about Tracey Sloane. You told everybody that the homeless guy killed Gordon. What are you trying to pull on me? I tried to be straight with you guys and cooperate. But now I get a lawyer."

94

Kate stirred. She felt a slight bump as whatever she was riding on got caught on something.

Where am I? she asked herself. Am I dreaming?

"The corner room," a voice was saying. "Number six."

Kate began to remember. She had met Gus in the parking lot. They had gone into the museum.

I smelled gas, she thought. I yelled at Gus to get out. It blew up. The museum blew up. Something heavy fell on us. I dragged him out.

Was Gus all right?

Why had he acted so nervous when I asked him to meet me there?

I think I'm in a hospital. My head hurts. I have tubes in my arms. I've been having the nightmare again over and over. Why?

She tried to open her eyes but could not. She fell back into a deep sleep . . .

The nightmare came back. Only this time she knew how it ended.

He caught me as I tried to run down the stairs. He grabbed me. I screamed, "You're not my daddy! You're not my daddy!" He covered my mouth with his hand and carried me into the bedroom. I was kicking him. I was trying to get away from him.

He threw me on the bed and said, "Watch this, Kate, watch this." Then he punched the mirror over Mommy's dresser and the glass went all over and his hand was bleeding. And he said, "That's what I will do to you if you ever say that again."

He picked me up and shook me hard. "Now tell me, what is it that you must never, never say again?"

" 'You're not my daddy.' " I was crying. I was so scared. "I promise. I promise. I won't say it again."

But I know I did say it again, Kate thought. I told him that when he was leaning over me after I got hurt and they brought me here. Then I heard him tell Hannah that I said that I was sorry about the explosion. But he was lying. I didn't say that.

I said, "You're not my daddy."

I have to tell Hannah. But I can't wake up. I'm trying but I can't wake up.

95

Confirming everything he suspected, Nick Greco studied the newspaper photo of the burial of Connor and Susan Connelly. The funeral had been delayed for three weeks so that Douglas Connelly could recover sufficiently from his injuries to be released from the hospital and attend the service.

Looking weak and devastated, his eyes swollen with tears, Doug Connelly stood at the foot of the two coffins, his left hand clenched as the final prayers were recited at the cemetery.

That was the hand that Connor had fractured so badly when he played football in college, Greco thought. That's what his brother, Douglas, meant when he said in that interview that when Connor had been injured, their father had insisted that he keep exercising that hand by flexing it so that it would be strong again. But then his father was furious because Connor had developed a nervous habit of clenching it that lasted long after his hand had healed.

Seasoned as he was, Greco was still shocked at what he was sure he was seeing. The figure beside the coffins had a clenched hand . . . Was it possible that it wasn't Douglas Connelly standing there? That Douglas Connelly was in one coffin and his wife, Susan, was in the other? Could it be that Connor Connelly was the only one who survived that accident and then he saw his chance? Could he have stolen his twin brother's identity and become Douglas?

The old man, with his old-world ways, had said in one of those articles that he believed that the firstborn son was destined to be the president and major stockholder of the business, and his descendants would own it after him. The second son would have a position in the company and a minor share of the family holdings.

Douglas had become the president of the company when his father, Dennis, died. I don't think Connor deliberately caused that accident, Greco reflected. But perhaps after it happened, in the hospital, he saw his opportunity and he grabbed it. He knew his brother and Susan were dead. He was not going to let the company pass to Kate and Hannah. He told them at the hospital that he was Douglas, and he got away with it.

Greco had in front of him the group picture that had been found in Tracey Sloane's apartment, the picture that, when Greco examined it closely, showed Connor Connelly's clenched hand on the table. Connor had been a fairly regular patron at Tommy's Bistro. He had been on the list to be interviewed when Tracey went missing but was taken off when it was realized that he had been killed in that accident a few weeks earlier. *Or so we had thought.*

Had Tracey Sloane somehow become a threat to Connor Connelly? How? The night she got into that van, she must have thought that the driver was his brother, Douglas. Somehow Connor must have become aware that she had noticed his habit of clenching his hand and he knew that she could ruin everything.

Greco pushed the speed dial button on his phone, connecting him to Detective Matt Stevens. "Matt, I think I know who killed Tracey Sloane."

Stevens listened, startled at what he was hearing. "Nick, it makes sense. Tracey Sloane would not have been nervous about accepting a ride at night from a Connelly, whose brother had been one of her friendliest customers. And twenty-eight years later, her remains are discovered on their property. We know that explosion was deliberate.

From what you're saying, I would bet that her body has been there since the night she got into that van."

"Matt, I would suggest that it is time to bring Mr. Connor Connelly, better known as Douglas Connelly, in for a chat. I only wish I was still on duty."

"I wish you were, too."

"Matt, I don't know why, and I don't know how, but my gut tells me that Tracey's death and Jamie Gordon's death and the explosion that killed Gus Schmidt and almost killed Kate Connelly are all connected."

"I think so, too, Nick. We'll find out. That I can promise you. As soon as I hang up, I'm calling Connelly. I want him here today."

96

Hannah's sense of uneasiness was turning into active distress. Something was terribly wrong. She knew it. Kate had been more than restless this morning. They hadn't moved her yet into a private room. Something or someone had frightened her. I shouldn't have left her, Hannah thought. I know I shouldn't have left her. She was trying to get through to me.

I wonder if Dad has been over to see her yet today. She reached for her cell phone and called his apartment.

Sandra answered on the second ring. Obviously upset, she said, "Hannah, I would like to know what's going on. Your father has been in a horrible mood since yesterday. Then not twenty minutes ago, some detective called. I answered the phone and he asked for your father. First, your father starts yelling at me for answering. Then he grabbed the phone right out of my hand. I guess the detective asked him to go down to the DA's office or something and speak to them and then your father started yelling at him, too. He was shouting that it was all a conspiracy to keep him from getting his insurance money. Then your father yelled, 'What do you mean that Jack Worth has been very cooperative?' Then he hung up the phone and rushed out. He didn't tell me where he was going. But, Hannah, he's losing it. It's been too much of a strain."

"You have no idea where he went?" Hannah snapped.

"I guess maybe he went to see those detectives. He repeated the address they gave him. I offered to go with him but he practically took my head off. Then he stormed out.

"Hannah, after we got back from the hospital yesterday, your dad was very upset even though Kate was doing much better and was going to be moved to a private room soon. You would think that he would be happy that she's going to wake up soon. Anyhow, I tried to persuade him to have Bernard drive us up for a nice lunch in one of those dear little inns near the Hudson River, you know, around West Point, but he wouldn't hear of it. He . . ."

Hannah couldn't listen anymore. She closed the phone and dropped it into her bag. She thought about the important executive meeting scheduled for four o'clock regarding the spring fashion show. She would have to miss it. She pushed back her chair, grabbed her coat off the rack in her small office, and threw it over her shoulders. She stopped momentarily at the reception desk as she rushed toward the elevator. "I have to go to the hospital. I have to be with my sister. Tell them I'm sorry. I just can't wait any longer."

It took ten long minutes to get a cab. "Manhattan Midtown Hospital," she said nervously, "and please hurry."

Alarmed, the driver looked back at her. "You're not having a baby or something, are you, lady?" he asked.

"No. No. Of course not. My sister is a patient there."

"I'm sorry to hear that, ma'am. I'll do the best I can."

Has Kate been moved yet? Hannah wondered, as twenty agonizing minutes later, she threw money into the slot between her and the driver, hurried out of the cab, and ran into the hospital. There was a line at the visitors' desk but, apologizing to the other people who were waiting, she rushed to the front of it. "I believe my sister was being moved from intensive care to a private room today. Where is she?"

"What is her name?"

"Connelly. Kate Connelly."

The receptionist checked the computer. "She is in room eleven-oh-six. Her father just arrived a few minutes ago. He should be with her now."

A sense of sheer panic consumed Hannah. She turned and began to run to the elevators. Not understanding why she was so frightened, she realized that she was pleading, "Let her be all right. Please, let her be all right."

97

$\infty\!\!\!\infty$

Connor Connelly stepped off the elevator at the top floor of the hospital. At the nurses' station he was directed to turn left and walk down the long corridor to room 1106. "It's the very last room, the nicest one on the floor, and the quietest," a nurse said cheerfully. "I just looked in on your daughter. She was quite restless earlier but now she's sleeping like a baby."

"I won't wake her up," he promised. "I just wanted to see her."

He was pleased to observe that the room was a good distance from the nurses' station and to be told that Kate was asleep. If the nurse had just checked on her, it was unlikely that she would come back soon. Being careful not to seem in too much of a hurry, he walked down the corridor to 1106. His mind was churning.

He knew that the caller who told him yesterday he had one week to pay up meant business. His only chance of putting his hands on nearly $4 million was to collect the insurance. He knew that the insurance company wasn't going to budge until Kate could be interviewed about what had happened that night.

If Kate was dead, they'd never be able to prove that she had anything to do with setting off that explosion. A good lawyer could make the argument that when she happened to call her old friend Gus, as she sometimes did, he laid a trap by asking her to meet him in the museum. Gus was the one with the technical know-how to set off an explosion and he was just bitter enough to do it.

The disgruntled dealer was smart enough to know that if he comes after me, he'll never get paid. If I can convince him that the insurance company will have to pay the claim in the next couple of months, he'll wait but he'll keep racking up the interest.

How could Jack and I have had the colossal misfortune to have timed that explosion for just when Kate and Gus happened to be there in the middle of the night?

And how could that antique desk have turned out to be a fake? It had been in the museum for forty years. Even my father was fooled on that one, Connor thought. And he bragged that he knew everything there was to know about antique furniture.

His mind jumping wildly, his breath coming in short gasps, he nodded to a patient whose door was open and who was looking directly at him as he passed by.

I planned everything out so carefully, he thought, almost bewildered at how everything had gone wrong. When I told Jack I was thinking of putting him in charge of the plant five years ago, I laid out my entire plan for him. It was so simple. One by one over the next five or six years, we would take a valuable antique from the museum and replace it with a reproduction. We'd do that until we had just enough left of the real stuff for the insurance investigators to find genuine remnants in the ruins of the fire that we would set.

"This way we make millions by selling the real stuff privately," I told Jack. "There are plenty of people in China and South America who will pay top dollar in cash for the originals, no questions asked as to which private collection they came from. So our records will indicate for the insurance company that all of the originals were in the museum when the fire destroyed it." I promised Jack 10 percent of every sale. He jumped at it.

But that was why we had to retire Gus. He would have spotted a reproduction in the museum with his eyes closed.

For five years, they had been removing the priceless originals at night and replacing those pieces with the fine copies that to an untrained eye were indistinguishable. It had been easy for Jack to manipulate the documentation showing the supply of stock in the warehouse.

I've gone through the money I made, Connor thought. I'll bet Jack has most of his in an offshore account.

They always met in the hours after midnight. After they made a substitution, Jack would drive a van containing the antique and deliver it to the middleman in Connecticut who worked for the dealer. We were careful, Connor thought, as he neared the end of the corridor. It was only one sale every three or four months.

That homeless guy must have been sneaking in at night at the very back of the parking lot. On the news they said he admitted that he was inside that van when that college girl tried to talk to him. He admitted punching her and then hearing her yell for help. They all think he killed her.

Connor put his hand on the door, that had been angled closed, of Kate's room. He thought back to when Jamie Gordon came running across the parking lot at three o'clock in the morning a few years ago and saw them carrying the antique table out of the museum. She was holding her jaw. It was bleeding. She was screaming, "Help me, help me!" and begging us to call the police. I grabbed her by her scarf and twisted it around her neck. I could see that Jack was panicking, but I had no choice. She was in the wrong place at the wrong time. But that was her doing. She was on my property. Jack was a wreck, but I told him to pull himself together. I made him tie up her body and put it in the van. He dumped it in the river on his way to deliver the armoire.

That detective said Jack was being cooperative. Did he tell the cops that I killed Jamie Gordon? How could he do that without burying himself? That cop was bluffing. Jack's too smart. He knows they have no real proof of what he did.

If Kate is dead, no one will ever know that I'm not the real Douglas Connelly.

No one will ever be able to prove anything about me, either. Tracey Sloane was dumb enough to write me that sympathy note after the boating accident and ask if I had injured my hand. She wrote that she had seen a picture of me at the burial in the papers and she had noticed that I had a clenched hand, just like Connor did. She wrote that when she was waiting on his table at Tommy's Bistro, Connor once told her the reason that he clenched his fist out of nervous habit was because his father insisted he keep flexing his hand to strengthen it after he broke it once.

It would only have been a matter of time before she figured the truth out or mentioned my clenched hand to someone who would have figured out what really happened. I couldn't risk it. I had to get rid of her. She thought she was getting a ride home from my bereaved brother Douglas that night. My big mistake was to take advantage of the fact that they were paving over the parking lot and extending it farther back. It was easy that night to dump her under all the dirt. I never expected that godforsaken sinkhole would open at that spot all these years later.

Taking care not to make a sound, he stepped inside Kate's room. Then he closed the door quietly behind him. The room had a small entrance foyer. Noiselessly, he moved the few steps to the end of it and looked into the spacious private room. It had a sitting area with a couch and chairs. He could see that the reason there was so little light was that the shades had been drawn. Kate was lying on the bed motionless. There was an IV in her right arm and what appeared to be some sort of monitoring device hooked up on the other side.

He would have to be quick. He had anticipated that when her breathing stopped, a dozen people would come rushing in. It wouldn't work to smother her. The only way to get this done would be to make her swallow the powerful sleeping pills that were now in his jacket pocket. By the time the monitors reacted, it should be too late for them to bring her back. If she died in her sleep, they might attribute it to the brain injury or to a mistake in her medication.

They'll know that I was here. Her loving father. I'll make sure that I say good-bye to them on the way out. I'll tell them she was still sleeping and thank them again for taking such good care of her.

I'll be only one of many people who had access to her in this room today. Maybe they'll even think it was one of those "angel of death" type nurses who did it.

Connor moved to the side of the bed. He reached into his pocket and opened the vial of sleeping pills. Realizing that she might have difficulty swallowing them whole, he broke all of them and dropped them into the glass of water that was on the night table. He watched as they dissolved and then placed his hand around the back of Kate's neck and raised her head several inches.

"Time for your medicine, my little girl," he whispered.

She opened her eyes and gasped with instant recognition that he was going to harm her. "Tell me one more time what you were never permitted to say again."

When she did not move her lips, his tone became harsh. "I told you to say it."

"You're not my Daddy," she whispered, now defiant.

"Why do you think I punched that mirror that night, little girl? I had to be sure that my hand was in a cast for a while so if I did ever flex it, there'd be a reason. It hurt a lot but it worked until I was able to get over that habit."

Connor reached for the glass. "Now drink this. It's not going to hurt. It's going to kill you . . . If you don't, I'm going to kill Hannah. You wouldn't want that, Kate, would you?"

Terrified, she began to open her lips, then as he held the glass up to them, her expression changed. She was looking past him.

"I heard you!" Hannah screamed. "I heard you!" As he spun his head around, he saw that she was standing directly behind him. Before he could react, she lunged for the hand that was holding the glass. Knowing that it was all over, he still tried to force the contents down Kate's throat, but she pursed her lips and turned her head, the contents of the glass spilling onto her neck and the sheet.

As Connor turned to attack Hannah and his fingers closed around her neck, Kate frantically groped for and then pressed the call button, which was covered by a fold in the blanket.

When the nurse responded on the intercom, somehow Kate managed to get out the words that eerily were almost the same as the last words Jamie Gordon had uttered. "Help us. Help us."

Fifteen seconds later a burly male nurse rushed in to find Hannah, now losing strength, struggling to claw Connor's fingers away from her neck.

Instantly, he lunged to pull Connor away from her and forced him down to the floor. As Connor continued to violently resist, other aides came pouring into the room. It took three of them to subdue him.

One of the nurses was tending to Hannah, who was desperately trying to pull herself up. "Is Kate all right?" she asked, sobbing. "Did he hurt Kate?"

"No. She's all right. Look for yourself," the nurse assured her as she helped Hannah to her feet. Kate outstretched her arms and Hannah let herself collapse onto the bed next to her sister.

Epilogue

One Year Later

Connor Connelly had chosen not to go to trial. He well understood the mountain of evidence against him. He pled guilty to the murders of Tracey Sloane and Jamie Gordon, the felony murder of Gus Schmidt, the attempted murder of his niece Kate Connelly, the aggravated assault upon his niece Hannah Connelly, and to insurance fraud.

He admitted that after the boating accident, when he was still in shock, he had heard the nurse call him Douglas. He realized then that he must have grabbed his brother's wallet by mistake. And it was his big chance.

When he went home, it was easy enough to slip into Doug's life. At first he pretended to have spells of forgetting names and details, and that covered him.

Hannah was just a baby. Kate became the problem. She was the only one who sensed he was not her real father. When he knew that he could not stop clenching his hand, he deliberately broke it again while she watched. And she had buried that memory until she was injured in the explosion.

As anguished and angry as they were, Kate and Hannah had

drawn some comfort from the fact that the pleas Connor Connelly had entered would ensure that he would die in prison.

When Jack Worth had abruptly ended his last session at the district attorney's office, after Detective Matt Stevens had as much as accused him of killing Jamie Gordon, he had understood that it was only a matter of time before he would hear the knock at the door that meant he was about to be arrested.

He had gone home, collected his passport, packed a suitcase, and booked a flight from Kennedy Airport for seven o'clock that evening to go to the Cayman Islands, where he had maintained his offshore bank account. He had been standing at the head of the line when the agent at the ticket counter of gate thirteen announced that passengers with first-class seats could begin boarding.

It was at that moment that he had felt the hand of Detective Matt Stevens grip his shoulder. "Not so fast, Jack. You're coming with us."

Connor "Douglas" Connelly had been only too happy to drag Jack Worth down with him when, crying and shouting that he had never been treated properly by his father, he admitted to all of his own crimes and to Jack's complicity in some of them.

Jack was now serving a sentence of twenty-five years to life.

Harry Simon pled guilty to the murder of Betsy Trainer, the young woman he had dragged into the courtyard in the Lower East Side. Reluctantly, the district attorney's office had allowed a sentence of twenty years to life, instead of the standard twenty-five years to life. Noah Green had effectively argued that Simon's information about Tracey Sloane getting into that furniture van had been invaluable.

It was obvious to the detectives that even if Clyde Hotchkiss had tried to help Jamie Gordon, he would have been too late to stop Connor from killing her and would have ended up dead himself.

A statement was given to the media exonerating decorated Vietnam veteran Clyde Hotchkiss from having any part in Jamie's death.

A grateful Peggy Hotchkiss phoned Frank to thank him and added, "Now Clyde can truly rest in peace, and I can go on with the rest of my life."

Lottie Schmidt had provided the last piece of the puzzle. Angry and bitter when he knew he would soon be forced into retirement, Gus had enacted his revenge. With consummate skill he had created a perfect replica of a small writing desk that had been in the Fontainebleau suite in the museum. He had made the substitution and had sold the antique through the underground market. With the $3 million that he had been paid in cash, he had bought Gretchen's house and the annuity to maintain it for the rest of her life.

That was the desk that Connor had unwittingly sold to the dealer who had later threatened his life, never dreaming that it was a replica that had been created by Gus Schmidt.

Kate and Hannah did not press charges against Lottie for her complicity in Gus's theft of the antique desk. They knew how much she had suffered, and they decided to allow Gretchen to keep her house.

Now Kate, her hair grown back to shoulder length, and, except for a tiny scar on her forehead, showing no sign of the injury that had nearly killed her, reminisced to Hannah, "I can't believe it's been a year already. As I told the police, I didn't understand why Gus was so nervous that night. I had been in the museum and suspected that the desk, which I had seen so many times over the years, looked a little bit different. That's why I asked Gus to secretly meet me at that hour. I thought that maybe Jack Worth was stealing from us and I knew Gus could tell in a minute if the desk had been switched. Now we know that it was Gus himself who had made the switch."

They were sitting on the couch in Kate's apartment. On the nearby table were the documents they had both signed relating to the final sale of the Connelly complex property.

The others were about to join them for dinner. Mark and Jessica, who had become inseparable . . . Mark's mother, in for a visit, who was lovingly pressuring him about how much she wanted a grandchild. And Justin. He and Hannah, whose own design line had proven successful, were planning their spring wedding.

In the kitchen, on the windowsill, the bromeliad plant that had brought Justin and Hannah together was blooming.